When Brothers Fight

For my Great-grandmother, May (Little Pimple)

Chapter 1

Arthur woke to the sound of the blasts and the thuds of shells dropping close by. He was face down and cold, and the agony in his head was immense. Opening his eyes hurt. They flickered, allowing some light back into his blurred vision. His body shivered, and for a moment, he thought he might be sick.

Thud. Another shell poured down small stones like hail, followed by heavier clumps of mud onto his already dirty uniform.

Gaining control of his limbs, he managed to roll over and sit up. The wet, muddy floor of the trench was cold. He moved onto his knees and looked up into the sky. He wiped his brow and ran his fingers through his brown hair. It was sweat that had dampened his hair, but Arthur checked his hands to make sure it wasn't blood. He patted his whole body, checking for wounds.

"Christ almighty, I'm alive!" he whispered to himself. "Where is my brother? Where's the battalion?" The realisation that he was alone worried him. He gathered his senses and stood up. Except for the shells that were being fired *from* someone, presumably *at* someone, there were no other sounds.

Where am I? he thought. He tried to remember, but his brain was only capable of acknowledging the unbearable pain piercing right through it from all angles.

Deliriously, he stood up, and his head spun sickly inside as if he were drunk. He put both hands on his temples as he tried to come to terms with the pain. He gritted his teeth and scrunched his face. He'd never had a feeling like it. His eyes managed to adjust to the light, and he began to walk.

The trench was shallow, only deep enough for him to stand up fully and barely wide enough for him to turn his body without wiping himself against the wet walls. He had no idea which direction he was going. He followed the trench the way he was already facing. Every few steps, he turned a corner, twisting left and right as if walking through the body of a giant snake. Several shovels were piled in a heap. A few feet away from them were some other trench-digging tools lying propped up against the trench wall, abandoned. A broken rifle butt and some spent cartridge shells scattered close by were lying on the floor amongst multiple boot-prints. There was a boot half-buried on the floor. Arthur walked up to it and bent down to pick it up.

"Jesus Christ!" he said out loud. The boot still had a foot inside, but there was no leg or body anywhere around. He dropped it, and as it hit the ground, another shell landed, forcing some mud from the top of the trench to collapse to the ground behind him. He stomped on. The earth beneath his feet was soggy and sticky, and his boots were making a sucking noise every time he lifted his feet. He turned another corner and instantly looked away from the sight before him. Again, he thought he might vomit. He retched, but his empty stomach had nothing to offer.

In front of him was a man with no legs lying on his back, mouth wide open. His soul-stirring white face hung like a statue while his fair blond hair swayed in the spring breeze. Hundreds of fat black flies were smothering his eye sockets, and his fists clenched tightly. Where his legs should have been was now merely a dark mixture of blood and mud. Accompanying this was a foul odour that Arthur lacked the words to describe. He didn't recognize the dead man's face, but he could tell from his muddy uniform that he was British. Arthur half stepped and half leapt over the body to avoid touching the corpse, then continued to make his way through the trench, balancing himself with his hands against the walls.

He had only gone about twenty yards, but it felt like more, and he needed a rest. His legs felt heavy. He leaned against the side of the trench, allowing his body to slump down. There he sat with his back against one side and his knees against the other.

More shells came. Arthur still had no idea where they were coming from or who they were firing at.

No one else was around. He knew that they were already firing before he was awake and correctly persuaded himself that he was not the intended target. Arthur closed his eyes and untensed his neck muscles so that his head dropped almost perfectly perpendicular to his body. Sweat dripped from his nose and ran down his face. Despite its annoyance, he didn't bother to wipe it off. He thought about the dead man who was lying there just around the corner. He was considering going back and checking his body for a paybook or a wallet or something that could identify him. He sat for a while and imagined the poor man's mother as she received the dreaded telegram that would soon be on its way to her.

Like the click of some enormous invisible fingers somewhere above him, Arthur suddenly remembered where he was, or at least where he was supposed to be. He was in Belgium, at a place called Ypres.

Arthur had lost all concept of time and so could not tell how long it had been since the battalion had left him down in the miserable hole. Although he tried to remember, he wasn't quite sure how he'd ended up there.

As he allowed his mind to drift, visions of his recent past started to spring into his memory. He remembered marching in line order across an open field. Puffs of brown smoke gently danced in the air above him, sending down shrapnel to disembody the limbs of his fellow volunteer countrymen who marched before him. He began to remember the fear of the battle that had led him to this mysterious wilderness where shells still landed with no apparent purpose. He envisioned his brother and his friends all down on one knee, aiming their rifles in the direction of an enemy that they could not see through the dust and smoke. Then his captain ordered them forward while flames of yellow and orange scorched with black heat pounced from the ground in front of them. Then he remembered the order to dig. Then nothing.

"They must have thought I was dead. Why else would my battalion have left me here?" He asked himself. His thoughts had become words, and Arthur realised he had been talking aloud to himself. He pinched the bridge of his nose and tightly closed his eyes. His head was still thumping furiously.

Arthur sat for several minutes before finally standing up and walking farther along the trench. After just one step, he immediately froze. He couldn't move. There were voices, and they were speaking in a different language. Fear gripped his body. All of his muscles tightened. If there had been any urine in his bladder, it would have spilled out uncontrollably, but he was dehydrated. Panic consumed him, a kind that meant he could do nothing but stand perfectly still, even though he wanted to run as fast as he could. He stood there frozen with nothing but the will to cry taking hold of him. He couldn't control his voice or his breathing, and he began to murmur and pant.

"Put your hands up, Tommy!" said a voice behind him in a strong German accent. Arthur tried to raise his hands, but his arms just shook. With saliva dripping from his mouth down his chin, Arthur turned around. His eyes met with the enemy standing over the trench, looking down at him.

"You can stop worrying, Tommy. I won't shoot you." The German spoke slowly yet oddly reassuringly. Arthur could see that he was an officer.

"I... I'm..." Arthur had no more words. The German officer's face appeared to pity Arthur. His thin eyebrows and pale forehead shaped themselves into an honest look of understanding that this pathetic boy in front of him was merely a helpless baby. He reached down and offered a hand to Arthur, who took it and climbed out of the trench.

The first thing Arthur noticed was that the shelling had stopped. Then he looked across the field. Ahead of him was a burning village with at least four smoke plumes coming from different sources. The buildings were houses that were peaceful homes during happier times. They had red roofs, reminding Arthur of the Victorian bungalows outside his training camp in Dorset. Every window had black burn marks rising from it. Some of them looked like faces. The windows glared like eyes, and their front entrances where doors used to be stretched like wide-open, harrowing mouths. They looked like ghosts or monsters, either smiling or in pain; it was hard to tell. Ghoul-like, they stood aghast amongst the graveyard of what was once a tranquil home to many.

As he stood beside the German officer, Arthur moved his eyes from the village and to the field in front of him. It was a mess. Shell craters were everywhere between patches of green where clumps of grass still clung on to some sort of existence. There was battle debris all over the place. There were different kinds of headwear, all sorts of weapons, water bottles, mess tins, pieces of clothing, wooden crates that not so long ago must have served some purpose. Then there were the bodies—so many corpses.

"Come," said the German officer as he put an arm around Arthur's shoulders. "Please forgive me. I would like to offer you a cigarette, but one of your shells destroyed my backpack, which my bat-man was carrying. It was a good shot!" he said with a smile.

Arthur still did not know what to say. His eyes were watering as he walked forward in step with his captor and tried to resist looking at the dead bodies around him. There were too many to count. Some of them looked at ease. Others didn't. Some of them looked like they had died writhing in agony, twisted like a child had been playing with plasticine and left it deformed. The expressions on their still, lifeless faces were scaring Arthur. He looked at one dead British soldier who had sergeant's stripes on his arm and a thick bushy moustache. The poor man's blue eyes glared into nothingness.

Arthur looked at another corpse. This one had no jaw, just a black hole with dried red blood splattered over his cheeks and neck. His torso was bloated. The top front teeth had been shattered, and the rest of his skin had turned a pale blue.

A few steps farther, and Arthur was guided into a shell crater where two other German soldiers were putting bandages on two unconscious British privates. The officer spoke to his comrades in German, which Arthur had no hope of understanding. One of the British soldiers was breathing heavily. The other looked like he was fast asleep, as if he were tucked up in bed.

"These boys of yours will survive," the officer said to Arthur as soon as he had finished speaking with his subordinates. "We will see to that."

Still, no words came to Arthur. He just nodded. The other German soldiers, each wearing a spiked helmet, looked at Arthur; he looked back and nodded at them as well. After a few more exchanges between the three Germans, the officer looked at Arthur and took him by the arm, once more leading him out of the shell hole.

There was no action where they stood, but they could hear sounds in the distance. It was the rumble of artillery firing, followed by their explosions and the distant crack of rifles and machine guns. It was far away, though; Arthur could tell that much.

"The rest of your boys," said the German officer, "are that way." Arthur looked at the officer in confusion. "Do you see that farmhouse? The broken building in that field?" asked the officer. "I think you'll find your regiment on the other side of it. We saw you come out from behind it yesterday when you attacked us."

Arthur nodded. About half a mile away, he could see the farmhouse in ruins across flat fields, strewn with lifeless bodies and all sorts of random objects. A mile or so behind the farmhouse was a more significant collection of buildings, leading Arthur to believe that this must be the city of Ypres. The sheer amount of smoke coming from it made it difficult to tell. There was an incredible amount of rubble from the damaged buildings that made it impossible for Arthur to discern their origins. Only the tall spire of the city cathedral was recognizable. Even that had flames emerging out of the top, which sent billows of black smoke rising hundreds of feet up into the sky. Arthur couldn't quite come to terms with the scale of destruction he encountered. He stood, confused.

"I'm letting you go," the German officer said.

Arthur's eyes began to fill with tears. He didn't understand why the enemy was releasing him. Was it some cruel trick? Were they going to use him for target practice? Was this the brutal Hun's way of dealing with prisoners?

The officer laughed before speaking again in a thick German accent. "I suppose you're wondering why I am doing this, aren't you?" He was smiling, making Arthur feel uncomfortable.

"I want you to go. I haven't got the time or patience to take you for a prisoner. Besides, I want you to deliver a message for me. Can you see what's happening here?" the German asked Arthur, looking at his comrades, who were doing some splendid bandage work on the two wounded British soldiers. "These are not medics or military doctors. These are ordinary German soldiers, volunteers. They have no personal quarrel with you English folk. You can see they're helping. They don't want you to die. You must have German casualties behind your lines, too, no? I want to think your men will help my men the same as my men have helped your men, don't you agree?"

Arthur finally found it in him to speak.

"Yes" was about as much as he wanted to mutter, but he had understood what the enemy officer was trying to explain. "You want me to go back to my unit and tell my commanding officers what I saw here today so that we will treat your wounded German prisoners well? That's why you're letting me go?"

"Exactly. You Tommies understand everything. A smart nation. A Germanic nation! God alone knows why we fight against each other and not side by side."

The officer smiled and held out his hand to Arthur, who shook it and tried to speak again. Only a tiny whisper came out.

"Thank you," he mumbled. Arthur understood how weak he looked and sounded.

The officer turned away and went back to the shell hole a few yards behind him before shouting to Arthur, "Go now; I will order my men not to shoot."

Arthur could hardly breathe. His chest tightened with fear. Shaking, he began to wend his way toward the farmhouse, expecting at any second to hear a shot and then feel the pain of a bullet entering his back. It never came.

Chapter 2

"Sir!" the private shouted. "Sir!"

"What is it, Private?" asked Captain Clark.

"There are some men, sir."

"Can you be more specific than that?" the captain said dryly. "What uniform are they wearing, how many of them?"

"I think there's one of ours, sir," the private said.

"Let me have a look." Captain Clark stood on an ammunition box and tip-toed just enough to get his eyes at the same level as the ground above the trench and peered outward through his binoculars. "One of them is ours, all right. What the devil is he doing?" He stepped off the box. "Here, Wilson, have another glance, will you? Your eyes are better than mine."

Private Wilson stood on the box and looked out over the top of the trench.

"Yeah, one of them is a Tommy. He's lost by the looks of it. He's chatting to a German, sir!" he informed Captain Clark.

"Are you sure the other one is German?" Captain Clark asked.

"Well, he looks like a German, sir!"

"He could be Belgian?" the captain suggested.

"Nah, he's Boche, sir. He's got Boche clobber on!"

"Keep watching them," Captain Clark instructed.

"The German is pointing at us, sir! He's showing our boy where to go; he's sending him this way, sir!" Private Wilson sounded surprised.

"What the devil is going on? Stay sharp, lads. This might be some dirty Hun trick!" the captain said over his shoulder to the other men of A Company, who were listening carefully.

"He's walking this way, sir. Shall I call him in?" Private Wilson asked.

"No, Wilson, don't draw attention to us. Let him wander here on his own accord. He'll see us soon enough. Keep an eye on him and call him in when he's a bit closer." Captain Clark ordered.

"Yes, sir." Wilson watched the man walking towards them. The uniform was clear, but the face wasn't, as he was still too far away. He wasn't walking like a normal person, as if he were confused or inebriated.

"There's a lot of bodies out there, Captain," Wilson observed as his eyes scoured the open field in front of him.

"Thank you, Wilson, keep that to yourself. Not everyone is as tough-minded as you," the captain replied. "How far away is our friend?"

"About a hundred yards, sir. Maybe less."

"When he gets to fifty, call him in. What about that German?" Captain Clark questioned the young private.

"The German's gone, sir." Private Wilson put his head above the lip of the trench but for no more than a few seconds for fear of a sniper picking him off. He watched the man walking towards them and wondered how nobody else had seen him. Not a single German was firing at him.

"Bloody hell, sir!"

"What is it, Wilson?" the captain asked.

"It's Greeny, sir!"

"What?"

"It's Private Green, sir!" Wilson stood up and shouted. "Greeny!! Over here!! Arthur!! ARTHUR!!"

"Get down, Private!!" the captain said sternly. "Are you sure it's Private Green?"

"I'm positive, sir!" replied Wilson, who then tried to shout out again. It took far longer than it should have for the man out in the open to hear him. Although the fighting was far away, the sounds were still loud enough to block Wilson's voice.

"He's seen me, sir!" exclaimed Wilson excitedly.

Arthur had made it. He had walked all the way across the field, which was in a dreadful state, not knowing which direction he was going. He was still delirious and subdued by his encounter with the German officer. The officer had kept his word and had ordered his men not to fire at him.

Arthur noticed Wilson when he was about thirty yards away and realised there was a trench in front of him. His pace quickened, and he jumped into the long, thin hole in the ground and slumped on the floor. A small crowd of friendly and familiar faces gathered around him.

"Somebody give me some water!" A canister from somebody's hand made it to him, and he drank half the bottle and poured the rest on his head.

"Let me through," said the captain as he brushed some of the other men aside. "Welcome back, Private! You've pulled through then?" The captain looked at Arthur and smiled. He was happy to see that Arthur was not hurt.

"Yes, sir," Arthur panted, still out of breath, partly from drinking so much water but also from the adrenalin fuelled by his situation's surreality.

"Hey Belly, go and get Trimmer—tell him his brother is alive!" said Wilson. Private Bell nodded and disappeared round the corner of the trench.

"Where the hell have you been, Greeny?" asked another private.

"Yes, Private, where the devil did you just come from?" asked the captain, who dispersed the gathering audience by waving everyone away and ordering them to get back to their positions. "Come on, up you get, Private." The captain held out a hand and pulled Arthur to his feet.

"Thank you, sir," Arthur said.

"Come with me, Private," the captain said, warmly putting an arm on Arthur's shoulder to guide him as he started walking.

The two men walked through the busy trench until they came to a small dugout that was only big enough for two at most. The dugout had been made very hastily by the looks of it. Some candles had been shoved into the thick, wet mud, offering a little more light. White wax had dripped down, giving the dugout entrance a strange decoration. All that the artificial cave had room for was two chairs.

"Sit down, Private." Captain Clark gestured to a chair. Arthur was thankful to sit down given his exhaustion, and as the cramped dugout was too short for the men to stand up.

"Yes, sir." Arthur sat down and noticed that both of his legs were shaking. The captain looked at him and saw the shaking too.

"Got the jitters, have we?" Captain Clark asked rhetorically.

"Yes, sir. I think..." Arthur couldn't finish the sentence.

"You'll soon get over that," the captain interrupted with a reassuring voice. The captain was a young man of twenty-five years, tall and slim, with a thick moustache and brown hair to match his brown eyes. He looked sympathetic towards Arthur. He was far more articulate than the rest of the lads, who were all from London's lower-working class areas. He was from Berkshire and had enjoyed a relatively privileged upbringing. That's why he was an officer. He had had an excellent education and was training to be a lawyer until the war broke out eight months before.

"Private?" he said, breaking the awkward silence.

"Sir," Arthur squeaked pitifully in reply.

"Private, where have you been?" The captain

pulled a cigarette from his pocket, tapped it on the metal case, and put it in his mouth. He took a candle to light the cigarette and then shoved it back into the wall, dripping more wax as he did so.

"I don't know, sir," Arthur replied sincerely.

"We thought you were dead, Private."

"No, sir."

"Yes, well, we can see that." The captain could tell that Arthur was not acting like his usual self.

"I think you might have a concussion, Private."

"Concussion, sir?"

"Yes, Private. Concussion. It's what happens when you've been hit on the head, and you don't really know what's going on. You seem very confused."

"Yes, sir. I'm not exactly sure where I was, and I have a pounding headache."

"You've just wandered from the position we dug yesterday before German resistance and later on counter-attacks forced us to retreat, and yet you don't have a scratch on you."

"No, sir. I woke up before, not too long ago, I don't think. There was a German officer and some other Huns, sir. They were patching up our wounded. He said I could go."

"I beg your pardon, Private?" The captain's face dropped.

"I tell it true, sir. A German officer found me in a trench up that way. Two German soldiers were patching up two of ours, sir, then he spoke to me in English. He pointed this way and said you were all here behind the ruined barn." Arthur became sud-

denly nervous, hoping the captain would believe
him.

"Do you realise the penalty for fraternising with
the enemy, Private?" The captain had changed his
position, and his tone darkened. He was now sitting
up straight and looking far more serious. The sympathetic look Arthur had once found in the captain
was no longer there. Arthur's legs were shaking
again.

"No, sir—I mean yes, sir, I understand the penalty,
but I wasn't frasternisi... I wasn't frraster... I wasn't
frastern..." Arthur could not say the word. His voice
was trembling again, as well as his legs.

He started to feel the sweat from his forehead and
heat coming up through all his body. He suddenly
realised how uncomfortable his clothing was.

"Fraternising, Private." The captain spoke for him.
"Yes, sir. I wasn't doing that! I woke up and found another one of our dead soldiers. And then a Hun officer got hold of me. He told me you were all over here
by the ruined barn and sent me on my way. He said I
should tell you that I'd seen it firsthand. The Germans bandaged up some of our wounded so that
we'd treat theirs in the same way, sir. He promised
to make sure none of his men shot at me, sir. He
didn't even ask my name or anything!"

"Taking orders from German officers, are we now?"
Captain Clark asked with raised eyebrows and a
look of intense assertiveness.

"No, sir! Not at all, sir!" Arthur answered, sounding
desperate.

The captain allowed his body to relax, which Arthur took as a sign that he had been believed.

"Very well, Private, but I would prefer it if you do not speak of this to the men."

"Sir," Arthur said, totally relieved.

"Patching up ours, you say? Well, at least that's something. We collected some wounded during the night, and they've been sent back to the casualty clearing station. Some of them will be okay at a guess, but I doubt many of them will be fit for active service. Believe it or not, Private, you are our only reinforcements."

"Sir?" Arthur spoke again, not quite knowing what the captain had meant.

"Did you recognize any of them out there?" the captain asked.

"Any of who, sir?"

"Any of them out there. The dead. They're all ours, lad." The captain spoke with profound sadness in his tone.

"Not really, sir. I saw them, but I didn't look, sir. There's a lot of flies out there, sir. I didn't really want to look at them, sir."

"I understand you, boy." The captain looked at Arthur in the eye and raised his eyebrows again. "Lost one hell of a lot. Your brother made it, though. I've sent him back into the city to see if he can locate our rations. God willing, he'll be back shortly. Okay, Greeny, you can take yourself back to the line. You are also exempt from sentry duty until your concussion is gone. It's seventeen hundred hours now, so get some food and some rest and we'll see how you are tomorrow. Dismissed."

The captain and Arthur stood up, saluted each other, and began to make their way out of the small dugout. Just as Arthur's head reached the daylight, the captain spoke again.

"Private?"

"Yes, sir."

"Not a word to the men about the German officer, okay?"

"Yes, sir. Thank you, sir." Arthur saluted again, but the captain had already taken his eyes off Arthur. Arthur walked away in the direction he had come after it became evident that he was not getting a salute in return.

A few twists and turns of the trench, and he was back with Wilson and the other survivors.

"Arthur!" Said Wilson. "Are you gonna tell us what the hell happened to you or what?"

Before Arthur could reply, he looked up and was filled with joy and relief to see his brother Charlie.

"Bugger me, it is true!" said Charlie, and the two brothers hugged. "Where the hell have you been, lad?"

Charlie was the slightly taller of the two, and at nineteen years old, he was a year and three months older than Arthur. They looked similar enough that one could tell they were brothers. They both had the same-shaped face and mouth, with the same bluish-green eyes and mousy brown hair that had once been blonde during their childhoods. Charlie was able to grow slightly more facial hair, which was starting to come out in a thin stubble since shaving hadn't been possible for the past couple of days. He had worked in a barber shop and had been given the nickname Trimmer by Arthur before they had joined up.

"I was about to write to Mum and Little Pimple saying you'd popped your clogs on day one!" said Charlie, patting Arthur on the shoulder as the embrace came to a natural conclusion. Wilson and Belly had come to join them.

"Come on, out with it," said Wilson. "Where ya been hiding?'" he said in his strong cockney accent.

"Honestly, I don't know," said Arthur. "Have we got any grub? I'm starving."

"We got shit on bread again," Charlie answered miserably.

"Trimmer?" asked Arthur seriously. "I honestly don't know where I've been."

"Bloody hell, mate, you've lost it," the elder brother commented.

"You mean you don't remember wallopin' that spike-helmeted bastard yesterday?" Wilson interrupted.

"Honestly, Wilson, I have not got a clue!" Arthur was perplexed. Walloping a German? What was Wilson talking about?

"Right, let's have a look," said Charlie. "I'll explain it best I can. Right?" Arthur nodded at his brother, and the four teenagers sat down in a huddle on some empty wooden crates. The sun was going down behind them, and the shadow of the trench wall darkened their surroundings. They could still hear shelling in the distance, but it was so constant that they had become desensitised to it.

"So it went like this," Charlie continued. "We got to Wipers, which was on fire and still is, and got this order to advance in open order across a field. There was no cover whatsoever, and suddenly, shrapnel shells started bursting above us. That's when I saw Sergeant Cunningham go down. Bloody awful, it was. A couple of others dropped out with wounds, and then Shakespeare - well, it's hard to describe. He just sort of disintegrated."

Arthur couldn't remember any of this, and he could see Charlie was struggling to retell the story of the previous day.

"Then we made it to a ditch and got in it, but there were already some of our fellas in it from the Connaught Rangers, I think. Then we were ordered to advance farther, and then their machine guns opened up. Watson got hit in the stomach and went down, and then it got a bit hazy. That's when we saw the gas."

"The what?" Arthur asked.

"Huns gassed the Froggies," Private Bell answered.

"Don't you remember the gas, Arthur?" Wilson asked.

"That big yellow cloud that just swallowed everything. Poor French chaps, and some of them were Indians too. They came staggering through it with foamy shit coming out of their mouths and their faces burning. The worst thing I've ever seen in my life." Charlie described it as best he could. "So we ended up in a mass panic. Clarky, and Captain Giles —you know, from B company—well, those two ordered us to move to the right, away from the cloud. That's when out of nowhere, these three Germans were hiding in a shell hole. You turned your rifle round like a cricket bat and clobbered one of them over the head with it! The other two ran away. I don't know if they made it to their lines or not. There was too much going on, but the one you hit must definitely be dead. After that, we got an order to dig a trench, so we did this under fire, and before we knew it, a shell came and knocked you down. We got another order to retire here, where we are now, and that's the last we saw of you. We all thought you were dead, Arthur!" Charlie exclaimed as he finished telling his version of events.

"Douglas is dead too," Private Bell added.

"And Buck," said Wilson.

Arthur sat in silence and looked at his two friends and his brother.

"You were fucking lucky, mate," Charlie commented.

He didn't feel lucky. Hearing his brother's account of what had happened the day before left him feeling disbelief and a sense that none of this was real.

"Wilko's alive, though, and so is Sergeant Wignell," said Wilson.

"What about Curwen?" asked Arthur worriedly.

"I saw him go down," said Charlie. "I saw Dan Williams get shot to shit too."

"Paul Denman made it back, but with only one arm, so he'll be in Blighty soon, no doubt," Wilson added again.

"Are you all right?" Charlie looked at Arthur.

"I didn't realise that so many of us were dead," Arthur replied. "I killed a man." Arthur suddenly looked up at his friends and brother. "His mother's going to be getting a telegram."

"Hey, just you look at it this way." Charlie tried to sound optimistic. "If you hadn't battered that kraut, then it could have been you, or me, or either of these two getting snuffed by them. Mum could be getting a knock at the door. But she ain't, coz you came here and did what you were meant to."

Arthur didn't entirely burst into tears, but he was close. His head still hurt, and now his frowning was getting the better of his forehead. He pinched the bridge of his nose.

"So here we are—the remainders of A Company. There are a few more of us wandering about somewhere, though. We got B Company up that way." Charlie pointed in the direction of where he had gone with the captain earlier, "And C Company on our left with D Company on the far left. Now, let's go find something to eat. I brought some bread back and left it with Sergeant Wignell up that way. He's got some ammo being brought in as well, so make sure you stock up. You got a rifle?" Charlie asked as he took on the big brother role.

"No," Arthur answered as if it were obvious.

"We'll find you something," Charlie assured him.

The two brothers left while the others stayed sitting down. They came back with a loaf of bread about half an hour later. The company cooks told them that it was to share between sixteen of them. There weren't sixteen of them to share it. They ate well.

The sun finally went down, but the sounds of distant shelling didn't. Private Ellmer and Private Yates came to join them after their stint as sentries. Two other surviving men from the company took up their unenviable positions. Ellmer and Yates both told Arthur their accounts of the battle, which he had no hope of remembering. They dropped a few more names of men that Arthur had known who were not yet accounted for and even more friends, whom Arthur knew he would never see again.

When Arthur had decided he had heard enough, he lay down on the cold trench floor. Wilson had given him a blanket and a dead comrade's overcoat, which Arthur used as a pillow.

The sleep that Arthur tried to get failed to materialise. He made numerous attempts but tossed and turned, trying to find a comfortable position. Now and then, soldiers stepped over him as they made their way to wherever they were going.

Many men who couldn't sleep just whispered to each other all night. Trying to get warm was impos-

sible; trying to get comfortable was even more chal-
lenging. Arthur covered his head with the blanket
and held his hands over his ears. The sounds of explosions didn't cease for one second. He squashed
up his legs so that he was in the foetal position and
lay there for hours.

Still, sleep didn't come. His mind was too focused
on hearing his pals' ordeals. He thought about the
German officer who had let him go and the two German soldiers who had been helping the British
wounded. He thought about them, but he couldn't
remember their faces. If he saw them in battle tomorrow, he wouldn't recognize them. Then he
thought about the dead soldier with no legs. Arthur
hadn't recognised him, for which he was thankful.
So many of his friends were gone already. He
thought about their mothers. Some of them he had
known. He imagined their tearful faces when they
received the telegram telling of their son's death.

Then Arthur thought about his mother, sitting at
home looking after his younger sister, May, who had
been nicknamed Little Pimple due to eczema making her face red. She was only two years old and
might not even recognize him now. He remembered playing with her on the road outside their
family home in Tottenham; he helped teach her to
walk on the cobbled high street. He wondered how
many new words she had learned and how tall she
might be now. Since she went to meet him outside
Shaftesbury recruitment centre upon joining up
several months ago, he hadn't seen her. After six

weeks in their training camp in Dorset, the order to depart overseas had come with only a twenty-four-hour notice, and Little Pimple had been ill. Their mother didn't bring her to the train station to see them off.

Arthur lay deadly still in the cold dark trench. He tried his hardest to remember the battle, but nothing came to him. His memory still held the long march to Belgium from somewhere in France, and he remembered seeing the glow of Ypres burning. Then he recalled marching through the rubble of the city with raw, red feet that morning after marching through the night. Then he recounted the arguments between some of the boys, most of whom were now dead, about how to pronounce the city's name.

"Wipers," one man called it.

"No, it is Eepers," argued another

"No, it's eye-peres," somebody else had told them. The spelling was easy, but nearly everyone had all called it Wipers in the end.

Arthur then remembered standing at a crossroad that had been dotted with shell holes. He remembered again some incoming fire that had forced them to spread out and quickly escape into a field nearby. Then, nothing. No battles, no dead men, no Germans. Nothing. He could not remember anything after that.

The sky was beginning to turn a pale blue as the

morning was approaching. Arthur took the blanket off his face and looked up into the sky, seeing some stars fading as daylight stole them away. The eternal sounds of shelling continued as he heard some other men talking.

"Officer coming through!" he heard. Some men towering over him stood to attention, and he got up too. He stood between the two men he didn't know but could see from their badges that they were London regiment.

Through the trench walked an officer. It was Major Burnett. Arthur knew the major well and respected him.

"At ease, men," the major said as he shimmied his way through the trench.
A few paces past Arthur, the major stopped and started to speak.

"Listen up, men. I have assumed command of the 4th Battalion. I have received instructions from HQ that there is to be an attack here in the coming hour." There was some murmuring among the men, and a tense atmosphere descended all around. "However, it's going to be a French division, and some of our Indian boys will be on the right flank, but you probably won't be able to see them from this position. Our job is to sit tight until they arrive. The French and the Indians will leapfrog us, so we've got to be ready for them. They're going to jump right over us. We're going to support them once they've gone ahead. Their objective is that village, St. Julien. You can all see it from the parapet;

you can't miss it. Our own objective is to re-occupy the trenches we dug yesterday at Canadian Farm, which are in front of the village. There will be some duckboards going across the top to help the French across, and we have got to be diligent and ready. Expect some shelling coming this way. Keep your heads down! Is that clear?"

The rhetorical question went unanswered. About twenty men had gathered in the small vicinity, including Charlie and Captain Clark, who had taken up a position next to the major.

"Captain Clark here will be issued his orders, and as always, we expect you to do your duties. Our French friends will be here in approximately half an hour, so be ready!" The major held up his arm, showing everyone his wristwatch as he spoke. "Half an hour. Dismissed."

The two officers walked through the trench to give the same talk farther down the line. Arthur approached Charlie, who had placed his cap on his head, deliberately tilting it to one side. Yates, Bell, and Wilson had come around him too.

"You get any sleep?" Charlie asked Arthur.

"Not really," he replied.

"Me neither. Ellmer's dead."

Arthur stared sorrowfully at his brother. Ellmer had been with them just a few hours ago; Arthur was shocked at how it could be that he was dead. The answer was that no one knew. Somebody had found him when it had started to get light. At first, they thought he was trying to sleep, but as the sun rose, it became clear that his face was in a pool of blood, and there was a purple, black and red matter that was covering the back of his head, neck, and collar which turned out to be his brains. A single bullet had gone right through his head. Everyone concluded that he must have shown himself to a German sniper, who had picked him off in the night. A couple of stretcher-bearers had been called and taken him away while Arthur was still under his blanket.

Twenty minutes later, the trench started to fill up with more unfamiliar faces. Men carrying duckboards on their shoulders were meandering through.

"Come on, lads, get 'em up," came the voice of Captain Clark. "Heave them over."

Arthur and Charlie took a duckboard from a couple of grateful soldiers and threw it above their heads, creating a makeshift bridge over the trench. Wilson and Bell did the same.

"Here you go, Private," Captain Clark said. Arthur didn't realise the captain was behind him but knew the voice. He turned around, and the captain was standing with a new rifle, which he gave to Arthur.

"Thank you, sir!"

"Let's hope we don't need it today, eh?" Captain Clark said with a smile. "Did you get ammunition from Sergeant Wignell?"

"Yes, thank you, sir. I've plenty," Arthur thanked the captain once more. As soon as he loaded the rifle, the first shell landed. Everyone got down on the ground or crouched as low as possible to avoid mud and other debris showering down on top of them.

"Okay, boys, stand firm. There's going to be more of that today!" shouted the captain.

Boom! The second shell landed just behind the trench, sending huge chunks of earth all around them. Then came the third and fourth, until suddenly they could no longer be counted. Arthur and Charlie huddled as close to the ground as they could. Seemingly everything was flying all over the place—pieces of splintered wood, hot metal, shrapnel, rocks, mud. Something landed on top of Arthur, but he didn't look up to see what it was. He had his ears covered by his hands and his eyes tightly shut. He could hear Charlie shouting over the top of the sounds of blasts. Even though the two brothers' heads were less than half a yard apart, he couldn't make out what he was saying.

Arthur managed to turn his head around and noticed his legs were stuck underneath something heavy. He tried to shuffle around so that he could see what it was. He saw it. It was a torso, a headless and legless torso. Blood was streaming out of the top of the shoulders where a neck and a head should have been. He felt the warm wetness seep through his uniform and onto his bare skin. After a brief moment of sickening shock, he eventually managed to wriggle out, only to look up and see two more dead men. One of them was flat out on the trench floor, face down. The other was leaning against the trench wall. The dead man's arm was missing, and blood was soaking the lower part of his face. The ground was shaking, and the sound of shells landing was deafening.

Private Yates came running along from Arthur's right. He hadn't seen Charlie, who was still crouching on the ground, and he trod on his foot. A shell came, filling the air with fire, spitting shrapnel down towards them. Arthur and Charlie were both missed, but Yates hit the floor screaming in agony. Arthur got down to help his wounded comrade.

"Where are you hit, John?" Arthur shouted. Yates screamed and screamed as he twisted and turned his body, which squirmed in excruciating pain. There was blood covering Yates's clothing, but it was difficult to make out where it was coming from. Yates moved one arm away from the other to reveal the source of the bleeding. He had no fingers. His right hand had been cut in half. His thumb remained but was broken and disfigured, and the hand as a whole was at an unnatural position, a perfect right angle to his wrist.

"Shit!" Arthur said. "Stay down, John. We'll get you some help!"

"He's got a fucking Blighty!" shouted Charlie, who was still in the same position. The thudding of shells was sending shockwaves in all directions and causing Arthur's nose to bleed. His head once again began to pound and throb as it had done the day before, and with it came the uncontrollable shakes which he had felt when he believed he was about to die. A shrapnel piece went straight through a water bottle that was sitting on a makeshift bench made from empty ammunition boxes. Water started spilling all over the floor, mixing with the blood as it did so.

Arthur looked up and saw two soldiers in blue uniforms jump over and run across the trench. He realised the attack had begun and tried to pull himself together. More and more blue soldiers in oddly-shaped caps carried long rifles with them as they jumped through the air and hopped across the duckboard bridges. Arthur knew that it was the French.

"Give 'em hell, you frog-eating bastards!" Charlie shouted. One French soldier leaped over the trench, but as he did, his body took six or seven bullets, immediately turning his blue tunic red. His body flopped to the ground. His feet dangled into the trench. His upper body twitched frantically, and blood ran down his legs, spilling out the bottom of his trousers. Out gushed the red liquid, as if a cork had been removed from a bottle of red wine.

Another French soldier tried to leap over them, but a blast knocked him sideways, and he flew into the trench, landing next to Arthur and Charlie. Yates was still screaming, but Arthur decided to help the Frenchman first, knowing that Yates was stable. The Frenchman gestured that he wanted help going back over the top of the trench, and so Arthur and Charlie both put out their hands to make a cradle for the man's feet. The Frenchman stood on their hands and jumped. The two boys thrust upwards with all their strength to throw the man over the top. He made it and continued to run, shouting, "Merci!" as he left.

Arthur turned back to help his friend. Yates had managed to get a bandage out of his pack and tried his best to wrap it around his fingerless right hand, which was saturated in blood. He was crying, and Arthur noticed that he had also soiled himself. The stench made Arthur retch, but he continued to help with the bandage.

"Just sit tight, John. You'll be out of here soon," he bellowed. He had to shout. The noise of the battle unfolding above ground level was indescribably loud. Arthur could not distinguish one sound from the other. The shelling now sounded like one continuous rumble, like a crack of thunder that just went on and on and on. Arthur, kneeling by his wounded comrade, felt two hands, one gripped onto each shoulder. He twisted his head round to see that it was his brother trying to force him to his feet.

"Let's go!" he shouted.

"Go where?" Arthur shouted back, rising to his feet unsteadily. He picked up his rifle, which was also drenched in Yates's blood. Charlie pointed along the trench, and Arthur saw Captain Clark blowing a whistle, standing on the parapet waving his men forwards. They were joining the attack. All the other men, including Charlie, had their bayonets fixed and were ready to go. Arthur had missed the order through all the noise and drama that was happening all around him.

Charlie attempted to scale the trench and immediately fell back down as the body of a British soldier who had just gone up before him fell backwards, preventing him from going up the muddy wall any farther. Both Charlie and the dead man landed firmly on the red and brown trench floor. The fall knocked the air out of Charlie's lungs and left him lying on his back, winded. He struggled to breathe as he pushed the crushing weight of the dead body off himself.

Arthur managed to climb up using what strength he had to pull himself out of the trench and onto his stomach. As he did, hundreds of pieces of dirt flung up into his face where about ten or twenty machine gun bullets had hit the ground a yard or so in front, temporarily blinding him. There was not even enough time for him to blink. His cheeks were stinging from the pelting of small stones he had just received. He rolled onto his back and reached around for his water bottle. Almost in a state of panic and unable to see, he clumsily fought the tightly screwed lid and poured water over his face. He then tried his hardest to open his eyes, but the pieces of mud and tiny stones caused him too much pain to open them fully just yet. There was nothing else to do, so he lay on his back with his hands over his face. He poured water over his sweating brow again and successfully washed away some of the dirt from his stinging eyes.

He lay there, still unable to open them for quite some time, and lost all orientation while the chaos ensued around him.

Lying amongst the blazes of shellfire and the whipping of earth as bullets sprayed, Arthur felt strangely at peace, helpless and redundant. He allowed his head to drop to one side and, finally, after some time had passed, began the process of slowly opening his eyes. They still stung, but it was just about bearable.

Arthur watched soldiers in blue, running, ducking, leaping, crouching, crawling, falling, squirming, bleeding, crying, and dying. Limbs were ripped from their bodies, and they seemed to take leave as if they had minds of their own. Arthur watched one man running across the horizon. There was an explosion in front of the man. His legs and arms stopped, the man fell to his knees, and his head rolled off backwards, leaving the body upright. He saw British men in khaki with their round caps run into a hail of lead, which split their bodies across their waists, red liquid splattering out of their backs as bullets passed through, leaving enormous exit wounds. The bodies lifelessly dropped to the ground, dead before they reached it. It was pitiful. Arthur noticed a dead man next to his feet. He thought he saw him move but soon realised that it was a bullet that was causing him to twitch.

Arthur decided that he wasn't safe lying out there, so he sat up and gathered his bearings, remembering that he had only gone about two feet from his trench, and rolled back into it. He stood on a ration box and watched across the bloody field.

Walking wounded had already started to make their way back. Some hopped, some limped, and some were crawling. Two men trudged together, arm in arm. All four of the shaky legs were blood-soaked. A third man appeared out of a shell crater; his legs looked fine, but he was still struggling to walk. The hobbling man put his arm around another one of the men to make three. In the blink of an eye, a burst of machine-gun fire tore through them, instantly reducing them to nothing but a pile of flesh and bone.

One man managed to crawl to the trench, and Arthur took his hand and helped him in. The man was bleeding all over his face and unable to speak. All of his front teeth had been smashed out, and only half of his tongue remained. The man's left ear dangled across his cheek, held on only by a thread of stringy tissue. He had no bottom lip at all. He was able to stand, though, and on dropping into the relative safety of the trench, the man with a broken face simply stood still. He stared into nothingness, his vacant eyes unable to focus.

Charlie, out of nowhere, suddenly appeared next to Arthur. "What happened?" he panted in a husky voice.

"What are you still doing here?" Arthur asked, relieved to see his brother. "Didn't you join the attack?"

"Didn't you?" Charlie asked in reply. "I couldn't get out of the bloody trench. I tumbled back to the floor with a dead man on top of me before I could get out.

Knocked the bloody wind out of me. When I got up, no one was here. So I didn't know what to do. I just waited."

"Are you wounded?" Arthur questioned his older brother.

"No. Are you?"

"No," Arthur said. "I got a load of dirt in my eyes, so I stopped going forward until I could see. When I opened them again, I saw all our men getting cut to ribbons. And the Frenchmen too, so I got back here." Arthurs' jitters had returned, and his whole body started shaking as if it were a freezing cold day.

The trench slowly began to fill up with wounded men returning from the disastrously failed attack. Arthur and Charlie did what they could to help some of their battered comrades, but they had so little in the way of medical supplies and training that they felt utterly useless.

The day went on hour by hour, minute by minute. Stretcher-bearers came and went, carrying those too badly wounded to walk themselves. The ruined, smouldering city of Ypres was behind them. As the trench had been hastily dug only the day before, there were still no communication trenches reaching back to the rearward lines. The soldiers had to make the trip to the city in the open ground. Luckily for those making the perilous dash, the Germans, for now, seemed uninterested in this section of the line. Most wounded could be evacuated safely.

"Officer coming through!" a voice boomed loudly.

Almost no one stood to attention or even attempted to acknowledge the authority figure the voice was announcing. Captain Clark came along the trench, his clothing dirty and his skin blackened, but he was unharmed.

"Ah, the Green brothers. You two made it back all right, then!"

"Yes, sir."

"Yes, sir."

"Shame about, Wilson, eh?" the captain commented unsympathetically. Neither Arthur nor Charlie knew what the captain was referring to.

"Beg your pardon, sir?" Arthur asked.

"Wilson took a bayonet through the neck. Didn't you know?"

"No, sir," said Arthur, while Charlie just shook his head silently. A lump started to grow in Arthur's throat. Charlie sighed massively. The news was bad for both of them, and they were uneasy with how complacent the captain was.

"I need able men. Are you both fit for duty?" the captain asked.

"Yes, sir."

"Yes, sir."

"Good. I've just had a runner from HQ; Major Burnett sent me the order to pull back on the morrow. We're to strengthen the trench immediately, get it suitable for front-line action by tonight, and by daybreak tomorrow, we'll be relieved by the Manchesters. I need you two and any other man capable of filling as many sandbags as possible, widening and deepening the trench. Get the wounded evacuated, erect some barbed wire, go on sentry duty, fight off potential German counter-attack, bring ammo forward, be the company cooks, bring up two heavy machine guns, man the howitzers and of course polish your buttons. You two think you can manage all that?" Captain Clark asked sarcastically, knowing that they had far too much to do.

"Yes, sir."

"Yes, sir."

"Well, you're both bloody mad." The captain put his hand on Arthur's shoulder. "We'll do what we can. I can't afford to lose any more men, so for God's sake, keep your heads down. Understood?"

"Yes, sir."

"Yes, sir."

"Right, find some shovels, and fill some sandbags. Then just keep yourselves occupied until the morning. We're getting out of here!"

"Yes, sir."

"Yes, sir."

Another night descended. The Green brothers had managed to get hold of a tin of bully beef each. Some troops who had come carrying duckboards for the attack earlier had left their packs in the trench. Their dead owners no longer needed them, and so the boys had no guilty feelings about rummaging through other people's personal property and stealing the edible contents. They also took clean water from abandoned water bottles, which now also belonged to the dead.

"I wonder how John Yates is getting on?" Arthur said with a mouth stuffed with bully beef.

"On his way home, probably. They'll all think he's a hero," Charlie said with a hint of jealousy. "While Wilson and Ellmer and all the others who copped it today will all be forgotten next week. Belly's missing too!"

Arthur knew it was true. There were so many dead bodies in the fields all around them that one Private Wilson or one Gareth Ellmer would make little difference to the long list of boys who would never be seen by their mothers ever again.

Still, the sounds of shelling persisted. If it stopped coming from one direction, then it started up again from somewhere else. The black night sky lit up with a flash every now and then. There were no stars in the night sky, just big, thick clouds that started to drizzle. Both the boys sat under overcoats as the drizzle turned to heavier rain. No one spoke, and before long, the rain became a downpour. The coats were useless.

Rainwater was drenching every inch of Arthur's body. He could feel the wrinkles on his fingertips where his skin had been saturated for too long. Soon the droning of the shells merged with the patter of giant raindrops, which mimicked the sound of battle as they smashed into his head. A lone trickle of water streamed off of his nose.

The trench floor began to fill up. An empty and hollow mess tin began floating next to Arthur's feet.

However, the rain soon filled the container, and when water from the ground poured over the edge, it quickly sank.

Several hours passed, and although Arthur had once more tried to sleep, the heavy April rains had made it impossible. He stood up and saw that the water was now up to the middle of his shins. His feet were numb with cold. He looked at Charlie, who appeared to be sleeping regardless. Arthur wished he could sleep through such discomfort as his brother could. He reached up and pulled down a piece of broken duckboard, which was roughly as long as Arthur was tall.

"Perfect," he muttered to himself. He found two crates and stood them on end so that they were above the water line and put the duckboard across them, creating himself a makeshift bed. It had worked. He lay down and closed his eyes. It was hardly comfortable, but at least his feet were out of the water.

"Let's go! Let's go!"

Arthur felt his body being shaken and opened his eyes to see his brother.

"Okay, okay. I'm up; I'm up. Get your hands off me!" Arthur didn't enjoy the rude awakening. His body ached from sleeping on the plank, and his feet were freezing in his sodden boots.

"You've been asleep, Arthur!" Charlie said, smiling. Arthur looked down from his wooden-panelled bed and saw that Charlie's feet were still underwater.

"What the fuck are you so happy about?" Arthur said. He could see Charlie smiling. "Where are we going?"

"We're getting out of here. The Manchesters are here. We're leaving!"

"Officer coming through," came the voice of Sergeant Wignell.

Captain Clark waded through the water and stopped amongst the men to speak loudly.

"Come on, come on, let's be ready; we've got hot stew waiting for us. Let's get started, let's go. Come on, Private Green, nice bed but time to leave it. Chop-chop, let's get marching!"

The march was sloppy, muddy, disorganized, and exhausting. The wetness of the ground sucked their feet into the mud. The remnants of the battalion spread out in the shell-holed field towards Ypres, which was still burning. Arthur looked back across the field to where the trench was hiding, by now about half a mile away. A German aeroplane, a Taube, was circling over it very low. Arthur had never seen an aircraft flying so low. It was silver and brown and had bat-like wings with the black cross of Germany on its fuselage.

A machine gun opened fire on the Taube, and so did an artillery battery, which was well hidden in the adjacent field to the left of Arthur's battalion.

Several flashes started to appear in the sky, with small black puffs of smoke emerging next to the aeroplane. It was less than three hundred feet high at a guess, easily within rifle range.

The engine started to sputter; black and brown smoke followed the aircraft. It banked to one side, gently at first, and then, while still being fired at, began spiralling downward out of control. Within a few seconds, the unfortunate pilot and his flying machine had plummeted into the ground, causing a sizeable booming explosion. A mushroom cloud rose from the billowing smoke. Even though it was probably about seven or eight hundred yards away across the flat ground, Arthur and his other comrades who had also turned to watch the spectacle could still see the burning wreck upon impact. The whole battalion cheered and shouted pointless insults across the field towards the plane wreck.

They finally entered Ypres and reached the crossroads Arthur remembered from their arrival. They covered their faces with scarves or handkerchiefs as they walked through a destroyed street past a pile of dead British soldiers. There were more than a hundred bodies by Arthur's reckoning. Maybe even two hundred. The smell was overpowering; the swarms of flies that tended to fill empty eye sockets were sickening.

Most of the bodies were dismembered. Bodies with only half of their legs still attached, torsos with no arms—a stomach-churning sight. Again, Arthur tried to avoid looking at their faces; the skin had turned a pale yellow. Many of them were frozen in the positions they had died in, as rigor mortis took over.

All the men walked past without saying a single word, feeling sorrier for any group of soldiers they met heading the other way into the salient that had formed around the city.

A few feet beyond the mound of corpses was another pile, this time of horses—a revolting assembly of equestrian body parts. The horses were so incomplete that bits of the mass looked like a collection of innards and limbs. Working parties were carrying dead bodies of both men and horses. It was not a coveted task. Arthur would much rather be under fire again than be here moving dead animals.

Ypres was brimming with activity. The discrepancy between the horror Arthur had just witnessed and the scene before him was unnerving. More horses than could have been imagined lined up with wagons of rations, ammunition, artillery pieces, horse-drawn ambulances, rows and rows of walking wounded, almost like a chain gang heading westward out of the city. So many fresh, clean-shaven, bright, smart-looking boys, all going the other way.

"What's it like up there, lads?" asked one boy who could be no more than twenty years of age.

"Bloody awful!" came an anonymous reply. It seemed to make the men laugh. Arthur thought it strange that the old British sense of humour had managed to survive.

"Okay, take five," shouted the captain, who was one of only three remaining officers. Captain Giles was still in charge of B Company, and Major Burnett was still the acting battalion commander. C and D Companies had no officers left and were under their NCOs' orders, who had to take some responsibility for the men.

The 4th Battalion dispersed by the side of the broken cobbled road, sitting down on a pavement underneath the ruin of an old school building that was now a casualty clearing station. In truth, they'd have preferred to have taken a break once they were for certain out of the range of German artillery, but the road had become clogged, and so they decided to aid the ration carts going forward towards the fighting by clearing the way and taking a short break.

The break lasted two hours as the city's soldierly congestion finally cleared enough for the battalion to get back on the road.

"Two more hours' march, and then we're there," shouted Sergeant Wignell.

He must have inside knowledge of where we're going, Arthur thought, because none of the men had any idea of their destination. The men of the 4th Battalion, London Regiment stood up and got into line, most of them carrying their rifles slung over their shoulders. The ones who had packs took them too.

The soldiers marched onward and out of the city, where Arthur noticed on the roadside that the buds of blooming flowers started to grow after two or three miles. He took it as a sign that somehow amongst all this madness, some hope still existed.

Chapter 3

"Where the hell are we now?" Arthur asked his brother, but Charlie had no reply. The battalion had marched for nearly three hours. They had had to leave the muddy road several times to allow horse-drawn supply wagons through.

Occasionally, there had been trucks coming from both directions at the same time. Major Burnett ordered some of the battalion to help push one of them out of a ditch after it had tilted too far to one side, trying to pass another vehicle coming the other way. One unfortunate soldier was in the wrong place at the wrong time and the poor chap was caked in mud after the wheel spin had flicked dirt several feet up into the air.

They had passed dozens of farms that their owners had abandoned. British officers had occupied many of them, and others were set up as various battalion or regimental headquarters. Arthur had no idea where his headquarters had been during the battle. Nobody had told him.

His mind began to drift as he reflected on the past few days. He had hardly eaten anything, and the last time he had passed water, he saw that it was darker than usual. Arthur knew that he had become dehydrated.

He was hungry. A nice hot meal would be welcome. He thought about some of his mum's roast chicken and potatoes with gravy, sausages from the local butcher on Tottenham High Street. He thought about home and the comforts he was missing.

"Fat chance," he whispered.

He imagined what his mother and sister, so aptly nicknamed Little Pimple, would say if they could see him now. His mother would probably embarrass him by trying to clean his clothes while he was still wearing them or licking a handkerchief and trying to wipe the dirt from his face. A smile emerged as he continued to think of the regular daily routines they'd be doing right now.

The march went on. Fortunately, it was not raining. Most of the men were used to marching and didn't mind it. There wasn't much thought required. The boredom of merely putting one foot in front of the other and watching the back of someone else's head bobbing along was quite welcome after the past few days of action.

Marching in the rain, however, was something that the men had come to hate. Arthur remembered his training in Dorset. A ten-mile march before breakfast for the first two weeks, then it stretched to twelve miles after that. It wasn't that bad once their feet became accustomed to the pain, and the blisters turned into hardened skin, tough and leathery. It was only drab and tedious when it was raining. It made the clothing heavier, more uncomfortable, and colder when they stopped, especially if it came accompanied by wind.

The unmistakable deep roar of Sergeant Wignell's booming voice rose above the sound of boots on the dirt track. "COMPANY, HALT!"

The marching stopped. Captain Clark stomped into the adjacent field so that all his men could see him. They had been marching in twos, which stretched back about one hundred yards.

"A Company gather round," Captain Clark shouted loud enough for everyone to hear him. The company stomped into the field and made a U shape around the captain. It was evident to anyone who had a glance around how small the company had become.

"That," the captain pointed forward down the road to a small cluster of houses. "That's a village called Ouderdom. We're going to stay there tonight and maybe for the next few days, until we get new orders. Some of you can set up a bivouac; some of you can find shelter and warmth in the houses' cellars. The houses themselves are empty and handed over to the British army, courtesy of the Belgians. Brew up, get yourselves comfortable, and the battalion cooks will have some stew made. We'll eat hot food tonight." The captain nodded towards Sergeant Wignell, who took that as his sign to give the order to fall out, which he did.

Ouderdom was barely a hamlet. It did have a tiny church, presumably used by all the surrounding farmers and the residents of Ouderdom in peace-time, giving it village status. In truth, it was about five or six houses built around a small crossroads.

The red-bricked houses were all relatively still intact, except for the windows and doors. On one of the houses, the chimney had fallen off, as well as several red tiles piled up next to the front door. Arthur went into the house. It was dark inside and empty. The wooden floors remained untouched, but there was no furniture in any of the downstairs rooms. Charlie followed him in.

"Well, this'll do nicely, methinks," he said and walked into what was once a living room. He leaned his rifle against the wall, took his cap off, and sat down on the floor. Arthur joined him.

"Look what I got," Charlie said as he pulled a packet of cigarettes from his top pocket.

"Where did you get that? You don't smoke! Or do you now?"

"I do now," he said, lighting a cigarette. "I swapped them for a packet of biscuits I found lying by the side of the road a few hours ago. I think they must have fallen off the supply wagon or something. Finders keepers, I say. I didn't want the biscuits, so I swapped 'em for some fags with Tim Harper in D Company."

"I didn't know Tim Harper smoked," Arthur commented.

"I think everybody out here smokes. Here, you try some." He handed Arthur the lit cigarette. Arthur took a drag and inhaled the smoke, and started to cough. He took another and coughed again before giving it back to his brother.

"Dad would pluck my eyes out if he saw me doing that!" Arthur said.

"Dad smokes all the time!" Charlie replied.

"Yeah, but he always told us not to. Said it causes the flu or something."

"The flu?" Charlie chuckled. "Dad doesn't believe that rubbish!"

"He does; he said if I ever started smoking, then I'd catch the flu. All right, maybe not the flu but something else. He said it's bad anyhow."

"Well, I don't believe that rubbish. This stuff puts hair on your chest."

There were some footsteps in the hallway. Sergeant Wignell walked into the room where the boys were sitting.

"Ah, the Green brothers," he said, looking down at both of them. "Are we comfortable?"

"Yes, thank you, Sergeant," Charlie replied.

"Good, right, well, the captain's got the cooks making the stew across the road in the opposite house. It'll be ready in an hour or so, but he says there's going to be an announcement. The major is coming too, so be on that village green in five minutes. We got supplies coming after that, and we'll need a hand unloading."

"All right, Sarge," Charlie said again, taking another drag of his cigarette.

Arthur stood up and had a glance out of the front window. All the other places were being occupied.

Groups of soldiers were also making their way towards the house where he and his brother had taken up residence. Arthur watched them walk up the small broken front garden path until he could hear their voices enter the hallway.

"In 'ere, lads," he heard someone say. Four soldiers entered the furniture-less living room, and others made their ways up the stairs or into another one of the downstairs rooms that Arthur and his brother were yet to explore.

One of the four men, a corporal, held out his hand to Arthur. "Corporal Lindsay."

"Private Green, Arthur. This is my brother Charlie. We call him Trimmer, but he's also Private Green."

"Brothers, eh?" said the relatively short corporal with thick black glasses and a full beard.

"That's right. But most people call me Greeny and him Trimmer," Arthur replied.

Charlie stepped forward and also shook the corporal's hand. "Hi, I'm Trimmer."

"Why do they call him that then?" the corporal asked.

"Coz he's a barber!" Arthur said, smiling.

"Gotcha!" said the corporal. "Well, we're from the 3rd Battalion. We're merging with you boys in the 4th."

"Merging?" Arthur asked inquisitively.

"That's right. We heard you boys had a bit of a hairy time up at Wipers, so they sent fifty of us from 3rd Battalion to join the 4th."

"Yeah, it was a bit rough. We lost a lot of good

chums. Have you been up there yet?" asked Arthur.

"We held the line for about three days, but our losses were quite light in comparison to you lot. Got gassed, you see. We got orders to piss on our socks and hold them over our pie holes. Stank a lot, but it did the trick. Krauts didn't want to advance into their own gas cloud, so we were let off, really."

"You did what?" Charlie asked in shock.

"We had to piss on our socks and hold them over our noses and mouths and keep our eyes tight shut," Corporal Lindsay explained again.

"Bugger me!" Charlie replied, screwing up his face in disgust.

"Anyway, we're with you lot now, so here we've got me; I'm Corporal Lindsay, and here are the boys in my section. That lanky bastard there is Private Scott Salt," Lindsay said, pointing to a tall man of about twenty with surprisingly little hair on a round head.

"That's Jimmy Steeples with the mole on his forehead. One hell of a shot, so we call him Holey Moley. He took down three Germans in three seconds back at Wipers. And that one there is Private Matthew Burnham. Amateur footballer scored a hat-trick against 2nd Battalion just before we left Blighty and hasn't stopped talking about it since."

Arthur and Charlie shook hands with their new friends. They all took off their packs and found a space on the floor to sleep.

"Well, welcome to the 4th Battalion, lads," Arthur said.

"Where's the rest of your section?" asked Corporal Lindsay as he scanned the room with his eyes.

"We're it," Charlie replied, sending the room quiet.

"I see," said Corporal Lindsay, who strategically avoided an awkward silence. "Well, actually, we had another one with us, but he bought it at the crossroads in Wipers. Hun shell finished him off. You remember the crossroads?"

Both Arthur and Charlie nodded as they remembered the pile of bodies they had marched past earlier.

"It's no wonder they've nicknamed it Hellfire Corner," Corporal Lindsay went on. "Well, anyway, that officer Captain Clark told us to be outside for an announcement in a few minutes, so we'd best get out there."

The six young men walked out and joined the rest of the 4th Battalion on the village green, although Arthur looked at it and decided it was more a village brown. Hundreds, maybe thousands, of soldiers continually walking over it for the past few weeks had reduced it to nothing more than a patch of mud.

The battalion formed another U shape around a wooden box which Major Burnett had stood on, with Captains Clark and Giles standing either side of him. Sergeant Wignell bellowed from the far-left side of the U.

"Battalion, attention!" All the soldiers immediately stood to attention, their parade ground training not being forgotten since arriving on the front line. "At ease for roll call!"

All the men stood at ease as Major Burnet took roll call himself, which he hadn't been in the habit of doing.

Arthur and Charlie stood listening along with the other men, and it became hauntingly clear at how many unanswered names there were as to quite how many casualties they'd taken. The brothers answered their names and continued to stand for another fifteen minutes listening to the ghostly silence that followed each un-answered name. There were too many to count. Arthur felt empty inside. The scale of the loss overwhelmed him.

"Jesus Christ, we've barely been here a week!" he whispered.

"Roll call complete," Major Burnett announced. "Now, I'd like to say that everyone at headquarters is very proud of the whole division and, in particular, the 4th Battalion London Regiment. You've held the line! Those brutes from Germania have failed. Their objective of taking the city of Ypres has been checked. With God's good grace, we shall see them off this year and put an end to this spectacle. Now, we are aware that you have suffered much and taken many casualties but let me remind you that the cost of such is worth it in the end."

There was a short pause, and Arthur noticed how the major had managed to pronounce the name of the city Ypres with particular ease. Everyone else amongst the ranks had pronounced it Wipers.

The major continued, "The 4th Battalion has received fifty men from the 3rd Battalion as reinforcements, so I trust you will all welcome them amongst our ranks, and we shall cooperate with the professional attitude which a British soldier must display at all times! Now, Captain Clark and Captain Giles have had the battalion cooks brew up a stew, so I want you all to eat well and get a rest. In a day or two, we'll be marching south. We're going back to France. Our job here in Flanders is done. That's all I have to say to you now. Thank you, Sergeant," he said, nodding to Sergeant Wignell.

"Battalion dismissed!" Sergeant Wignell bellowed again.

The men dispersed, and most of them went back to where they had gone before. Sergeant Wignell marched across the brown village green towards Arthur and Charlie.

"Private Green!" he spoke loudly.

"Yes, Sergeant." Both brothers spoke together.

"Not you, Arthur, the other one, Trimmer."

"Yes, Sergeant," Charlie answered.

"Captain Clark wishes to see you in Company HQ."

"Oh, right then. Where is it?" Charlie asked.

Sergeant Wignell pointed to one of the other houses in the hamlet-sized village, situated right next to the picturesque church.

"It's that one, the Vicarage. All the officers are in there. Captain wants to see you before you eat, so get yourself over there pronto."

"OK, Sarge," said Charlie. "I'm on my way."

Charlie turned to his younger brother and raised his shoulders as if silently asking a question. He didn't know what the captain wanted with him. Maybe he would be charged for not handing in the biscuits he had found on the road earlier.

"See you for stew later then," Arthur said and turned away. He marched back to the red brick house with Corporal Lindsay and the boys from his section.

Charlie knocked on a white wooden door frame and stepped into the Vicarage through the doorway where the door once was. He wasn't sure where Captain Clark was. A high-pitched voice answered, which Charlie followed.

"Looking for Captain Clark, sir," said Charlie when he discovered the voice belonged to a young lieutenant he didn't recognize.

"Upstairs, Private, second door on the right."

"Thank you, sir."

Charlie went up the stairs and followed the lieutenant's instructions into the second door on the right. Again, he knocked on the door frame due to the absence of a solid door.

"You wanted to see me, sir?" Charlie said, looking at the captain, who had seated himself behind a desk and found a wooden chair to sit on from somewhere.

"Yes, come in, Private, stand at ease." Charlie did. "Private Charles Green, your lot were quite in the thick of it back there."

"Yes, sir. Glad to have had you with us, sir," Charlie complimented the captain.

"Well, we had six hundred men in the 4th Battalion upon our arrival in Belgium last week." The captain looked up and stared Charlie in the eyes. "We've got two hundred and thirty-five men now." The captain took off his cap and ran his fingers through his hair. "We're not going to win this war with no men, Private."

"No, sir," Charlie agreed.

"We're going back into the line soon, and we will probably be receiving a draft of men from London as well as the fifty we've got from 3rd Battalion. I am therefore obliged to promote you."

"Pardon, sir?" Charlie raised his eyebrows at the unexpected news.

"You are now Lance Corporal Green. We've got a few trucks of supplies coming up for us with new rifles, ammunition, and clothing. I want you to find the company quartermaster and get yourself a stripe before we march to France. Can you do that for me, Lance Corporal?" Captain Clark asked with a congratulatory smile.

"Yes, sir!" Charlie replied excitedly. "But why me, sir?"

"Because you've got what it takes!" The captain stood up and shook Charlie's hand vigorously. "We need men like you, Lance Corporal Green; you've been in battle and survived. Fresher troops need someone to look up to, someone to be the big brother. You indeed are a big brother, aren't you? Arthur is still with us, so you fit the role naturally."

"Thank you, sir!" Charlie was genuinely pleased

with his new rank.

"Right, well, off you go. Go and tell your brother. I'm sure he'll be pleased for you."

"Yes, sir." Charlie saluted and turned to walk out the door.

"And Lance Corporal, this might be a good time to get letters home. Try to encourage the others to put pen to paper," Captain Clark advised.

"Yes, sir. Will do, sir."

The night was warm inside the abandoned Belgian house, and all the men managed to get a decent night's sleep. The stew had gone down well, and the two brothers had been able to write home to inform their mother and little sister that they had both seen action and were both still unharmed. Charlie was happy to speak of his promotion, and Arthur was delighted for him. They both agreed not to mention the considerable danger they'd both faced. They did not want those at home worrying about them, as they surely would be. They knew all too well that postmen would be bringing the telegrams to their deceased friends' mothers, and the newspapers would be printing the lists of the dead. It made them feel too uncomfortable to mention their friends who were no longer with them. Arthur struggled to hold the pen properly. His handwriting looked like a child had written it due to his hand shaking as he thought of the losses.

They had managed to spend quite a few hours getting to know their new pals. They were all Londoners, and they had all grown up close to the same streets as each other. Arthur and Charlie were from Tottenham, Scott Salt from Enfield, Matthew Burnham from Islington, James Steeples had moved to the Angel district as an early teenager, and Corporal Lindsay was from Fulham. They all shared their stories of how and when they had joined the army, and over a hot brew, they all told each other of their lives back home.

They talked about their fathers' jobs, where their schools were, what jobs they had intended to do before joining the army. Arthur spoke about his little sister. With his father working most of his time on the London underground maintenance and his older brother getting a job in a barbershop, it had fallen on Arthur as a teenager to spend most of his time helping at home. This meant looking after their younger sibling while their mother did the housework and went to the market. It was not really what Arthur had wanted to do, it being an unnatural and unmanly role for a teenage boy, but he had grown close to Little Pimple, perhaps closer to her than his brother and father had been. He missed her terribly. Speaking of her made him want to go home more than anything else in the world.

The next morning, the battalion rested. Most of the men appreciated not having their feet in their boots. Cooks and quartermasters distributed some bread and plum jam, and there was a huge water tank with clean drinkable water that had arrived sometime during the night. Later on, the promised supply trucks arrived too. There was a mild scramble for new caps, rifles, and other equipment that had been left behind after the fighting at Ypres, such as mess tins, mugs, entrenching tools, belts, webbing, overcoats, bayonets, and a few lucky men at the front had managed to get hold of some goat skins.

Eventually, the quartermaster and two of the logistics officers had managed to calm the rush and ensure everyone that they would all get what they needed. Of course, Charlie managed to get his hands on his stripe and was now officially a lance corporal.

The lazy day dragged on. Some of the men had set up a football game or two, but apart from Private Matthew Burnham, none of the men camping in the living room Arthur and Charlie had commandeered were interested. They were all quite content to sit and do nothing unless an officer or a higher-ranking NCO came along with a job to do, but they had received no orders so far.

"What's the date today?" asked Steeples. "I'm writing another letter."

"It's the first of May," replied Corporal Lindsay, "But don't date it. It won't pass the censorship. Just your name, rank, number, company, battalion, regiment, and you can write that you are in Belgium if you like but not where."

"OK, thanks, Corporal." Steeples sighed.

"What was that guys' name, the one from 3rd Battalion in B Company who wrote the date in his letter? His commanding officer gave him a right old bollocking. He took the letter, tore it up, and then drowned the ripped-up pieces in a puddle and forbade the man to write it again," Corporal Lindsay asked.

"It was Matthews," answered Salt.

"Pardon?" asked Corporal Lindsay.

"The guy's name, the one from 3rd Battalion."

"Ah yeah, that's right, Matthews. So don't put a date on it, Steeps."

Suddenly, Sergeant Wignell entered the room. No one had heard him enter the house or his footsteps in the corridor outside.

"Hi Sarge," Arthur greeted him.

"Good afternoon, lads."

A chorus of "Good afternoon" from the other men in the room followed.

"I'll get straight to the point. You need to be clean-shaven, buttons polished, boots polished, uniforms clear from dirt, all equipment clean, ready, and packed by nineteen hundred hours this evening. There's to be a briefing on the village green at that time, followed by an approximately four-day march south to France."

A few other men from the other rooms in the house had gathered in the corridor behind the big blonde Sergeant.

"You all got that? Nineteen hundred hours. We're leaving Belgium. All heavy equipment is going on the wagons to be taken by train. We'll get it when we arrive; if you need anything, get yourselves to the quartermaster pronto coz once we leave you ain't gonna be able to get it for a while. Any questions?"

"Where are we going, Sarge?" one man behind the sergeant asked.

"France, lads. France. That's all I know."

No one had any more questions to ask. The sergeant spun on his heel and walked out of the house across to another. He gave the same talk again as he informed the next group of soldiers of their marching orders.

"Right, you heard the sergeant—clean-shaven and buttons polished. Let's get on with it," instructed Corporal Lindsay.

At precisely one minute before the nineteen hundred hours deadline, the entire battalion lined up in fours. The line stretched the whole length of the small village. A Company heard the boom of Sergeant Wignell's voice giving the order to march. Simultaneously the company marched away, leaving Ouderdom behind them.

They went on and on, through one small hamlet after another, past fields and ditches, farms, and churches. Arthur would have liked very much to have stayed for at least a few more days at Ouderdom. He liked the house that he'd stayed in there, and he was a little sad to be leaving the haven of a home. To the west, the sun began to set. Looking over his shoulder, Arthur could see the distinct silhouette of British soldiers on the horizon and the flashes and the fires of the battle that was still raging at Ypres.

Chapter 4

For four days and nights, the battalion had been marching. They had occasionally stopped for a short rest and had slept by the side of the road each night for barely a few hours. On the second night, Arthur and his pals slept underneath a broken-down supply truck. Then daytime came again. They enjoyed a breakfast of plum jam on bread, accompanied by a weak tea with no milk, before another hard slog along the Pas-de-Calais. On one occasion, a German aircraft had flown overhead, prompting the officers to give the order to take cover. They had spread out in case the pilot was able to attack them with a small bomb. Nothing had happened, and after the aircraft had flown back in a north-easterly direction, there had only been British aeroplanes in the late blue spring skies above them.

The fourth night was approaching, and that would be the end of the long, hard yomp. Relief that the march was coming to an end amalgamated with the anxiety of re-entering the front line.

The ground had gradually hardened and become less muddy as the days had gone by. The earth beneath their feet was dry. It hadn't rained for the

entire march. The farther south they walked, the
drier the soldiers got. Here the soil was more like
chalk, which suited the men's marching much more
than the thick sludge which sucked their feet into
the ground at Ypres. Arthur was thankful to the
weather for the absence of rain. Marching in even
the mildest shower could have added another day
to their journey.

"Not much farther, Trimmer," Arthur said to
Charlie.

"How do you know that?" came an exhausted
reply.

"It can't be. It just can't be."

Onward they went—one foot in front of the other
as they dragged their boots along the dusty road.
Not one man, including the officers, was spared the
agony of two painful feet. Still, they continued mile
after mile, field after field, farm after farm. When
the order to stop finally came, one man at the rear
of the line collapsed in a heap. He couldn't wait for
the order to fall out. He just took himself down by
relaxing all muscles at once, allowing gravity to be
his body's master.

The light of the sun was also on its last legs, cast-
ing huge, eerie shadows beside each man. The temperature had begun to drop.

Yet again, the whole battalion went into the irrigation ditch next to the road. The men sat down,
removed their caps, their packs, their webbing, lay
down their rifles, and then lay down themselves.
Some of the men removed their boots, but Arthur

didn't. He knew that it would hurt more trying to squeeze his swollen feet back into them.

"Why couldn't they give me boots that fit?" Charlie asked as he removed his tattered footwear.

"It's your foot that doesn't fit the boot, not the other way round, Trimmer," Steeples joked.

Corporal Lindsay made a brew and served it out to his section, which now included Arthur and his newly promoted brother.

Distant sounds of war had dominated the eardrums of all the marching men, of which there were now millions in all directions on either side of the static front line. An explosion, a heavy gun firing, or a machine gun rattling—there was no end to it. All the men could sense they were getting closer, and the look of fear was beginning to appear on their faces.

The constant streams of supply trucks and horse-drawn artillery and the long lines of walking wounded gave them an idea of what they were about to head into. Men with arms in bloody slings, men who limped, and men with rags tied around their heads were all making their way to the trains that would take them home and out of this horror.

"Gentlemen," Captain Clark announced as he appeared behind Arthur, who was sipping his tea. "As you were, chaps. You enjoy your brew. We're almost there, and we're going in tonight. Each section commander will be given trench maps of our sector, and it will be their responsibility to get their men to the correct post. So a meeting of all NCOs—that's you,

Lindsay, and you, as well, Lance Corporal Green—will be held promptly at the head of the column in a few minutes. So could you please go there now and wait with Sergeant Wignell? I will be over there in just a few moments, along with our new officer."

"New officer, sir?" asked Corporal Lindsay.

"Yes, Lieutenant Chapman. I'll introduce you all to him during inspection later on, before we head off. See you in a few minutes, you two," said the captain, pointing at Charlie and Lindsay before walking away.

"New officer—let's hope he's not a hero," Steeples mumbled. "We knew a hero once, didn't we?" he said, nudging Private Burnham.

"Aye, we did. Graveyards are full of them heroes. He wanted a medal that badly. I'm sure his sweetheart back home will be pleased to receive that after she gets the telegram of how heroic her lover was," Burnham said sarcastically.

"Who was that?" asked Arthur.

"That was our Lieutenant Rogers. Not a bad chap, not a lousy officer from our point of view. Just too eager. That first day back at Wipers, he was far too keen. He decided to be a hero and take on the entire German army all by himself. Found himself riddled with lead before he had time to blink," Steeples answered.

"Rather him than me," Burnham commented.

"I'll second that," said Steeples. The two boys chinked their tin mugs and sipped down the now semi-warm watery brew.

"Right, let's go, Lance Corporal," Corporal Lindsay spoke, prodding Charlie with his index finger. They walked away towards the head of the column, leaving Arthur, Burnham, Steeples, and Salt in the irrigation ditch to finish their teas and enjoy any relaxation they could.

"So Arthur, how much of the other action have you seen, then?" Salt asked with an intriguing smile.

"Well, we've been overseas for six weeks, pulled a stint in the rear of the line somewhere in France, then got marched into Belgium where we fought at Wipers. I got a concussion, you see, so I don't even remember that first day..."

"No, you wolly. The *other* action," Salt interrupted him. "The *other* front line. Guarded by the panty line, not the Huns' front line!"

"Oh, I see." Arthur understood but became embarrassed by his naivety.

"Well?" said Salt with a huge grin. The others were all looking at him with eager anticipation. Arthur couldn't understand why they were all so interested.

"That's a private matter; I can't tell you!" Arthur felt his face turning red with embarrassment.

"That's right, and you're a private! So come on, out with it, lad!"

His new friends were all grinning from ear to ear. The truth was that Arthur once had a girlfriend called Florence and had even been to bed with her. But he had performed so poorly and had been sent away to his training camp so soon afterward that he had not had time to see her properly after the awkwardness which followed both of their first times. She hadn't answered any of his letters in the first few weeks, so Arthur stopped writing and assumed that his brief attempt at love was a lost cause. Arthur, therefore, decided that he would redeem his masculinity after returning from the war. He had barely even thought of her since being deployed overseas.

"Well?" Steeples prompted impatiently. "I've got a girl back home. Haven't you?"

"No, I haven't," Arthur replied sternly, "and it's none of your business, so fuck off!"

"All right, all right. I was only asking, don't get so touchy!"

"Sorry. I had a girl once. She stopped writing," Arthur admitted.

"Ah, chin up, boy, there'll be thousands once we get home. Just you wait and see!"

"We've got a war to win first," Arthur said miserably.

"And after we've clobbered these bastards thinking they can take over the world, we'll all be heroes then!" Steeples said, patting Arthur on the back.

Arthur was getting more annoyed and lashed out. "Not Wilson, or Ellmer, or any of the others. Me and my brother are the only ones from our section who came out of Wipers alive. All the officers except Clarky and Giles are gone. Are they heroes? No, they're not. I don't want a girlfriend; I just want to win this war! What's more, I want to survive it!"

"Of course, we'll win," Steeples spat back viciously.

"I know. I'm sorry." Arthur sighed. "I just don't want to get my hopes up, that's all. It bothers me. I'm not scared to fight. I just don't want to go home with no legs and have to be pushed around in a basket for the rest of my life. What girl is gonna want me then?"

No one spoke. They all knew that Arthur was right. There would be no girls back home for those who became amputees. There was nothing heroic or manly about being pushed around in a wheelchair by your mother. A wound that left the body intact; that was sometimes more desirable than not being hurt at all—a nice flesh wound, a scar that they could show off, proof of one's duty to King and country.

A few more minutes passed, and the two NCOs returned.

"Okay, listen up, lads," said Corporal Lindsay. "I've got this map here, you see?" He showed them a map of a trench system going around a village. It was very well detailed. Farm buildings, wooded areas, and even a pond in the shape of a duck's bill were all labelled. Arthur looked at the map and read aloud the name of the village.

"Nooveey Chapel."

"It's pronounced Neuve-Chapelle," Charlie corrected him.

"That's right, Trimmer," continued Corporal Lindsay. "Now, we're going to follow this road here. It's called La Bassee Road. We're going past this

crossroads that's called Rouge Croix. There's a casualty clearing station there, and we will be setting
out headquarters there, too, should you have any
need for it. After we've gone past the Rouge Croix,
we're going into the line here." He pointed at the
map and made sure everyone was paying attention.
It would be dark when they got to the front line,
silence was to be enforced, and they would have to
get to their posts on time and without getting lost.

"These lines here, the black ones in front of the
village, well, those are our trenches. These lines
here in the red ink defending the woodland, that's
the enemy. Where the La Basse Road meets Euston
Road is where our trench line starts. Take note, all
the trenches here are named after streets in London.
We're going to follow the trench at Euston Road
until we get here, Sign Post Lane. Now it runs along
the road here, Rue Tilleloy, and into an old orchard
on this farm called Moated Grange Farm. We'll be
in the second line; the first line of trenches will be
about fifty feet in front of us to our immediate East.
Any questions?"

In the few days that Arthur had known Corporal
Lindsay, this was the first time he had seen him acting professionally. He had all of the six men under
his close watch paying full attention and was displaying why he had been made a corporal despite
only being in the army a matter of months after
joining as a Private.

At dusk, Major Burnett had made an appearance,

and the men had lined up for inspection. The men themselves complained throughout the arduous task of polishing buttons and boots when the same officers ordered them to drag themselves through the mud in the first place. They managed well enough, though, and Captain Clark introduced the men to the new arrival, Lieutenant Chapman. Then the captain made it clear that he was more interested in the rifles and bayonets being clean than the buttons and boots. The men were very grateful for their fortunes in being allotted such a kindhearted company commander. Other officers could be sticklers for petty infractions, such as muddy sleeves or unclean boot laces. When they had first enlisted, they had heard stories about how an officer might make a meal out of recruits purely because they felt like it. Other rumours circulated, always from someone who had heard it from someone else, who in turn had heard it from someone else. Even at the training camp, Arthur felt no reason to hold any grudges against his officers.

His first impression of Lieutenant Chapman was a good one. He was in his early twenties and had enjoyed a nice enough first meeting with the men of A Company. Time would tell what they would make of him.

The men received the order to march just as the sun ducked down below the western horizon. The men walked silently in single file along the La Bassee Road and on past the Rouge Croix. At this junction, a field hospital and a casualty clearing station were waiting eagerly to fill with the inevitable casualties that were soon to be on their way. Each man had a rifle slung around his right shoulder, packs were full, webbing was complete, ammunition was plentiful, and the silence was maintained as well as it could have been. It was impossible to mask the sounds of hundreds of boots marching on the road, the clattering of small pieces of metal on metal. There would be a cough here and a whisper there, but mostly no one spoke a word. As Corporal Lindsay had shown on the map, a wooden sign spelled out "Euston Road."

Into the dark, deep crevasse they went, slowly lowering themselves in and following the man in front as best they could. This trench was deep, much more so than those they had dug at Ypres and much more in-depth than those they had practiced on back home in Dorset. Sandbags and barbed wire ran parallel along the top of the trench, which slowly curved left and right. It was wide too. Easily wide enough for two or three men to stand side by side.

The dark occasionally caused Arthur to lose his footing and stumble, but the ground was mostly steady. Deeper into the trench and closer to the front line, the company walked. Arthur suddenly realised he didn't know where Charlie was. He did not know and could not see who had gone in before him, and he had not turned around to see who was behind him either. He felt strangely alone, considering he was amongst thousands of other men.

Now and then, he passed other men who had dug themselves little cubbyholes into the side of the trench and were using them to sleep in. Eventually, there was a junction in the jagged trench system. One sign which had been carved into the shape of an arrow read *Oxford Road* and pointed to the right. Another, which read *Sign Post Lane,* was pointing to the left. A sergeant stood on the junction beneath the two signs. Arthur knew which way he was going, but he still decided to ask the Sergeant for reassurance.

"Sign Post Lane?" he whispered.

"That way, laddy," the sergeant whispered back and pointed to the trench which was going to Arthur's left.

He continued into the trench named Sign Post Lane and came into a stream of men coming the other way.

"Good luck, lads," they said, and "Welcome to the front," or "Give 'em hell boys." One man patted Arthur on the shoulder and said, "You fucking give it to 'em!"

"Yes, sir." Arthur nodded as he replied but realised he was speaking to a private, so he didn't know why he had added the "sir" at the end. He was nervous. An exciting kind of nervous—or was it a nervous kind of excitement? He couldn't tell. He wasn't hungry, but the constant tensing of his stomach muscles began to give him a cramp. It was not controllable. He had too many mixed emotions, which now included fear as well.

The sky turned red from a bright very light that

had shot upwards.

As they fumbled their way past Arthur on their way out of the line, the men's faces were glowing red too. The mixture of the light, the mud, and the sweat reflecting off their skin gave a reminder of what they might expect now that they were back in the battle zone.

It took a decent hour for all the men to switch places. The 4th Suffolks had left the trench in a 'lived-in' state. They had left much of their cooking equipment behind. Arthur could see where some clothes still hung upon a makeshift washing line.

Who could have left their clothes behind? he thought. *Someone who didn't make it!* came a voice from inside his head. Arthur felt a sickening shiver shoot up through his spine. He continued through the trench until chancing upon Steeples and Burnham, who hadn't been far in front of him the whole time. Salt managed to find them after another ten minutes had passed. He brought with him the news that one of their company, a man called Private James Stewart, had been killed on the way in, but he wasn't sure how he'd died or who he had heard it from. Rumours being passed along the lines of men in the dark conditions often turned out to be nothing other than untraceable gossip.

"Well, I'm not standing about here all night. We might as well get comfy," said Salt. He sat down in the trench with his long legs pushing his back against the muddy wall from one side to the other. Arthur joined him. Steeples and Burnham chose to stand.

"Well, this is fucking cosy, don't you think?" Salt joked. "Very fucking cosy indeed."

"I wouldn't get too comfy if I was you," came a voice which made the boys jump. It was from Charlie.

"Where the Hell did you come from?" asked Salt.

"Took me a while, but I found you. A bit of confusion coming in; one of the Suffolk lot needed help being carried out, so me and another one of them had to carry him. We didn't take him out the way we came in, though, did we? So I had to ask quite a few chaps the way to Sign Post Lane. Got here in the end."

A machine gun rattled close by. All the men stopped and looked in the general direction it was coming from. There was some shouting which followed.

"We're in a hot spot," said Charlie. "And I need two men; Sergeant Wignell sent me to get some volunteers."

"What for?" Asked Burnham.

"Engineers are coming up to the front with some replacement barbed wire. We need a wiring party. They want it done now while it's dark. If Boche finds out we've got fresh troops here, then he might try and attack us with patrols, so someone, I dunno who, has ordered more barbed wire up the top. It'll mean going to the front trenches. The new Lieutenant Chapman is going with you to reccy no man's land and get a decent look around if possible. Can't do it in the daylight; Fritz is too close."

"I'll go," Steeples volunteered. "Fat chance of me catching forty winks tonight anyway. I'd rather keep busy than sitting here shivering."

The weather was not particularly cold for this time of year, but sweat often gave the men the chills when they stopped moving.

"Anyone else?" Charlie asked.

"Fine, I'll go," said Arthur.

"You sure?"

"Yeah, sure, why not?" Arthur replied, hoping Charlie wasn't going to attempt being the protective big brother.

"Fine, come with me; we've got to find the sarge. Leave your packs here; weapons and ammo only."

It didn't take long to find the sergeant. The engineers and carrying parties had already brought up vast rolls of barbed wire, long steel twisted stakes for them to be entangled to, and some giant mallets to hit them into the ground.

"Right, are these my volunteers, Lance Corporal Green?" Sergeant Wignell asked.

"Yes, Sergeant. Private Steeples and Private Green."

"Good, where did Smithy go?"

"Who, Sarge?" Charlie had no idea who Smithy was.

"That engineering chap. Sergeant Smith, he's going over with the wiring party to supervise, make sure it's in the right place." The big, blonde sergeant looked at Arthur and Steeples.

"Right, do you two know what you're doing?"

"No, sir."

"No, Sarge."

"Don't sir me, Arthur, I'm not an officer," Wignell sternly reminded Arthur.

Arthur didn't know why he suddenly started saying sir to people he knew weren't officers. He put it to his nerves lapsing his usual concentration.

"Right, you two are going to keep a watch on the Bosch ahead of the wiring party. You can't be having men working in the open while Hun patrols are going on, so they'll need some protection. Lieutenant Chapman is going with you for a spot of reconnaissance," Wignell instructed the two nervous boys.

"Sergeant Smith is here, Sarge," said Corporal Lindsay, who also appeared out of nowhere. No one had seen him for hours. Where he'd been was anybody's guess, but he seemed to know what he was doing.

"You two off on a wiring party then?" Corporal Lindsay asked Arthur and Steeples.

"Yes, we are," Arthur replied confidently.

"Bring yourselves back, all right? No heroes, Steeps, got it?" He looked Steeples in the eye as he said it.

"Got it," Steeples replied.

Sergeant Wignell gathered the party around him and a line of engineers standing there the entire time holding their equipment.

"Right, let's be off. Silence now, lads."

Arthur and Steeples followed the sergeant out of the trench the same way they had come in, only a few minutes ago.

"Arrival at the front and straight into the action. What would my mother say?" Arthur whispered. Through a deep but relatively straight communication trench to the forward line, Arthur thought about Little Pimple and what she might be doing right now. Probably sleeping safe and sound, he reassured himself. It was strange to him how she popped into his thoughts whenever action was imminent. It was comforting to have thoughts of home and his little sister in particular, but he knew it distracted him from the task at hand. He tried to concentrate as best he could.

The 2nd Battalion occupied the front row of trenches. The men themselves seemed to be trying to relax, only one of them on sentry duty with a rifle and a fixed bayonet. Arthur was surprised to see Lieutenant Chapman was already there.

"Evening, sir," Arthur said as they arrived.

"Good evening. Green, isn't it?"

"Yes, sir. Arthur."

"Who's the other one—Charles, is it?"

"Charlie. Yes, sir. That's my brother, but we call him Trimmer coz he worked in a barber shop, you see, when we were -"

"Very good, Private, let's keep the small talk to a minimum. Who else have we with us?" the young lieutenant interrupted him.

"It's Private James Steeples, sir," Arthur answered.

"Ah, hello, Jimmy, come for a look around, have we?" Chapman asked.

"Yes, sir," came a hushed reply that broke out from a whisper into a tiny yet audible voice.

"Well, let's not get too keen; let's keep it sensible and quick. We'll get up there, have a look around, let the engineers get this wire up, and hopefully, Fritz will leave us alone, then we'll all be back for a cup of hot tea. I've got something stronger, too, if we get the job done well."

"Yes, sir. Sounds good to me, sir," Steeples answered nervously but with a grin.

"Sound good to you, Private Green?" Chapman asked him.

"Yes, sir. Very good, sir. Let's get it done, eh?"

"That's the spirit. Right, let's go." Chapman turned to the engineers. "Come on, then, let's get this over with."

Chapman went up and over the parapet first, then Arthur and then Steeples. They crawled forward with their rifles in front of them. Chapman only had a revolver with him, but he had it drawn, and he was ready to use it. They had gone about ten feet when another very red light hit the sky, illuminating them. Arthur could see right across no man's land. He could see a similar amount of rubble to that which he had seen at Ypres. Twisted metal, broken weapons, shell holes, and of course, one or two bodies could also be made out.

Then he saw the most frightening sight he could have imagined. The enemy wire. There it was, sandbags neatly placed behind the wire, which was all coiled in several rows—twisting, curling, reaching out like a steel bramble bush of death. They were far too close. Arthur's heart raced. He began to pant and sweat, and then his jaw started to wobble unsteadily with fear.

They went forward a few more yards until the very light slowly faded and darkness regained control of the night sky. Although it was difficult to see, Arthur made out the back of Chapman's head as it dipped into a shell hole. He followed him in, and Steeples came next.

"Okay, you two, rifles at the ready and fix bayonets. Don't show too much of yourselves. Shoot anything that moves or doesn't speak English!"

The two privates aimed their rifles across the muddy field. There was no way of seeing much unless another light went up. There was a little bit of moonlight, but clouds had begun to obscure its potential, so visibility was low.

They could hear the engineers getting to work behind them. They were supposed to be silent, but that was impossible. The engineers had to talk to each other to get the job done right. Any form of sign language was useless in the dark. The tapping of mallets and trench shovels on stakes began, and the vocal strains of men carrying, hitting, lifting, pulling, and mostly struggling with the enormous coils of heavy barbed wire could have been heard a mile away.

The temperature had dropped enough for Arthur

to see his breath as he slowly released air from his lungs to be as still and quiet as possible. His jaw was still shaking. He lay there, flat out against the side of the shell hole, pointing his rifle aimlessly in the dark.

The first shell landed harmlessly to their left, but the orange and yellow flash was enough to expose the unmistakable, fear-inspiring outline of several German soldiers. It was only for a split second, but ahead of them, crouching, was the enemy, who had come to see what all the noise was. The second and third shells landed closer, and one of them sent two of the engineers to the ground dead.

Bullets started to whiz past Arthur. He couldn't tell where they were coming from or if they were aiming at him or the wiring party behind. He was clueless as to what he should do and nearly panicked.

"Return fire!" Chapman ordered. That was easier said than done. Arthur could not see a thing, but Steeples had started firing, so Arthur followed suit, sending five or six rounds in the general direction of his invisible foe.

A few more shells dropped behind them. They could feel the heat of the blast on their backs, and more Germans were exposed for a few moments of light. Arthur fired again and again but was never sure if he had hit anything. Suddenly someone jumped into the hole, startling them.

"Bloody hell!" shouted Chapman. "It's Smithy; keep firing, lads." He fired his revolver towards the

Germans ahead of him.

"I haven't got a weapon!" shouted Sergeant Smith. "Get me a rifle!" he shouted at Lieutenant Chapman. He started to panic, grabbing hold of the Lieutenant's free arm.

"Oh fuck, what's up with you?" shouted Chapman as he looked down at the sergeant.

"I need a weapon, sir!" the hysterical sergeant shouted back.

Just then, a strange object flew past them and landed in the hole on top of Sergeant Smith, who stopped moving and stared at it, mouth gaping and eyes as wide as they could go.

"Oh, fuck-fuck-fuck!" swore Chapman when he realised what it was. "It's a grenade!" he screamed. "Get out of the hole!"

Steeples fired a shot and down went a German who had come too close to them. He was so close that he was an easy target, even in the pitch dark.

"Got the bastard!" Steeples shouted as he fired another shot.

"Get out of the hole!" Chapman screamed again.

"It's a dud, sir!" Smith shouted as he regained control of himself. Men from the trench behind them had started firing too.

"Oh great, we're gonna get shot from our own fucking side. Get down!" the lieutenant yelled, grabbing Arthur as he ducked his head.

"We've got to get out of here, sir!" Arthur shouted.

The four men crouched in the shell hole as bullets from all directions stormed over their heads ferociously.

"We'll wait for a lull," instructed Lieutenant Chapman. He breathed heavily before gearing himself up for a dash to the trench. Another potato masher-shaped grenade dropped into the shell hole. This time the four men all jumped out and scrambled in the direction of safety without waiting to see if it would go off or not.

"Okay, fuck the lull, let's go!" said Chapman as he stood up and ran. Arthur watched the lieutenant make it into their trenches safely. He'd made it look easy.

The German grenade in the vacant crater behind them exploded, sending a bright flash followed by smoke out of the hole.

"Here I go!" Arthur shouted as he stood up and bolted for safety.

"Wait for me!" shouted Steeples, who also pushed himself off the ground and ran.

"Oh, shit! Greeny! Help me! Help me!"

Arthur turned around to see what had happened. Steeples had caught himself in the new barbed wire.

"Oh, shit!" Arthur shouted. He impulsively conquered his fear and went back to help his friend. More bullets went past the pair of helpless soldiers, who both wondered how neither of them had been hit.

"Hold still, Jimmy!"

"Get me out of here, Arthur!!"

"Hold still; I can't get you out if you keep moving!"

Arthur struggled but eventually managed to rip Steeples' trousers along the knee until he wiggled free. Blood trickled down the bare leg where barbs had pierced his skin.

A figure appeared out of the darkness behind them.

"Shit!" shouted Steeples as he picked his rifle up off the ground. It had its bayonet attached. Steeples thrust the cold steel blade into the stomach of the figure who had startled them, causing him to scream in agony. The unknown figure clasped his hands around the rifle. Steeples pulled the trigger, which sent a bullet straight through the body before he was able to yank the bayonet out. The screaming man fell to the ground and continued to yell in immense pain.

"Oh, shit-shit-shit!" Steeples looked at the man. It was Sergeant Smith.

"Oh God. What have you done, Jimmy?" yelled a panicked Arthur, who had also turned around to see the sergeant's face staring back at him. "Let's go, Jimmy, let's fucking go!"

They turned around, leaving the dying sergeant on the ground to his fate. They both slid into the trench. The alert men of the waiting 2nd Battalion helped them down.

"Holy shit, Arthur! Are we alive?" Steeples asked, the pain in his leg starting to make itself known.

Arthur looked across to him and nodded. "We're alive, mate!"

A shell exploded above, sending them both to the

ground. A cacophony of incoherent voices invaded the air, and the trench filled with calamity and wild, unthinking behaviour from soldiers who ran away from the blast. Part of the trench collapsed. Arthur looked up to get a face full of dirt.

Lieutenant Chapman fell to his knees. He became wedged between two huge piles of sandbags, which broke his ribcage, crushed his lungs, and snapped his spine. Life was slowly squeezed out of him like air out of a tire. He struggled pointlessly for a few more dying breaths before his body leaned forward, lifeless and still.

Quietness descended. Arthur stood up and brushed the dirt off himself before giving a helping hand to Steeples, who had an equal amount of soil on his torn clothing. They both looked at the dead lieutenant.

"I need to be sick." Arthur retched, but only a mouthful of bile came out.

"Let's get back, Greeny. We've done our job. Let's go back," Steeples whimpered, and his whole body was shaking.

They walked back through the communication trench to the second line, where they found the rest of their friends sitting and drinking tea. Corporal Lindsay had found a comfy-looking cubbyhole that someone had grooved into the side of the trench.

"Hey, look, the heroes are back!" said Burnham.

"Christ, you both look awful; what happened? We could hear some shooting up there, and we had a few German shells sent our way," Charlie informed the returning boys.

"Charlie?" Arthur said.

"Yes?" Charlie replied.

"I want to go home," Arthur cried as his teeth chattered.

The next few days were quiet. Arthur spent most of them sitting on a box in the reserve line trench and replaying in his head the tormenting action he'd faced with the wiring party. He felt numb with the horror of it all. He had refused food for a while but had accepted half a hundred cups of tea throughout each day. They didn't have a lot to do, so having a cup of tea was one of the few things that helped to pass the time.

They had dug a fire hole into the wall of the trench. They had done this in training and were experts. They filled the hole with small wood and kindling and got a fire going before sliding a tin kettle, filled with dirty water for the brew, on top. The fire hole effectively stopped smoke going up over the top of the trench, which the Germans would see.

"Tea's up," said Charlie, taking the kettle off of the fire. Steeples, who had also hardly said a word for days, held his tin cup out and received his tea gratefully, nodding at Charlie. He sat down next to Arthur.

"You all right? Your brother has made tea. Give us your mug. I'll get you another."

"Thanks, Jimmy," Arthur replied.

They sat next to each other, gently sipping the

hot watery solution. Corporal Lindsay had managed to get his hands on some powdered milk, which felt like a luxury.

"Poor ol' Chapman," Arthur groaned. He'd said it plenty of times over the past few days. He chinked his mug against Steeples' as if to give cheers to the deceased lieutenant.

"Aye," was all the reply that came back. "I killed one of our own men!"

"I know. It wasn't your fault. It was dark."

"I just forgot he was behind us."

"Me too. Seriously Jimmy, if you hadn't killed him, then I would have. I thought he was a German just as much as you did." Arthur patted Steeples on the back and sipped his tea. They'd had the same conversation more than enough times already.

"I'll tell you what, though," Arthur said.

"What's that?"

"You got a German too, didn't you?"

"Yeah, I did. But he was a Boche, and they fucking deserve it. I'd kill every last one of them if I could."

"How many is that you've plugged?" Arthur asked.

"He got three at Ypres in three seconds. Best soldiering you ever saw. It was bang. Dead. Bang. Dead. Bang. Dead. Just like that. Three shots, three seconds, three dead Germans." Corporal Lindsay joined the conversation. "It's a well-known fact that you're just as likely to get snuffed by your own side in a battle."

"What do you know about fighting a battle, Corporal? You've scarcely been in one," Steeples commented.

"It's what they said about Waterloo and Crimea. I read about it one time. And my Granddad fought in Natal against the Zulus."

"I'm not sure them Zulu warriors had forty-two-inch howitzers that can lob a shell ten miles, to be honest!" Steeples said again, this time lowering his tone to one more like sarcasm than resentment.

"Well, that's not the point. So don't go getting yourself down in the dumps over it."

"None of us are likely to make it out of this alive anyway, so you probably did him a favour," Burnham added, lowering the tone.

"Steady on, mate, that's not helping!" Lindsay replied to Burnham.

"Sorry. I'm only joking. We'll be all right. We've got Holey Moley on our side!" Burnham raised his tin mug, and the others raised theirs.

"To Holey Moley and surviving this war!" Burnham raised a toast. It put a grin back on Steeples' face, and Arthur decided that they were right. It was no good moping or dwelling. They had a job to do, and they were here to get on with it. There would be more action to come, and none of them knew what was going to happen.

Chapter 5

Except for a few shells landing somewhere out of sight and not being any danger to the entrenched men, the next few days passed uneventfully. Smoking had become a new hobby now that boredom had taken over. Arthur soon lost count of how many cups of tea he'd had.

Trips to the latrine were becoming more frequent. Some of the men were coming down with diarrhoea due to a lack of clean water. The only water available to them was from the rain. Either it fell into their mugs, or they were able to scoop it out of puddles on the trench floor.

The latrine which the company was to use lay towards the end of an adjoining trench. It was little more than a hole in the ground about four feet deep. Fortunately, none of the officers had given Arthur latrine duty yet, but he was aware that it would come one day. It was such an unenviable job. The stench overpowered everything else around Arthur as he took himself there one more time to urinate. He couldn't help but think of the mildly amusing scenario in which a shell would land right in the middle of it. Hopefully, no one would be around if it were to happen because the explosion would throw filth all over the place. The thought made him chuckle.

On the seventh day of their stint in the reserve line, the weather took a turn. The nights had been getting longer and longer as mid-May approached, but that afternoon Arthur saw the darkest and gloomiest skies he had seen since leaving England. A huge black cloud hanging low over them, stretching for miles and miles, opened up, lashing down an ocean of heavy rain. The wind picked up too, which blew the downpour sideways, so the trenches were able to offer little if any protection.

It was a long, cold, sleepless, arduous night that left the men miserable as they huddled in the mud. Just as it had done at Ypres, the trench began to fill up with rainwater. Very soon, each man in the company was drenched and cold. Arthur sneezed. His eyes turned red and dark rings appeared underneath them. He sneezed again. Before long, the entire company was sneezing. As the storm intensified, the exposure to the elements started to take its toll, and soon everyone was rife with chills and a shivering fever.

By daybreak, almost all of them complained about swollen glands, sore throats, and rivers of mucus flowing out of their nostrils. The more dramatic of the men were convinced they had influenza or pneumonia.

Due to the sudden sickness, those at the top

ordered the entire battalion from the line by mid-afternoon. Although the wind had died down and the worst of the awful raging weather was over, the rain continued, which meant a march to the rear with saturated socks, wrinkled fingers, heavy clothing, pack, rifle, and webbing.

The march had been shorter than anticipated, and it felt strange to be above ground again. Arthur was suspicious about the amount of artillery lined up on the road going towards the battle zone. That amount of heavy firepower told a soldier only one thing - a big offensive was looming. Mere privates like Arthur were not entrusted with such delicate information, but the men were not stupid. Arthur was not the only one to observe the tell-tale signs of a coming battle.

"That's gonna blow them to kingdom come," Burnham said to Arthur.

"How many guns do you reckon they're going to use on this one?" Steeples queried.

"I don't know, but I do not envy the Krauts' position. There are bloody hundreds of them. Each sending what is it, one shell every five seconds?" Arthur asked.

"Something like that," Steeples replied.

"Eight rounds a minute for those eighteen-pounders," Corporal Lindsay spoke to the two men in front of him as they marched.

"Eight rounds per minute? So if one gun fired non-stop for ten minutes, what would that be?" Steeples questioned the corporal.

"Well, what's eight times ten?" replied Arthur rhetorically, as if it was obvious.

"I do shooting, not maths! I can read, and I can write, but maths was never my strong point" Steeples defended his lack of number abilities.

"You get an eight, and you times it by ten, right?" Arthur went on.

"Right, so if these cannons can fire eight rounds a minute, and there are ten of them..." Steeples paused as he struggled to complete the sentence due to the confusion he'd created for himself.

"Right," said Arthur, listening attentively.

"Actually, the howitzers can fire one round every two seconds," added Corporal Lindsay.

"Is that more than eight rounds a minute?" asked Steeples.

"Yes, a lot more. It's thirty rounds a minute," Lindsay sighed.

"Wait, what? You said they fire eight rounds a minute."

"No, I said the eighteen-pounders could fire eight rounds a minute, which is one round between every eight and nine seconds."

"So hang on, if a howitzer can fire two rounds a second, and an eighteen-pounder can fire a round in eight seconds, then why don't we just replace all the eighteen-pounders with howitzers to increase our rate of fire?" Steeples put to his bewildered comrades.

"No, Jimmy, a howitzer can fire ONE round every TWO seconds. Not the other way round! There isn't a gun in the world that can fire two rounds in under a second."

"But you said they could!"

"No, I didn't," Corporal Lindsay said, giggling.

"Yes, you did; you said that the howitzers could fire two rounds in one second."

"Oh my God, Jimmy, think about it. Can any gun shoot that fast?" Arthur commented.

"No," Steeples agreed.

"This is painful, Jimmy, come on. Do the maths to the original question," Burnham interrupted. "If you have one cannon, and that cannon can fire eight rounds in one minute, how many rounds will it fire if it continuously fires for ten minutes?"

"Eight hundred," said Steeples. The men around him erupted with laughter.

Even though they were all mostly still sneezing and coughing, it was incredible how quickly their morale had improved since the previous evening after just a few hours walking away from the trenches. The battalion marched to a camp where they slept in hutments, which offered substantially more protection from the weather. Even though they all knew that they were not out of range of enemy heavy artillery, the men were content to be inside something which resembled a building.

That night the men slept well. The thin wooden walls of the hutments, which held four men each, did not do well to prevent the sound of a hundred men snoring in unison. Arthur was one of the last men to sleep. He drifted away slowly into the darkness, re-emerging in Slumberland, which happened to be in Tottenham with his mother and his beloved sister, Little Pimple.

There was hot food, roast chicken, gravy, potatoes, and homemade lemonade from his neighbours. The kitchen was hot from cooking, and everyone was happy and laughing. There was no war and no hunger, no cold, no marching, and no fear. It was just a simple, happy life at home amongst family. Charlie was there too. The boys' father walked in and drank a pint of ale in a glass with a handle. Engraved on the glass was a unicorn on a red background. It was their father's favourite glass. Little Pimple sat on the kitchen table, her face red with eczema. In her hand, she held a half-eaten carrot. She turned to Arthur and smiled. The smile became a chuckle, which then became a laugh. She laughed and laughed and laughed, and Arthur started laughing too. Then his brother, mother, and father began laughing.

Arthur couldn't remember how the dream ended. He woke, unaware of where he was due to unfamiliar surroundings, and he was sad that the dream had ended. He had enjoyed being back at home, even if it hadn't been a reality.

It was light in the hutment, and Arthur could hear people speaking outside. The door opened, and there was the smiling face of Sergeant Wignell.

"Right, come on, let's get up, clean-shaven, buttons

polished—you know the drill. We got inspection in one hour."

"Got it, Sergeant," Charlie groaned unreassuringly.

"Good, you too, Arthur, and who is this?" the sergeant said, pulling back the covers of the nearest bed to reveal who was lying underneath.

"Private Salt, up you get, lad," Wignell instructed.

"Yes, Sarge," he grumbled.

"Who's in that bed?"

"Steeples, sir," Arthur replied.

"Come on, Steeps, up you get. Private Green, please stop sirring me. I am not an officer!"

"Yes, Sarge," Arthur answered the big blond sergeant, who was himself clean-shaven and ready for inspection. Arthur noticed some of his hair appearing more grey than blond just above his ears. He was sure it wasn't like that the last time he had seen him up close.

"There's fresh water outside in big metal containers. Don't be selfish, though; the whole company has to use it."

"Thank you, Sergeant," Charlie called out as Sergeant Wignell left to attack the next hut with the same news.

The door had been closed less than a second when it opened again, this time by Corporal Lindsay.

"Morning, lads!" he said with a huge smile right across his face.

"What're you so happy about?" Arthur asked.

"Well, it's good news," the corporal answered him.

"Well, what is it?" asked Trimmer.

"We've got....mail!"

"What?" All four of the lazy lads, who hadn't attempted to get up even when the sergeant had come in, suddenly shot out of their bunks.

"Where is it?"

"Right here!" Corporal Lindsay pulled out a sack that he had hidden behind the door. "I got summoned to HQ earlier, and there was a truck from the GPO. They'd managed to find us all right—a great big lorry load just for the 4th Battalion. So let's have a look. Burnham? Where's Burnham?" Lindsay asked as he held a letter in his hand with 'Private Matthew Burnham' written on it.

"In the next hut," replied Arthur.

"OK, I'll give that to him in a sec. Steeples, you've got a letter; here you go."

"Cheers, Corporal," Steeples said, taking the letter.

"And here, a package for Private A. Green and a letter for Private C. Green." Lindsay handed the parcel to Arthur.

"What?" said Charlie. "You got a parcel? Is it from Mum? Where's my bloody parcel! I always knew you were her favourite!"

"Calm down. You've got a letter, haven't you?" Arthur fired back at his unhappy brother.

"That's not as good as a parcel. And look, the letter has Private. C. Green on it. I'm a lance corporal now! I did write and tell them, but they must have sent this before they received mine," Charlie concluded.

"Well, come on," Arthur impatiently fumbled with the string on the package, "open the letter; let's have some news from home."

Charlie opened the envelope. Although their mother had addressed the envelope to Charlie, the letter inside had both their names on it.

To Charlie and Arthur,
My Dear boys,
Here's from all of us at home, wishing you are both well. May is always asking about you, and so are all the neighbours. I also sent you a parcel that you should receive soon if you haven't already, and Mrs. Kiddle insisted on putting one of her muffins in for each of you and sending her regards.
We were sad to hear the news of your friend Teddy Wilson, who was killed the other week. I went to see his mother, and she is in a dreadful state. Christine Yates also received a telegram that her little John had been wounded and is on his way home. She's one of the lucky mothers. I dread it every time the postman comes, but as of yet, he has brought me only good news.
Dad tried to quit smoking to save some money, but as always, that only lasted a day and a half. Uncle Bill won a decent hand last week in The Red Lion and treated us all to some fish and chips on Friday. The house is empty without you, but I must say I don't have half as many clothes to wash now. I trust you are both keeping clean and eating well?
Well, boys, it's bye for now. Stay out of trouble, and don't forget to write when you can. I know you are busy and doing a splendid job, but don't forget about us, as we have not forgotten about you.

We will, as they say, keep the home fire burning.

All my love,
Mum
P.S. 'Little Pimple' is talking a lot now.
xxxxx

"You see?" said Charlie. "The parcel is for both of us; open it up. I want one of those muffins."

Arthur ripped open the package and sure enough, inside were two muffins wrapped in paper. One of them had an A on it and the other a C. There was also a packet of biscuits, two combs, a bar of soap, and two pairs of hand-knitted gloves, both green and with the fingertips missing.

"Aw, thanks, Mum!" Arthur tried on a pair of gloves. "These'll come in handy when it's cold at night, and we've got sentry duty. Look, the fingertips are missing, so we can pull the trigger!"

"I bet that was Dad's idea," Charlie replied and took his pair of gloves and put them into his pack without bothering to try them on.

They took the muffins out of their paper wrapping only to the disappointment of finding them a blue-brownish colour covered with mould.

"I'm eating mine anyway," Arthur said. He took a bite and immediately spat it out. Everyone else in the hutment started laughing. Such simple measures had again raised morale, and miraculously one night indoors had suddenly cured nearly all of them of their colds.

"Right then," said Corporal Lindsay, "I'll dish out the rest of this mail. Get yourselves sorted. There's fresh water outside in those metal containers, didn't you know?"

The inspection took place on a green, grassy fallow field adjacent to the one with the huts in it. There was a farmhouse with part of the roof missing, and a rumour had circulated that the farmer himself had been angry with how the British soldiers treated his field. Major Burnett raised the issue, and he had given a lengthy, unwelcome speech about the need for British soldiers to refrain from helping themselves to the crops. Anyone caught from now on would be tied to the wheel of a cart for two hours a day for twenty-eight days.

Except for A company, who remained in the field with Captain Clark and Lieutenant Tyers, Major Burnett dismissed the battalion. Lieutenant Tyers had been transferred from 1st Battalion to replace the late Lieutenant Chapman.

Sergeant Wignell marched the men to the end of the field and pulled back a large canvas cover the size of at least three or four bedsheets tied together. Under the sheeting was a model of a landscape.

"Gather round, men," Captain Clark ordered. "Who is going to be the bright spark to tell me what this is?"

"It's a map, sir," Arthur called out.

"It is. Well done. It is a model-map of the trenches which we left yesterday. To the edge here, well, that's the village Neuve-Chapelle, and as you can see, this is our trench system." He pointed to the little squiggles in the model with a long brown cane.

"Now, some clever chap has had this model-map made from our aerial reconnaissance photographs. You will all get a closer look, and you will find that it is superbly detailed. This over here is the ruin of Moated Grange Farm, and this area here, well, this is the front line that you will be occupying tomorrow night. It's not far from where we left off yesterday. We're going to try something new."

The sixty or so men of A company had surrounded the enormous map and were all paying attention to every word the captain was telling them.

"We're going to try a night attack. All of our efforts in this area have so far been checked. The French have been attacking to the south of Neuve-Chapelle at a place called Festubert. Now, the Germans hold an area of particular importance, this high ground here known as the Aubers Ridge. Also, just to the north of the ridge where it plateaus is a village called Fromelles. That ridge and that village are our two objectives. It is an area perfect for the Hun artillery, and they're using it to a particular effect. Once we hold the high ground and the village, then our French allies will be able to advance unmolested towards this here." He pointed the stick to a different part of the map. "This is the La Bassee Road, and it's the gateway to Lille. Why is Lille important?"

There were a few murmurings until, eventually, one voice spoke up. "Don't know, sir!"

The captain went on, "Lille is important because of its rail network. It goes from here right across the remainder of occupied France and into Germany itself, right into the industrial Ruhr."

The men looked at each other with an expression of confusion on their faces. "You lot don't know what the Ruhr is, do you?" The captain studied the looks on his men's faces and realised that it was apparent. "The Ruhr is the industrial heart of Germany. That's all you need to know, and the railway line goes straight into the city of Lille, allowing the Germans to concentrate and move troops and heavy weapons and machinery with particular ease. However, right now, they're bogged down in the East by the Russkies, so the time is ripe for us to strike while their backs are turned, so to speak."

"They won't know what's hit them, sir!" came another anonymous voice.

"Well, not quite," the captain went on. "We're going to lay down a barrage: a short one but a heavy one. No doubt you saw the number of guns yesterday making their way forward. They will begin at about twenty hundred hours. It will be a give-away that an attack is pending, but we're quite certain they won't expect it at night. Typically we'd fire through the night or even for a few days before attacking in the morning, so we'll catch them unawares for sure. Any more questions thus far?" No one spoke; they either looked at the map or the captain.

"OK. So it's up the ridge, capture the guns, then

move into the village Fromelles. We depart here tomorrow at midday to be in the line by dusk. A short bombardment, then it's kickoff at twenty three thirty. Study this map and make sure you get another good sleep tonight. I have one more thing to tell you. Listen carefully; this is important."

The captain struggled to keep back his smile. "There is a water tank over by the farmhouse. It's just for you, lads, and it's full of beer! Two pints each —help yourselves!"

There was a raucous cheer, and suddenly Arthur felt like he was a horse in the Grand National as a great stampede took hold of the entire company.

The resting battalion spent the remainder of the day quite peacefully in the comfort of the hutments. Private Burnham joined a football match, later on, set up between A Company and B Company. Arthur watched for a while, but as sports were not his thing, he spent most of the evening in conversation with his brother and Corporal Lindsay. They sat up for a few hours after dark, in their candle-lit hutment, talking about home and swapping stories of their childhoods. Arthur and Charlie came to loggerheads about memories that they both seemed to remember differently. One such memory was the time when Arthur was ten and Charlie eleven. They had gone to a river for a family picnic and had taken the train. Arthur was sure it was the Thames in Oxfordshire, but Charlie was sure it was the River Cam near Ely.

Such pointless conversation dwindled the night away. Eventually, as the candles reached the limit of their wax, the young boys climbed into their warm, soft beds, each of them knowing this would be their last pleasant night for some time, if not their last night on Earth of their short-lived lives.

Chapter 6

The march back to the front line had been much quicker than when they'd pulled out. The weather was once again favourable, and morale had returned to the battalion. In step and singing boisterously, they went, with a Union Flag flying brilliantly in the spring breeze for all to see.

The clues of the coming battle became apparent as they got nearer to their trenches. Thunderous roars were rolling a storm on the eastern horizon, and the main barrage wasn't even due to start until later that evening. The boys could feel their heartbeats against their chests. Fear and excitement played through their emotions like a joker whose face couldn't be read.

"This is gonna be a big one," Arthur commented to Charlie as they marched on. "I can feel it."

"Rumour has it this could be it, the breakthrough we've been waiting for," Charlie replied.

"Over by Christmas! Remember that?" Arthur smirked. "All done and dusted before we get our chance, that's what they told us, didn't they?"

"Well, I'm glad we got to play our part." Charlie smiled.

They were given hot beef soup with half a white cob between two before entering the rear trenches. They had bully beef with them too. Some of them chose to eat everything they had, knowing it might be their last meal ever. Others decided to save it, knowing that they could be without supplies for a while. Many of the men had chocolate and other things that had arrived in their parcels from home. Arthur had his new gloves stuffed into his webbing so that when he needed them, which he was sure he would, they would be there at the ready. It gave him a sense of home comfort, as if his mother or Little Pimple were going into battle with him like a guardian angel perched on his shoulder.

Right on cue, the artillery laid down an enormous barrage. The unknown number of guns they had walked past had all lined up and were firing furiously. Now and then, a heavy cannon would fire directly over their heads, ripping through the air and shaking the ground as they stood waiting.

"I would not like to be on the receiving end of that!" Charlie remarked.

"Well, I fucking hope as many Germans as possible are on the end of each and every one of them!" Steeples replied as he force-fed himself another mouthful of bread. "I mean, I know that they have to do the same job as us, fighting for their king and country and all that but seriously, sod 'em. I don't give a hoot. I wouldn't give a single shrug of my shoulders if every German, Austrian, Hungarian, Turk, or Russkie suddenly dropped dead from some killer disease tonight."

"Russians are on our side, Jimmy," Arthur put in, rolling his eyes.

"I don't care, sod 'em."

"Have you ever met a Russian?" asked Arthur.

"No, but I knew someone who had," Steeples answered, "and they said that he was a right 'orrible bugger."

"So no then, you've never met a Russian," Arthur stated.

"No, when I worked on the underground in London, there was an engineer type fella, and he said he had worked with a guy who had been Russian," Steeples explained.

"Been Russian?" Arthur asked.

"Yeah, or had been to Russia. One of the two. Anyway, he said he was a right old bastard."

"Well," said Arthur, "it sounds like a right load of tosh to me. Sure, hate the Germans; you're fighting them tonight, so you've every right to hate them, and it's them that dragged us into this. But you ain't never met any Turk or Hungarian."

"Are you on their side?" Steeples asked angrily.

"Yeah. Why the sympathy for the enemy?" Charlie questioned his little brother.

"No, I'm not on their side, but why the hatred? You're off to go and kill a load of guys you ain't never met. Don't you have any feelings about that?"

"Nope. I ain't got a shred of sympathy for any of

'em," said Steeples, shaking his head and finishing off the last of the bread.

"That's why we're glad he's on our side. Now, Arthur," Corporal Lindsay put a hand on Arthur's shoulder.

"Yes, sir. I mean Corporal," Arthur answered.

"When we get out there tonight, you don't go showing no compassion. Them 'ere Jerry bastards ain't gonna show you none, so you ain't gotta show them none neither! You shoot to kill, and if you shoot a German and he ain't dead, then you fucking reshoot him. Even if he's dead, you fucking kill him again!"

"That's right, Corporal!" said Steeples. "That's what I intend to do. Do you think they give two hoots about you and me? It's them that dragged us here, and it's them that thinks they're gonna send us back to Blighty in coffins? Well, not me! I'm gonna be making a few more holes tonight, I tell ya!"

"Okay, Jimmy," said Arthur, looking him right in the eye, "I'm with you. I'll take down any German I see in my sights."

"Here, here, boys!" said Steeples, looking round to Burnham, Salt, and Charlie. "You with us, lads? Let's kill every single one of 'em!"

"Every single one of 'em," Charlie repeated. All six of the boys in the section repeated the sentence several times each and chinked mugs.

A few more minutes passed before Lieutenant Tyers and Captain Clark came over and told them to move onto their starting points further forward.

"Right then, lads. We're off," said Corporal Lindsay as the officers gave the signal. Another clumsy walk through several communication trenches led the men to the very front line, where the boom of the guns was matched by the explosion of the projectile it had fired. They were landing far too close for comfort. It was ceaseless and sobering.

The men lined up along the zigzagged trench. White paper markers fluttered on the sandbags of the firing bays, signalling where gaps in the barbed wire were so that they knew where to climb out. A machine gun nest lay a few feet off to their right to give supporting fire. Arthur couldn't understand it. It seemed to him that it was more likely to shoot most of their own men in the back. Then he remembered what Corporal Lindsay had said about Crimea and Waterloo, how you're just as likely to be killed by your side. The thought made him shiver.

The sun had gone down without Arthur noticing. His mind was too fixated on the imminent task at hand.

"How long we gonna stand here for?" Charlie asked.

"Till the guns stop firing, I guess," came his younger brother's unhelpful reply. The waiting seemed endless. It was a warm evening in the middle of May. Standing there, waiting, made most of them sweat. Minutes seemed like hours, and the anticipation had become unbearable for some. Arthur noticed one boy standing alongside the others, rifle at the ready but shaking almost uncontrollably. The poor boy's eyes were closed, and he was whispering something inaudible to himself. Another voice cried out impatiently, "Come on; let's get on with it!"

"Silence!" came an authoritative shout. More minutes passed, and Arthur decided to lay down his rifle and put his gloves on. After all, he might not have time to put them on once he got out there, or he might get wounded or lose them and have to go home having never worn them. Then came the sickening thought of a German taking them off him. His mother and Little Pimple would have made the gloves only for the benefit of the enemy.

"Are we going to be standing here all Goddamn night?" Charlie asked with frustration.

"I don't know, Trimmer; we're gonna be here 'til they tell us to go!" In turn, Arthur was frustrated by the question, not because his brother was annoying him by asking, but because he didn't know the answer. He didn't want to think about it. Finally, an order came.

"Fix bayonets!" shouted Sergeant Wignell, whose voice was unmistakable. "Wait for it, lads!" the sergeant shouted again.

"We've been waiting bloody hours. Come on, let's fucking go!" Charlie said to Arthur but not loud enough for the sergeant to hear him. Then the whistle went. Two more whistles joined immediately, and simultaneously, the whole body of men started clambering up the crude and untrustworthy ladders in front of them. Getting out of the trench was slow. At least four or five men managed to get onto the ladder before Arthur did, but eventually, it was his turn. He grunted as he heaved himself over the parapet, but the chorus of shouting from the charging battalion soon drowned out his voice.

The machine gun from the nest close by opened fire and tracer rounds flew over their heads into the blackness beyond. Arthur looked over his shoulder to search for a friendly face. He saw Charlie and Corporal Lindsay both bent forward, with bayoneted rifles aiming ahead of them. Hundreds of men poured through the gaps in the barbed wire and into the open field of mud, craters, and army clutter. Several flares shot up into the sky, which illuminated the entire area, and then, as if by clockwork, the whole of hell was let loose.

The air became fire as enemy artillery rained down amongst the British advance. Men scattered in all directions. An infinite amount of flashes, cracks, whizzes, thuds, booms, and rattles filled the field all at once, sending nothing but confusion through Arthur's mind and body. Panic-stricken and in shock from the sudden plethora of merciless violence, Arthur got down on the ground. Men all around him began to drop. Whether they were taking cover or if the enemy had knocked them down, Arthur couldn't tell.

Suddenly he felt blinded. Not like at Ypres where dirt had sprayed into his face, but the sudden and random inability to open his eyes. Whatever was happening in front of him, or indeed all around him, he didn't want to see it.

It wasn't long before the screams of wounded men joined the sound of shots and explosions. High-pitched squeals and pathetic cries for helpless mothers stabbed the night sky, which had become an inferno of blood and fire.

Arthur couldn't take it much longer. Lying there with his eyes closed and not knowing what was happening made him even less comfortable than he thought possible. He could smell blood. A body had landed next to him, and silently the dead man bled a warm lake of red which seeped through Arthur's clothes and onto his skin.

Arthur decided to go forward into the raging fire fight ahead of him. Having conquered part of his fear, he stood up, took hold of his rifle, and went forward, clumsier than a newborn calf. His legs were unable to carry him more than a few paces at a time. Again and again, he tripped on a body or an unidentifiable object, but each time, he got up and continued. Following his instincts, he jumped down into a shell crater where he could see a few British heads bobbing up and down in the light of the flares.

Two of the men turned to look at Arthur. He recognized neither of them, and they instantly seemed to forget he had joined them.

"There, right there!" one of them said, spotting the enemy. The two other men fired in the direction he was pointing. Then one of the men with a rifle turned round and looked Arthur in the eye.

"Arthur!" he said. The face looking back at him was

covered in sweat and mud, and it took a while for Arthur to realise who it was.

"Jimmy!" Arthur said.

He had stumbled into the same shell hole as Steeples, a minor miracle considering the number of soldiers and craters.

"Every single one of them, Arthur, remember?"

"Every single one of them!" Arthur replied. He stood up and checked his weapon—loaded and ready. He lifted his head above the lip of the crater and aimed. They were very close to the German trenches—less than twenty yards. Hundreds of thousands of flashes made themselves visible to the small group of men, who seemed unnoticed. Arthur squeezed the trigger and fired. There was no telling where the bullet went. He fired again, reloaded, and fired again and again. He crouched back down in the hole and grabbed hold of Steeples.

"What are we supposed to do?"

"Kill the bastards!" Steeples shouted back.

"We're supposed to be taking the ridge! We haven't even got to their front trenches yet! Where are the rest of us?"

"I don't know," cried Steeples, taking another shot. The noise of battle didn't seem to die down at all. Any signs of an advance had disappeared, though. Shells were falling in front of them, and the familiar screech of metal tearing the sky was dominating.

"That's our artillery!" Steeples shouted. The other two soldiers in the hole with them also got down.

"Let's go back!" one of them suggested frantically.

"No, we're too close to the Germans; they'll see us. We need to wait for the fighting to stop and crawl back in the dark when they're not looking," Arthur said.

"When they're not looking? They're always looking!" the other man cried. "Look, I don't know who you are, but I'm going back; you can stay here. I'll tell your mother you love her very much!"

With that, the two soldiers scrambled out of the hole, and Arthur never saw them again. He liked to think they had made it, but he would never know.

Arthur tried to tap his fingers together in time with the shells landing ahead of him towards the enemy. Eventually, there were just too many, and he couldn't keep up. He tried blinking his eyes lids as fast as he could, but it was useless. Lying there in an open crater alongside Jimmy Steeples, Arthur felt a deep sorrow. Sooner or later, one of the shells was bound to hit them. He panted, knowing some had come close already. Maybe the Germans would counterattack, and then they'd be for it. They'd be spotted and shot immediately.

What would be better? Arthur thought to himself. *A shell directly hitting you so that you never knew about it, or a fatal wound so that at least you were prepared for the end and could say goodbye or get a message of love home before you went?*

Time went by, but still, death didn't come. Neither Arthur nor Steeples spoke. There was nothing to talk about. They'd have to shout to hear each other anyway, and the end of their short young lives was approaching, so Arthur didn't see the point.

Maybe we're dead already, and we just don't know it?
Arthur thought. *"Maybe I am a ghost, and my destiny
is to spend eternity in this hole being shot at by our own
side. Maybe I'll be hit thousands of times over and die
and re-die every day until the end of the universe.*

For Arthur, there was no belief in the afterlife. The
concept of a great creator preached about in his
school wasn't something he had ever accepted.
With death being such an inevitable outcome in
this longest of nights, there was a sudden feeling
within him that perhaps there could be heaven after
all.

"Surely I haven't lived such a bad life that I might
miss out on eternity in paradise?" He whimpered to
himself. Arthur soon lost track of time. The second
barrage which he had so impossibly lived through
came to an abrupt stop. Each gun fired its last round
for the time being. The night sky lit up, and once
more, the sounds of machine guns, rifles, small
arms, and a thousand voices charging broke the
temporary lull.

"That's our boys!" Steeples shouted. "We're attacking again. We're doing it, Greeny, we're attacking
again!"

Soon after the second attack had begun, Arthur
saw dozens of British soldiers running past the shell
hole. It seemed that the artillery had done its job
and silenced the Germans, allowing the British advance to get across no man's land.

"Let's go, Jimmy! We've got to the Kraut front line.

Let's go!" Arthur said as he watched British troops dropping into the German trench. Steeples nodded and straightened his cap, making sure it was on correctly. The pair scrambled out of the crater. They were much closer to the German trenches than they'd both thought. After only a brief few seconds in the open, they reached the wire, which had plenty of gaps, and they both managed to slide into the trench safely.

The enemy front line was filled with their dead. Twisted and breathless lay hundreds of young, bloodied, and terrified faces with no ounce of life amongst them. It was almost impossible for Arthur to put his feet on the ground; there were so many bodies, limbs, and indistinguishable pieces of flesh and bone. He stared in awe and disgust as he discovered what happened to bodies on the wrong end of heavy shelling. The Germans had suffered the wrath of the British barrage, and it had ripped them up like a child playing with a piece of paper and scattered their entrails like confetti. Arthur removed his cap, pulled out his water bottle, and drank.

"Stay alert Private. I wouldn't get comfortable if I were you!"

Arthur turned around to see a captain who was filthy from head to foot in mud. He was panting and holding a wounded arm, which still gripped a pistol tightly.

"The Jerries are going to try to re-take this position soon; put your cap back on your head, and be ready!"

"Yes, sir," Arthur said. He stood up, put his cap back on, and saluted the officer. The captain saluted back.

"As soon as they realise that we've got this position, they're going to try to re-take it. Are there any other officers around here?"

"I don't know, sir," Arthur said, shrugging his shoulders.

"Maybe it would be better to fall back and let them shell an empty trench. We've not got the men to hold this if they try a counter-attack tonight." The captain spoke but not to anyone in particular.

He seemed to be uncertain of what to do. He stood thinking for a few seconds, and Arthur did not envy being an officer in this most critical of moments. He could see the position of responsibility weighing heavily on the young captain's shoulders.

"OK, I need a runner, any volunteers?" the captain asked. Arthur pretended not to hear him, and Steeples just shook his head bluntly.

"Okay, you!" The captain pointed at a private who was standing behind Arthur. "I'm giving you an order. You are to run back to our front line and give this to the first officer you see, do you understand?"

"Yes, sir," the horrified private said with a face like a frightened schoolboy about to receive the cane.

"Let them know that Captain Johnson of the 1st Battalion has the German front trenches but needs reinforcements urgently. We cannot hold this position with what we have. Ammo and men required, repeat the order back to me please private!" The private had turned green with the sickness of fear.

"Captain Johnson, with the 1st Battalion, needs men and ammo. We have the German front line but can't hold it," he said timidly.

"That'll do. Off you go. Good luck, Private, you may be carrying the order that wins the war. Now's your time to be a hero. Get going, lad!" The private smiled excitedly at the thought of such an honour, saluted the captain, and hastily climbed over the trench to make his way back across the battlefield to the British lines.

The boy had barely gone two steps when several bullets pierced his back and sent him to the ground in a heap. The pointlessness of this teenager losing his life so unfairly filled Arthur's blood with rage.

A grenade dropped into the trench and exploded, tearing apart the stomach and arms of Captain Johnson, whose eyes rolled back into his head as his fractured frame flopped and flayed to join the corpses of the enemy beneath their feet.

Arthur had no time to think. The German counter-attack had happened much sooner than he could have imagined and with no barrage.

Several German soldiers descended on top of the ill-strengthened, ramshackle British troops. Fist-fights broke out, and a battle of knives, clubs, spades, and any object one could get their hands on seized the brutal night. A German soldier in a yellowy-green uniform raised his rifle against Arthur's neck and pinned him against the trench's wall, choking him. The German screamed and thrust all of his strength into making sure that Arthur would die. Arthur felt his neck muscles tighten. He tried his hardest to use his arms against his enemy, but the German had the upper hand and was too strong for Arthur. Another German came from Arthur's left and started punching Arthur's ribs. He picked up a bayonet and was about to put it to Arthur's throat when a bullet went straight through his forehead. It splattered out the back of his head like a flower blooming in fast motion.

Whoever had fired the shot put his revolver against the rib cage of the German who still pinned Arthur against the wall.

"Nicht Schisen! Nicht Schisen!" the German screamed, but the revolver fired twice, and two bullets penetrated the German's side, forcing their way through the vital organs and out the other side. The German's screaming face scrunched into pain and sadness as it became apparent to him that his life was over. Arthur felt his neck become free from the force of the German's arms, and another body slumped into nothingness.

"Private Green?" The man who fired the pistol spoke. Arthur turned his head and saw Captain Clark.

"Captain Clark, sir?" Arthur said.

"Bloody hell, Private, where have you been?"

"Fighting Germans, sir!" Arthur answered as if it wasn't obvious.

More Germans dropped into the trench, but the captain and Arthur had a different idea. They weren't going to stick around to take on the entire counterattack alone. The captain aimed his revolver and sent another German soldier to an early grave. The remnants of the British soldiers in this forsaken patch of God's Great Earth either fought on to their deaths or scrambled out of the trench and sprinted into no man's land. While on the move, Arthur unstrapped his webbing, left his rifle, threw off his cap, dropped his water bottle, and ran and ran and ran. A million bullets must have whizzed past him, but not a single piece of lead entered his body.

On finding himself on the British trench floor, Arthur, breathless and exhausted, panted, sweated, and pleaded for a drink. Soldiers stood all around him, rifles lined up and ready. A whistle blew, and the troops who surrounded him climbed up the ladders, and again the British army sent more men into the onslaught. Arthur closed his eyes and screamed.

"Oh God, let it stop!"

The morning came, and with it, a thick, heavy mist that put the fighting on hold. An eerie silence drifted along the shell-shattered crevasses. Every so often, Arthur heard the whispers and mutterings of other soldiers in the trench. Then there were the clicks and flicks of one young boy opening an ammunition box and the scraping of a spoon on the bottom of a mess tin as another boy ate.

Arthur followed the trench system all morning, trying to find his unit. He searched until his feet could barely take the agony anymore, and as noon approached, he chanced upon a familiar face. It was Corporal Lindsay. Arthur hadn't seen him since going over the top the previous evening, and he was happy to find him unharmed.

"Oh my God, the captain will be glad to see you!" Corporal Lindsay said to Arthur. "Are you hurt?" he asked with genuine concern.

"I got punched in the ribs by some bloody German arsehole, but the captain shot him with his pistol. They hurt a bit, but I'm all right. What happened to you?" Arthur asked.

"Oh, you know, this and that. Come on, let's get you to the captain; he's going to be happy to see one of you Greens alive," the corporal said to a stunned Arthur.

"What?" Arthur asked and stopped walking.

"Oh, you didn't know?" Lindsay said, looking into Arthur's eyes.

"Didn't know what?"

"Your brother."

"Where is he?" Arthur began to panic.

"We don't know."

"Is he dead?"

"We don't know. He was with me when we went over the top, but I found myself lost and in the middle of a fight with the Krauts. I don't know what happened to him. But you've been reported as missing too, so he might show up."

"Right," Arthur worriedly replied.

"Come on, follow me," the corporal instructed. Arthur did not know where he was going, but fortunately, Corporal Lindsay knew the way. He led Arthur back to his companions, and they were both pleased to find Private Salt sitting on a box smoking a cigarette.

"Hey, another one!" he said. He stood up and shook Arthur's hand.

"We had you as missing at roll call; the captain is gonna be happy to see you, mate."

"So I've heard. Are you all right?" Arthur asked Salt.

"Oh, I'm okay. I ended up losing my rifle, though. I stuck the bayonet into a German and couldn't get the bugger out. Then so many of them appeared that I had to leave it! What about you?"

"Ended up being rescued by Captain Clark himself after I nearly got strangled."

"Still no sign of your brother though, Arthur," Salt said with sympathy.

"Yeah, Lindsay told me. He'll be all right; he's tough as old boots. Has anyone else from the company made it back?"

"Wignell is around somewhere, Clarky, Lindsay, you, and me. Others have started coming back in dribs and drabs, and we've probably got some wounded lying about. Bloody confusing last night, though, wasn't it? I didn't know where I was for most of it. Got caught in the middle of the lines desperate for a piss, so I just did it in my pants."

"Tell me about it. I was with Steeps for most of the night but lost him when the German counter-attack started. I hope he's ok," Arthur said.

Corporal Lindsay pulled up a kettle.

"Let's have a brew, eh?" They didn't attempt to hide the smoke from the fire that boiled the tea's water. The mist above the trench was so thick that one couldn't see more than five feet, and they were back in the reserve line now. Slowly but surely, as predicted, men from the company started to re-appear. The numbers soon reached the twenties. It was still not an impressive number considering there were one hundred and fifty to each battalion company when they had first left England. Half of them were left behind in the mud at Ypres, and now another large fraction of them was unaccounted for.

"Such a friendly sounding name, isn't it?" Arthur put across to Corporal Lindsay.

"What's that then?"

"Neuve-Chapelle. It sounds peaceful. I think it would be a pretty place if it weren't for the war."

"I think you're probably right," Lindsay agreed as he tended the boiling water of his mucky kettle.

Arthur thought about writing home. How could he explain Neuve-Chapelle? It sounded like they were on holiday in the countryside, not in the bloody, battered fields of the largest war the world had ever known. He remembered he wasn't allowed to say where he was anyway. He decided he would wait a short while before writing to his mother and Little Pimple until he knew for a certainty the fate of his missing brother.

More men were still coming back every hour as the day passed, but none of them were Charlie, to Arthur's ever-growing concern. He was just as glad to see that his friend Jimmy Steeples had somehow survived the fighting in the German trench, and just like Arthur, had somehow made it back to their lines alive.

"Oh my God, you've made it!" Arthur exclaimed. The two friends embraced each other.

"What the buggering hell happened to you?" Arthur asked.

"Well, after that officer sent that boy to his death and then copped it himself, a load of fucking Huns jumped us, didn't they?" recalled Steeples.

"Yeah, they did. I got strangled and punched, but out of nowhere, Clarky came along with a revolver and shot two Germans who were about to kill me!"

"You were lucky. I ended up head-butting one German, but he still had his bloody helmet on, and I cut my own head, see?" Steeples lifted the fringe of his scruffy brown hair to reveal a short but deep scar running along his hairline. "I busted him up good and proper, knocked him down and stamped on his neck. Don't know if he survived, but then there were Germans everywhere, so me and a couple of these Indian fellas legged it back. I ended up about half a mile that way with the Meerut division!" Steeples was laughing at himself as he told his story.

Just as the boys perched themselves on a broken crate, two stretcher-bearers came through carrying the corpse of a man. They put him down in front of the four boys and asked them if they knew him.

A clean-looking captain who obviously hadn't been involved in any recent fighting barged past the stretcher-bearers and scowled at the mud-covered boys, turning his nose up at their deteriorated state.

"Who is he, Corporal?" the captain asked as he pointed a long bony finger at Corporal Lindsay.

"I don't know, sir," Corporal Lindsay replied, shrugging his shoulders.

"Well, he's one of yours; he's got your shoulder badges."

"Do you know who he is, Private?" He said to Steeples. Steeples frowned back at the captain angrily.

"You what?" Steeples asked, deliberately showing disrespect to this desk officer who had never spent a day in the front line before. His uniform was smart, and even his fingernails were spotless.

"Excuse me?" the captain said in shock at this mere private's insolence.

"I said you what?" Steeples answered again and slouched further.

"I am an officer in the British Army! You will refer to me by my rank or by sir, and if you did not understand me or hear me properly, you would say, 'I beg your pardon,' not 'You what?'"

Steeples stood up and lit a cigarette. Arthur, Salt, and Lindsay watched silently to see what Steeples was going to say.

"You what?" he said for a third time, causing giggles from his on-looking friends.

The captain was going red in the face, but before he could burst out his fury at the private, Steeples attempted to redeem himself.

"I beg your fucking pardon, your royal fucking highness, but I can't tell you who this man is, can I? He doesn't have a fucking face!" Steeples exhaled the smoke slowly.

The officer looked at Steeples with real anger and wafted the smoke away. "HOW DARE YOU SPEAK TO ME LIKE THAT?!"

Arthur tried to suppress his smile. Steeples took a drag of his cigarette and sat down. Salt and Lindsay began chuckling at the insulted and embarrassed captain.

"Sir?" Arthur butted in.

"Yes, Private?" the captain said.

"Maybe I can check his pockets for his paybook or a wallet or a letter or something."

"I think that would be a good idea, Private." He turned to Steeples. "I see you're not all as stupid as this cretin, then?"

"Sir," Corporal Lindsay interrupted, "please forgive Private Steeples. We were doing a lot of fighting last night, and we're not altogether in the usual frame of mind. He didn't know you were an officer, sir."

"That man, what did you say his name was? Private Steeples will be punished. Discipline will win us this war, not scoundrels like him," the fresh-faced captain hissed.

Steeples threw his cigarette on the floor and stood up. He was more or less the same height as the captain, and he spoke to him somewhat sternly. "Beg your pardon, sir. But can I ask you how many Germans you've killed? I got three up at Wipers, I

went out on a wiring party last week and shot another one, and last night I've gone into battle and
had half my mates killed. I broke another German
bastard's neck by stamping my foot on him after I'd
knocked him out with my fucking head! It is men
like that me that is gonna win us this war. Not
poncey, fucking smartly, dressed twats like you, sir.
Go on, punish me. Let's see how many Germans I can
kill when I'm in the fucking stocks or some military
prison."

None of the boys could believe what they were
hearing. No one had ever spoken to an officer like
this before. The captain stood tall and stared at
Steeples, their noses touching.

"Private. Steeples. Those are the only two words
I'll be needing. Thank you, Private." The captain
squinted and smirked.

"His name is Private Matthew Burnham, sir," Arthur spoke quietly. The four boys looked at the
body of their friend. With no face and uniform so
completely bloody and torn, and with his body in
an unnatural position, it had been impossible for
them to tell who it was.

The unsympathetic captain turned to Steeples.
"Knew him, did you?"

Steeples didn't say a word. A solitary tear rolled
down his face, and his bottom lip started to wobble.

"I see," said the captain. "Well, take a lesson from
me - "

"Fuck off, you prick," Steeples said without letting the captain finish his sentence. Steeples walked

away, brushing shoulders with one of the stretcher-bearers. The captain stood with his mouth gaping open as he watched the private walk away. He looked back at the other three, who stood staring back at the captain in defiance. Nobody was laughing anymore. The stretcher-bearers, who had a look of guilt on their faces, carried the body away, and the captain followed.

The boys sat down again, and Arthur picked up his tea, now cold. A lump had grown in his throat, and tears began to fill his eyes.

Later that afternoon, Sergeant Wignell, looking weary with red eyes lined by thick black rings and with a husky voice instead of his regular strong boom, came and joined the boys.

"Steeps?" he said to Steeples.

"Yes, Sarge."

"Captain Clark wants to see you." Sergeant Wignell sat down and nibbled on a stale biscuit. He looked different. His eyes were deep pits of sadness.

"He wants to see you too, Arthur."

"Yes, Sarge," he replied.

"Come on, Jimmy, let's go."

They both entered the captain's dugout. Oil lanterns hung on the walls, giving ample lighting. It was tall enough for them to stand up straight in. There was a desk and a wooden board covered in blankets, which was the captain's bed. Hanging onto the walls with crude and rusty nails was a poster board. Rigid wooden beams made a ceiling strong enough to hold the ground above. Arthur's first impression was that the engineers had done a fantastic job of creating such a sturdy living space that could withstand the sheer amount of activity above them. It smelled somewhat, but there wasn't anything around in the trenches or above them that didn't smell, so it wasn't overpowering in any way. The boys stood to attention.

"Hello, lads," the captain started.

"Sir."

"Sir."

"Right, first things first. Arthur, your brother. He's still missing. I can't confirm his death without a body, but he's not yet missing, presumed dead. We've still got men coming in. Only God knows how many wounded we have managed to bring back. I can't write to your mother confirming his death. I can only say that as of this date, we are unaware of his whereabouts, so I would like you to do something for her."

"What's that, sir?"

"I want you to write to her, letting her know he is missing, but at least one of you is still alive."

"Yes, sir. I will write it tonight."

"Good, bring it to the dugout for censorship when you've done it."

The length to which his company commander was going to look after even his men's mothers inspired Arthur.

"And you, Private Steeples," the captain went on.

"Yes, sir."

"I understand you've been in some serious action?"

"Yes, sir."

"I understand you've been killing Germans?"

"That too, sir."

"I also understand that you called a staff officer by the name of Captain Godwin a twat and a prick."

"Yes, sir."

"What in the name of God almighty prompted such a reckless outburst, Jimmy?"

"I was tired, sir. I have been up fighting all night. Didn't mean to, sir."

"Well, that may be so," Captain Clark continued, "And as it happens, I know Captain Godwin fairly well, and I can assure you that he is both a twat and a prick, and he won't be seeing any more action than a second-line trench because his war is not about the front. It is about being behind a desk at General HQ. He'd been sent up here for the morning so that he can claim to have seen the front line and report on last night's action to our top brass. He's going back to them with reports that we have the toughest fighting soldiers in the world with the foulest of mouths!"

Both Arthur and Steeples were smirking. Captain Clark had seen the funny side of their encounter with the desk officer that morning, but he had to show that he would do something about it.

"So what am I to do? I don't have a single officer to work alongside since Lieutenant Tyers is now missing too, and all other officers are being called twats and pricks by my men. I'm supposed to punish such behaviour, but right now, we're entirely under-strength, and I need you here in the line. You'll probably both be glad to know that since we're somewhat short of men since last night, we won't be going into action for a while. Our orders are to remain in the reserve line until further notice. We have got fresh troops arriving, but our commanders won't try another advance until this bloody mist has gone. So, Jimmy, I'm going to do you a favour. You're going to be strapped to a wheel of a cart for only ten minutes this afternoon. I'm going to make sure that Captain Godwin sees you himself, and then I'm going to lie and tell him that you have been given two hours a day for twenty-eight days!"

"Thank you, sir!" Steeples replied.

"You're welcome, but let this be the last time I have to speak about your ill-conduct in front of our own officers. Save it for the Germans, boy!"

"Yes, sir, will do, sir," Steeples gratefully assured the captain.

"Right, dismissed, the pair of you."

"Sir."

"Sir."

Chapter 7

Three days after the disastrous night attack, the mist disappeared. Fighting erupted immediately, and it raged for countless days and nights. Arthur and his three friends took no part in it since the battalion was now so thin. They stayed to the rear and waited for an order to reinforce the frontline, but it never came.

There was a constant stream of wounded men who needed carrying. Arthur's only orders were to assist walking wounded to the rear. If the battalion couldn't fight, they were to find a way to be useful elsewhere. They found themselves often carrying a wounded man to the rear, dumping him with the others to be picked up by someone else later, and returning to the front trenches with ammunition or other rations. It was tedious work and not by any stretch safe. The threat of being killed by a stray shell or a German aircraft dropping something on them was a persistent concern. Helping wounded out of the line could easily result in one's death. None of them complained; it was merely part of the job.

An entire week passed before the atmosphere changed. Captain Clark came with a report that the advance on the ridge was over. It was becoming increasingly evident that success was not imminent and therefore, news that the attack had failed came as no surprise.

The piles of dead were mounting, and the lines of wounded were getting longer and longer. While carrying supplies to the front stations, Arthur had spoken to a few wounded men about the situation in the casualty clearing station they had seen. Arthur had never been inside one, but it sounded ghastly. Continuous rows of beds occupied by screaming and dying men. More casualties sprawled on the ground, filling corridors, window sills, kitchens, and washrooms. Ambulances of all kinds, mechanized or horse-drawn, went back and forth as if on a conveyor belt. Combined with the supply trucks and wagons going forward and men marching in long lines, it spelled disaster for the traffic. Many men were lifted out of the ambulances upon arrival and dumped straight onto piles to be taken away by those on burial duty. They had not been able to get there in time before they bled to death or their bodies shut down from the wounds they had received.

There were stories of bodies being slung from ambulances halfway through their journeys before the drivers pulled a U-turn to go back to the death factory that was the front line. There was no point in continuing to the hospital with a dead body when somebody else might stand a chance if they got to him in time. It made sense to Arthur, but it instilled a fear within him that if he were to die during this war, he'd rather not have it happen in the back of an ambulance and be lobbed on a heap halfway to the hospital.

He cast his thoughts back to the night of the battle when he had pondered about his own death while cowering in the shell hole. He concluded that he'd rather not know about his coming end.

"You don't hear the one that gets you!" went the common saying about shells.

There was still no sign of Charlie. Arthur told himself to hope for the best, but that was no longer possible. It had been more than a week since he had gone missing. Arthur hadn't received any mail from home since the parcel and letter they'd both received before the battle. He'd written the letter that Captain Clark had suggested he wrote and sent it with only a vague sentence mentioning that Charlie's whereabouts was unknown.

The very thought of his mother opening the telegram that told them of Charlie's death was enough to make Arthur cry. Blocking it from his mind was impossible. He felt strange about not being sad for his brother, who had presumably lost his life, but more for his mother, who had lost a son. At least if Charlie were dead, then he'd not know anything about it. Their mother would go through the rest of her life never knowing what happened to her eldest son, and Arthur doubted it was something that she would ever get over. Life at home would never be the same.

As May turned to June and the fighting died down, the battalion moved half a mile south to a large redoubt. The company meandered its way into an enormous breastwork fortification built of earth and sandbags leading on from the trenches they had just departed. Arthur was impressed by its size. There were tunnels deeper than anything Arthur ever imagined possible, filled with thousands of men who had made this their home. There were tables and benches with an adjacent field kitchen. In one corner, there was a bucket with holes, which one man was using to shower. Crudely erected camouflage netting protected them from aerial observation.

"Welcome to Lansdowne Post Redoubt lads," Captain Clark said upon their arrival. He gave them a brief talk about getting settled. Arthur had a look around and discovered the main trench going forward with a sign saying *Front Line This Way*. Underneath were two more notices that read *To Forresters Lane, Rue de Bois, Main Street, and Port Arthur*. He was happy to have a trench that shared his name. There must have been fifty other Arthurs in the London Regiment, let alone the entire British Expeditionary Force, but still, he felt it meant something to him personally.

Sergeant Wignell came in his usual unexpected

manner and, he told the men to be ready for inspection within the hour. The monotonous routine of making themselves presentable took place, and Captain Clark did his part in pretending the men were clean as they lined up in the redoubt. Clark instructed them to make themselves comfortable, as they would be here for some time. The 4th Battalion London Regiment were to swap shifts with the 4th Suffolks, who occupied the front line ahead of them, swapping places every twenty-four hours.

Their first twenty-four hours off had begun upon arrival, and therefore, on the morrow, they would be going to occupy the front line. While not occupying the front trenches, they would be put to work in other menial tasks just as they had been doing for the past week. Last, they were to be joined by some Indian troops from the Meerut division, which they would work with. The captain made a small joke about how the men must not act surprised to see that the troops from India would have a different colour skin.

Arthur spent a lazy afternoon in the redoubt, during which he decided to reorganise his pack. He found his paybook and opened it up. Inside was a photograph of his little sister, and on the back, he'd written Little Pimple, August 1914. Behind it were two more photographs, one of his mother and one of himself and Charlie on the day the company had their pictures taken. That was in January. Five months ago, it now seemed a lot farther back in time than it was.

Later on, Arthur joined his friends sitting amongst some rectangular hay bales to throw onto the trench floors if it were to rain. He sat down and let out a large sigh.

"I'm bored," he said

"Go fight Jerries then," Corporal Lindsay replied lazily.

"I'd rather.....Holy mother of God, what is that?" Arthur looked up, unable to finish his sentence. The four boys each sat up and stared in disbelief at what had just walked into the redoubt. A company of Indian soldiers marching perfectly in step lined up and then came to attention, facing right with immaculate timing upon receiving the order, standing to attention and then at ease. It was a perfect parade ground performance.

"I saw several dark fellas working on the underground, but what on earth is this?" Steeples blurted.

The Indians spread themselves around the redoubt after their officer permitted them to fall out. Two of them approached the boys. As one of the Indian soldiers reached out his hand to introduce himself, he said in a very thick accent, "Hello, pleased to meet you."

The four boys couldn't mask their smirks. The Indian stood with his arm stretched out, smiling, and Arthur couldn't contain himself.

"What's that thing on his head?" he laughed.

"How is that rag going to protect him from shrapnel?" Corporal Lindsay giggled.

"And what's with that moustache?" Steeples said,

pointing to the Indian's face.

The Indian himself simply stared and smiled at the boys laughing at him. His moustache was enormous and curled up at both sides. Many of the British had similar style moustaches, but it just didn't seem to suit this particular man's look for some reason. He had a thick bushy black beard, a khaki jacket, which was normal, but his trousers' belt went around the top of his ribs, just under his armpits, not in the typical place a belt would go around one's waist. The laughing went on for longer than it should have, and eventually, Arthur stopped and shook the man's hand.

"Hi, I'm Arthur."

"Do you find my attire amusing?" the Indian asked. The boys started laughing again, this time at the accent. They'd not heard one like this before. Arthur was familiar with Irish, Scottish, Geordie, Scouse, Brum, and his strong Cockney, but this was like nothing he'd ever heard.

Arthur shook the man's hand and stood up. It was only after Arthur stood up that he realised how big the Indian man was. He was taller and broader than Sergeant Wignell, who was easily the largest man in the 4th Battalion.

"When you came to my country, we laughed at you too," the Indian said.

"I'm sorry," said Arthur, "but what's that on ya noggin?"

"On my what?"

"On your head," Arthur said, pointing at the Indian's headdress.

"Oh, this is my turban."

"Can I try it on?" Arthur asked.

"No," the Indian said abruptly but with a smile. It took Arthur by surprise; he was expecting the man to say yes. An awkward moment passed between them, but still, the Indian continued to smile.

"Right, well, I'm Arthur, and this is Steeples, Salt, and our section leader, the right honourable Corporal Lindsay."

"I am very pleased to meet you. My name is Arshpreet. It means I love the sky."

"Why ain't you flying with the Indian flying corps then?" Steeples asked.

"I don't love it that much," Arshpreet said, still without breaking his smile. "Arshpreet is the name my mother and father gave to me on the day I was born. My friends call me Ash."

"Who's ya pal, Ash?"

"I'm sorry?"Ash said. "My Palash?"

"Yeah, your mate, who is he? He got a name too?" Steeples asked.

"Please forgive my rudeness, good friends - "

"We ain't ya friends," Steeples interrupted.

"I beg your pardon, but we are not enemies. The enemy is one which we share. You might not like me despite not knowing me, but to be side by side in the very same place against the very same enemy makes you my friend, even if I am not yours!" said Ash.

Arthur, Lindsay, and Salt looked at Steeples, who

had no comeback to the wise words.

"And my mate's name is Hari."

Upon hearing his name, Hari dressed exactly like Ash, stepped forward and shook everybody's hand.

"Would you like an orange?" Hari said, pulling an orange out of his pocket.

"Bloody hell, where did you get that?" Arthur asked in surprise. It had been a long time since Arthur had seen an orange. Plum jam was the closest thing to fruit he'd eaten for weeks. Arthur accepted the orange and shared it out. It was sweet and juicy, and they thoroughly enjoyed eating it. Ash and Harry joined the four English men on the hay.

"So Ash," Arthur spoke, "what brings you to this quarter of the globe?"

"Well," Ash replied, "it is an interesting question. You may or may not have noticed that there is a war on, and I, along with my fellow countrymen of India, have come to help you fight it! You can't do it on your own, you know!" Ash said, still with a grin. "Although we are a conquered land and we must bow down to his majesty King George, we also believe that the powers of Great Britain and France are fighting the good fight—in this instance, at least. We believe in democracy. It will do us no good to see our British masters simply replaced by German ones. Your army will train us to use weapons and master modern tactics. Then, when we have helped you win this war, we will turn on you and win our freedom. Does that answer your question, Private Arthur?"

"Private Green. Arthur's my first name," Arthur said, half-confused by the unexpected answer from his new Indian comrade. "Well, thanks for the orange," he said before shifting his attention back to his friends, who were all slightly baffled by what they'd just heard the Indian man say.

A night in the redoubt passed noisily as random shelling flared up and died down sporadically through until morning. Arthur had slept comfortably on straw and blankets, using his pack as a pillow.

After a typical breakfast of plum jam on hard white bread, washed down with a hot tea and powdered milk, the company was guided past the sign Arthur had observed the previous day that read *Front Line This Way.* All the men were surprised at how close the front line was to them.

They were even more surprised after Captain Clark allowed each man in the company to have a glance through a box telescope, and they saw how close the enemy was. It was less than sixty yards. Any German could run into the middle of no man's land, lob a bomb and be back in his trench before it exploded. Whoever was on sentry duty needed to be paying attention. Once more, the boys made themselves as comfortable as possible, finding whatever was available to sit on, and each man bagsying their places to sleep when night came.

"Officer coming through!" The boys stood to attention as Sergeant Wignell, ever faithful to his captain, had come to see the boys.

"Good morning, chaps." Captain Clark greeted them with a warm smile.

"Good morning, sir," they replied together.

"Bit of bad luck for us, I'm afraid."

"What's that then, sir? Being sent home already?" Corporal Lindsay joked.

"Well, I like your spirit," the captain said, understanding the joke. "But sadly, no. We have a bit of a job to do, direct order from regimental headquarters. They asked Major Burnett as the head of our battalion, who in turn asked me as the head of our company to do something, as we just happen to be in the line today. So, as I said, it's just bad luck."

"What's he want then, sir?" Arthur asked impatiently.

"Prisoners," the captain replied bluntly.

"Come again, sir?"

"Prisoners, Private Green, prisoners."

"Prisoners?" Arthur repeated.

"Prisoners!" the captain stated one more time.

Corporal Lindsay sighed and intervened. "Burnett needs prisoners, and we've got to go and get 'em. Right, Captain?"

"To put it plainly, yes, you do."

"And it can't happen at any other time or place; it has to be here and now. It can't possibly wait until tomorrow. Right, Captain?" Corporal Lindsay added.

"You are a smart one," the captain said sarcastically. "Now, I could have chosen other people to do it, obviously, but I need a team of people who have experience and are likely to get the job done and are least likely to be killed. Lindsay, you're an excellent section leader; Steeples, you're a great marksman; Salt, you are very tall and imposing; and Arthur Green has a knack for staying alive. So this afternoon, after you've had your lunch at about thirteen hundred hours, you're going to take a stroll across there, aim your weapons at a couple of unsuspecting Germans and bring them back. Our reconnaissance says that there's not a machine gun position directly opposite us, and the trenches are only lightly manned right now. Whole sections of the line have hardly anyone in them. One of our planes flew over this morning; maybe you saw it." Captain Clark had made it sound like a walk in the park.

"Just the four of us?" Corporal Lindsay asked.

"No, not quite. You're going to scare the shit out of the Germans by taking along a couple of those big Indian fellows."

"You fucking what?" Steeples rose to his feet.

"That would be 'You fucking what, sir,' Private Steeples," answered the captain. "Have you heard of a chap called Khudadad Khan?" The boys all shook their heads. "Well, he's an Indian chap. The name at least would suggest so, but he is incidentally the first Indian employed within the British army to have received the Victoria Cross. He got it back in October defending Ypres. The government now believes that given a chance, more of these Indians might be gallant enough to go seeking medals and help our recruiting offices in India."

"So we gotta take darkies with us, sir?" Steeples asked again.

"Private Steeples!" the captain barked. "Do you know how many people live in India?"

"No, sir. A lot, sir."

"That's right—a lot. Now we might recruit a few million if we can persuade them to enlist, and medals are now one of our tools to do that! The Indians will have a big part to play if we are to win this war, and I will not have you calling them 'darkies' or belittling them in any other way. They are of use to us, and you will respect them! Do I make myself clear?"

"Yes, sir," Steeples said, standing to attention.

"Their commanding officer has asked for four volunteers, and a man by the name of Arshpreet stepped forward, as he said he had spoken to you lot yesterday. He's quite keen to join you. He'll be coming through with three others, and the eight of you will get the job done. Have I made myself clear?"

"Yes, sir," the boys again spoke in unison.

Sure enough, at precisely twelve fifty-nine, as Arthur and the boys finished their last mouthfuls of bully beef and biscuit, four Indians shimmied into the trench.

"Hello. Do you remember me?" asked Ash.

"Yes, we remember you," Arthur replied. "Are you ready?"

"Oh yes, very ready, thank you. Here we go then, yes?" Ash said enthusiastically as he stood on the parapet.

"Whoa, hold your horses." Corporal Lindsay put a hand on Ash's chest, preventing him from going up any farther. "We gotta go through the plan, right?" The four Indians looked at Corporal Lindsay blankly.

"Sit down, lads," Corporal Lindsay instructed them. They all took a knee or sat on an empty box. "Right, you each gotta go with a mucker." The four blank expressions continued to stare at Corporal Lindsay.

"I'll speak plainly," Corporal Lindsay went on. "Right, we will go over in twos, ok? As soon as we get through the wire, we're going to spread out. Salt is going left, then me centre left, Arthur centre right, and Steeples on the right. We're going to be about three or four yards apart. Behind each of us will be one of you Indians. We must be quick, so we're going to run, and we're going to run fast. Straight through the gap in their wire, directly onto their sandbags, and aim your weapons. 'Hande hoch' is German for hands up. It would help if you had all remembered that they told us enough times in training. Do any of you have any questions?"

"Yeah," said Steeples. "What are these guys' names?"

"My name is Arshpreet. It is only the name my mother and father gave to me the day I was born; my friends call me - "

"Ash, yes, I know who you are; who are these clouts?" Steeples said rudely.

"My name is Aanand. I will come with you!" said one of the Indians to Steeples.

"Very well," said Corporal Lindsay.

"I will go with Arthur," said Ash.

"That's fine by me if it's ok with you, Arthur?" Corporal Lindsay asked Arthur, who nodded.

"I am Balram," said another, "and I will go with the tall fellow. He looks handy in a fight!" he said, standing next to the tall and lanky Private Salt.

"That means I am with you, Corporal. My name is Jaidav." The last Indian spoke.

"Right, now that we're all acquainted, let's get on with it. Silence as we go; we've got to surprise them and hope to God or whoever you guys worship that they aren't savvy to us before we get to them," Corporal Lindsay told them.

Lindsay was the first to go over, followed by Arthur, then Salt, and then Steeples. They each crouched and jogged past their barbed wire and spread out exactly as the corporal had instructed. The Indians did precisely as they were supposed to and followed accordingly. The enemy wire was close enough to make Arthur's heart pound.

The silence of the still air was far too eerie for his liking. They got closer to the enemy wire without a single shot being fired. There were no Germans on sentry in the enemy firing bay opposite them. As their jogs gradually turned back into a walk, they made their way through the easily spotted gap in the enemy wire. They got to the lip of the enemy trench, and all four of the boys lined up and knelt down as if it were a training exercise, pointing their rifles at the dumbstruck German soldiers below them.

The first three put up their hands in silence. Arthur counted the Germans nervously. There were four more to his left and another five to his right who had yet to respond.

He noticed how remarkably similar their trench was to his own. Mess tins, pots, and pans were lying around, empty crates and boxes everywhere. There was a pile of cutlery and a packet of playing cards on the filthy floor. Just as in the British trenches, straw was on the ground for when it rained.

"Hande hoch, lads!" the corporal shouted. The Indians appeared behind the four kneeling boys and immediately aimed their weapons into the pit below them.

"Germans!" Ash said as if he was shocked.

"What do we do, Corporal?" Arthur asked.

"Hande hoch!" Corporal Lindsay said more assertively. Two more of the Germans put their hands up, but that was it. An enemy officer moved a few paces forward, and with not a shred of fear, he raised a pistol and fired. The Indian on Arthur's right, Balram, took the bullet between the eyes and fell forward into the trench. Arthur squeezed his trigger, and a German who had refused to put his hands up spun around as the bullet hit him in the chest, sending a limb of blood reaching out as if to grab hold of something. As the body dropped, two of his friends knelt to help him. Steeples fired, and the German officer collapsed. No one else moved. Arthur thought this the most bizarre situation. None of the remaining Germans were holding weapons or even trying to reach for them, but they still hadn't put their hands up. They just stared at the British troops above them.

"Are they surrendering or not?" Arthur confusedly whispered to himself. The four boys with three remaining Indians behind them now faced the larger group of Germans, who didn't know what to do any more than anyone else. Corporal Lindsay pointed at the enemy with their hands up and spoke to them in German with a terrible accent. "Ein, zwei, drei, you three are coming with me. Come on."

"What do you want?" One of them spoke.

"You three, you're coming with me!" Corporal Lindsay spoke again, loudly and aggressively.

"We must come with you?" the German said again.

"That's right, pal. Let's get going, or I'll blow your fucking head off!"

The German spoke something in his language to the small band of soldiers before offering his hand to be pulled up.

"Ash, get this kraut out!" Corporal Lindsay ordered. The great big Indian put his rifle down and pulled the German up.

"Keep your hands up!" Arthur said to the German. "Hande hoch, got it?"

The German nodded.

"Good. Ash, get the next one," Corporal Lindsay

ordered again.

Once more, the giant of a man bent down and lowered his hand to pull the next German soldier out of the trench, but the German had other ideas. He grabbed hold of Ash and pulled him into the trench. As Ash hit the floor, the rest of the Germans standing around suddenly sprang into action. Two of them started kicking and beating Ash while the others grabbed their weapons. Arthur fired and hit a German in the arm. The wounded man went to the floor, holding onto his arm with blood seeping through his fingers. Salt and Steeples both fired, sending two more of them to their deaths, but bullets started coming back the other way.

Corporal Lindsay stood up, gripped the German by his clothing, and started dragging him away from the trench.

"Let's go!" he shouted. Arthur, Salt, and Steeples immediately turned and ran for their trench, forcing the German to run with them. The remaining two Indians carried on firing, ignoring the order to fall back.

Halfway across the muddy space between the two lines, Arthur turned round to see the two Indian men. One was lying down in front of the German trench completely still and probably dead, but the other was kneeling and had one hand in the air. Suddenly a bullet ripped through his body, opening up his sternum. His arm flopped, and he was instantly dead.

A few rounds whizzed past Arthur, but they had

managed to take the Germans completely unaware, and only a few of them had plucked up the courage to raise their heads above their parapet. A few yards ahead was Private Salt, and Arthur noticed him limping. He caught up with him, put his friend's arms around his neck, and helped him the short distance back to the trench. Corporal Lindsay and Private Steeples were already back with the one German prisoner they had managed to capture. Arthur and Salt slid into their trench, and Salt immediately lay himself down on the floor. Arthur bent down and ripped his friend's trousers open to reveal quite a clean wound. A single bullet had passed through his lower thigh, fortunately missing the bone.

"Well, Salty, I think you've got a blighty, you lucky bastard!" Arthur said. Quickly, two stretcher-bearers appeared as if by magic and carried Private Salt away. Arthur bade him good luck and ruffled his short hair, smiling. Salt himself managed a smile, but also tears were running down the sides of his face. He was clearly in a lot of pain.

Turning back to Corporal Lindsay and Private Steeples, Arthur caught the German's eye; he was in a state of total shock and fear. His eyes were wide open, and his hands were trembling terribly.

"What do we do with him?" Arthur asked.

Other members of the company had gathered round to take a glimpse of their prisoner. Some shouted insults at him, while others said they should empty his pockets.

"Back off, you lot. Where's an officer?" Corporal

Lindsay pushed two men away.

Captain Clark made a sudden appearance. "Aha! What's this then?" he questioned with a proud grin upon seeing the German.

"Dickhead kraut, sir," said Corporal Lindsay.

"I knew you boys would be up to it. Right then, he'll be sent off with the MPs if Sergeant Wignell can take care of that?" the captain said, turning to the sergeant, who was ever-present at his side.

"Aye, sir." Sergeant Wignell nodded.

"Escort him back to the redoubt and stay with him until the MPs arrive, got it?"

"Got it, sir." Sergeant Wignell turned to the German prisoner. "Right then, let's be having you!" He took the German by the scruff of the neck like a stray cat and dragged him off to the redoubt.

The captain turned back to the three boys. "Only three of you?"

"Yes, sir," Corporal Lindsay replied.

"Who didn't make it?"

"Salty got a blighty, sir. Medics already took him," Arthur informed.

"And the Indians?" asked the captain. None of the boys spoke. "And the Indians?" the captain asked again.

"The fucking Indians can't follow a simple order, sir. I told everyone to fall back here once we'd got our German, but they decided to keep fighting. All four of them are goners, sir," Corporal Lindsay explained.

"I see," said the captain. "I'm going to have to have

a written report, Corporal Lindsay. Are you up to that?"

"Yes, sir."

"Good man, you may use my dugout."

"Now, sir?"

"Now is as good a time as any!"

"Yes, sir."

The corporal and the captain marched away around the trench corner, leaving Arthur and Steeples still slightly lost for words at what they'd just done.

"Well, what do we do now?" Steeples asked.

"I dunno. Keep our eye on those ugly Huns, I suppose. They might come and try to get their man back!" Arthur guessed.

As had been expected by most of the men, the Germans stepped up their artillery fire. Unhappy with what had happened, the Germans had ordered some extra shelling. Arthur and Steeples kept their heads well down, both of them taking what shelter they could in the corners of the trench whenever a shell landed. Most of them hit the ground on either side of the trench, but the shrapnel shells were of danger to the men here, bursting thirty feet above the men and sending hundreds of metal pieces towards the ground at hundreds of miles per hour. They received very few casualties for the number of shells fired at them. Only two or three more men needed to be carried off by stretcher-bearers, who Arthur thought were doing a splendid job.

The shelling came to an abrupt ending late in the afternoon. After a minute or so of silence, there was an almighty bang, and the earth shook. The men of A Company turned towards the giant charge. They were deafened and awed by the boom's enormity, which took several minutes before the smoke and dust settled. That was the last of the shells. Nothing more came after that. Later in the evening came the sad news that the massive final blast had been a direct hit from a giant forty-two-inch shell that almost wiped out D Company. The single explosion had caused twenty-seven deaths, twelve wounded, and a section of the line so severely damaged that its remaining occupiers had no choice but to abandon it and dig a new trench around the back of the crater which had emerged.

"And then there were three," Corporal Lindsay said as he sat back down in the redoubt the next day.

"Salty'll be on a train home in a few days, no doubt," Arthur said.

"Lucky bastard. Let's hope he doesn't get gangrene," Steeples added.

"Well, the wound was clean. I saw it. The bullet went through one part of his flesh and straight out again. One hole, no bits of the bullet left in his leg."

"Maybe he'll be back then?" Steeples asked.

"Not if he's got half a brain, he won't," Arthur answered.

Sergeant Wignell appeared and joined the three boys. "All right, chaps. Anyone fancy a cigarette?"

All three of them obliged. "I took 'em off that German bugger you lot got yesterday. A little bird told me that he's been completely useless an' all. Poor sod doesn't know anything. Just that he's a Prussian, and he's part of a dismounted cavalry regiment. He doesn't know where he is, where he's been, where he's going. The bugger didn't know what had hit him. Still, he's a lucky bugger. He'll sit out the rest of the war. He's a survivor!"

"Well, if you think I'm going again, Sarge, you better think twice. Someone else can go next time," Corporal Lindsay told the sergeant.

"Hey, don't you worry. We're going to sit tight in this quiet sector for a while. Battalion's got no strength left. Even less since D Company got clobbered for a six yesterday."

Arthur sat smoking his German cigarette and watching a group of clouds as they formed strange and amusing shapes. One of them was just like a German helmet, and the other seemed to be the face of a monkey. He hoped they might merge so that the monkey would wear the helmet, but as the clouds moved, the shapes turned into other things.

"Oh. My. God!" Corporal Lindsay sat up, wide-eyed.

"What is it?" asked Arthur, still fixating on the clouds.

"Look who it is!"

Arthur lowered his head and put his hand over his eyes to shade them from the sun, forcing its way through the clouds. "What? You can't be serious!" Arthur said. He stood up. "How on God's green

Earth…?"

"Hello, Private Arthur!" Ash said with a smile on his face, which was complemented by several bruises and red eyes where the whites should be. Steeples was yet again dumbfounded, and Corporal Lindsay just gawped at the big Indian in total disbelief.

"Don't worry. I am not a ghost!" Ash said.

"I don't know what to say, Ash!" Arthur exclaimed. "How are you not dead?"

"Yes, you certainly left me for the wolves!" Ash answered him, still smiling.

"How did you get here? What? I'm in shock, mate!" Arthur spoke with genuine conviction.

"Well, after you ran away, I was beaten by the Germans, but they didn't kill me. Then I managed to convince them that I am from India, and many of us want to overthrow our British masters and desert to the other side. I told them that if they allowed me to come back, then I would persuade many more Indian soldiers to cross over to their lines tonight to join the fight against Great Britain."

"And they believed you?" Arthur asked.

"These Germans are not so clever!" Ash started laughing, and the others listening to his story joined in.

"I say we should have a drink to that!" said the sergeant, who pulled out a bottle of rum from his pack and passed it around.

"Unless, of course, your real intention is to desert tonight with a load of your cronies?" Steeples questioned the giant of a man.

"Do not worry, my friend, if indeed we are friends now. I will be by your side all night!" Ash said with a warm smile. Everybody, including Steeples, was glad that Ash was alive. They spent the night in the redoubt quite comfortably in the warm June air. It didn't get dark until quite late, and so under the circumstances, they did enjoy it the best they could.

Chapter 8

By the middle of June, the nights were long, and the sun rose earlier each day. Arthur was awake at four o'clock every morning, unable to sleep in the light. Wooden beams had been shoved into the earth a few yards apart across the top of the trench. The men had used whatever covering they could get their hands on, including their clothing, to keep the daylight out, but it was very ineffective for the most part. Covering the trench tops was useless for sentries and inconvenient should they be attacked.

The front line trenches had been receiving very little attention from the enemy, who were only sixty yards away. The 4th Suffolks were removed from the line to another theatre of operations, which meant swapping shifts every twenty-four hours hadn't happened. The trench slowly turned into something the men called home.

It was typically a messy place to live, with mud being inescapable and the typical erosion taking place whenever it rained. The soldiers hadn't helped themselves, either, making the area more comfortable. Arthur didn't see the point in cleaning his cooking equipment. He would only use it again in a few hours, anyway, or someone else would likely use it after him. The same went for his boots, overcoat, khaki jacket, and pretty much all his worldly possessions. He had found a pair of spectacles that someone had left on top of a loose sandbag for at least three days. It was clear that they no longer belonged to anybody, so he wiped them and used the lenses to spread jam onto his bread. His knife was dirty, and the effort to fetch clean water, a rarity, was too much hassle in any case. So a clean, smooth piece of glass would suffice.

Offensives were taking place elsewhere in the war, and most of the battalions in this sector were too under-strength to be used in any attack, so sitting here watching the line was their only role. Therefore, Arthur found himself spending days on end at the front and never knew when he would be pulled back to the redoubt or the safety of the rear.

He drifted in and out of homesickness. As news of his brother still hadn't materialised, Arthur spent a lot of time thinking about home. A newspaper had arrived informing the men of zeppelin raids on London, German u-boats sinking an American passenger liner, and British soldiers fighting in lands they'd never heard of.

He remembered being in his classroom back in London and staring at the huge world map on the wall. England seemed very close to France, but that's not how he felt. He belonged to a different world now. A world where everybody lived underground. A world where mothers no longer existed

except in the backs of people's minds and in parcels
and letters from places that were becoming distant
memories. A world of strange and intoxicating
smells, harrowing sights of death and desolation.

Another day at the front had begun in the usual
fashion. After about an hour and a half of actual
sleep, Arthur had sat up from his cubbyhole, which
was cramped and protected by a border of half a
dozen sandbags. He rubbed his eyes, covering his
cheeks with more mud, and sat up. Sergeant Wignell
sat opposite him, already awake and splashing
brown water over his face from an empty ammunition box. Arthur leaned over and took a handful of
water and sprinkled his face.

"Cheers, Sarge," he said. "What we doing today
then, Wiggers?"

The sergeant shrugged his soldiers. He looked awful. He was dirty, smelly, and continually scratching
himself, as he'd become infested with lice. All of the
boys had lice living with them, but it had been
pointless to fight a war against them. After a few
days of trying to kill them, they stopped bothering
and learned to accept it. They had tried all sorts of
techniques, from burning their clothes' seams,
smoking their clothes, and washing them in boiling
water. Steeples had even urinated on his clothes,
thinking it would poison the lice. It didn't work,
and he was just laughed at by the entire company.

"I don't know what to do today," the sergeant said
in a very croaky and dispirited voice. "We'll sit here

again, most likely. I'm going to take a working party for more food rations, and then I have a good mind to go over the top and end this war once and for all, all on my own."

Corporal Lindsay and Private Steeples had both woken up, but neither of them had spoken. They both sat up and did nothing.

"When are we going to be sent for some fucking rest?" Arthur asked. No one answered. Not even the captain or any of the officers were able to answer that.

A strange shuffling noise had begun above the trench, making their ears prick up. Strangely, a bird had started singing, which was something they had not heard for a long time. The shuffling noise became a little louder, prompting the sergeant to take a periscope and have a look. There was nothing out there. Just mud, a battered field, the enemy wire, sandbags, and several visible dead bodies that were becoming rotten in the summer heat.

"Nothing out there," he said as he sat back down. "Let's have another hand at whist. Who's in?"

Suddenly a big red onion flew over the lip of the trench and landed right in the middle of the four bewildered men.

"Who the bloody hell threw that?" Steeples also asked in a croaky voice. He sounded still half asleep.

Then came another one.

"It's raining onions, Sarge!" Arthur said.

"Don't touch them, lads!" Sergeant Wignell warned. "Jerry might have poisoned them. Harry

Hun is up to something!" He stood up and gestured everybody to keep still and be quiet.

Arthur looked for his rifle and prepared himself mentally for an imminent fight. His fighting equipment was behind him. He quickly took himself through the motions if there were an attack— rifle, and ammo with webbing and a trench club. *Where's my bayonet?!* the voice inside his head asked.

"Englishmen!" a voice drifted over the field.

"What was that?" Steeples asked.

"Quiet, lads!" the sergeant replied, gesturing everybody to stay still.

"Hey, English!" came the voice a second time. Sergeant Wignell looked through his periscope. This time he saw a hand waving, and the voice came again.

"Hey you, English!"

"A German officer is waving at me! Get your rifles ready, lads," Sergeant Wignell instructed. There was a sudden scramble for equipment. "Corporal Lindsay, alert the rest of the company. Get everyone up now! Get the captain!" Sergeant Wignell ordered.

Lindsay picked up his rifle, checked that he had it loaded, and stumbled through the trench waking everyone up. Most of their first words were unpleasant obscenities aimed towards the poor corporal, but as soon as the men realised why he was waking them, they all jumped up and reached for their weapons, whether they were appropriately dressed or not. Some of the men had flung their jackets onto the beams, and some were not wearing their boots.

"Fix bayonets, everyone!" Sergeant Wignell ordered. Arthur still couldn't find his. From the direction of the waving hand came another onion flung by a different body.

"What the devil is going on out there? What are they up to?" Sergeant Wignell asked himself as he continued to stare into the slanted mirrors of the periscope.

Captain Clark appeared behind him. "Mind if I take a look, Sergeant?"

"Not at all, sir."

Captain Clark saw the German waving. "What are the bastards doing now?" he asked.

"They've thrown some onions at us, sir," Arthur told the captain.

"Onions?" he asked in reply.

"Yes, sir, onions."

"Ammunition must be low for them if they've resorted to using onions!" the captain commented. "I think they're trying to make contact." The captain stepped down from the firing step and handed the periscope back to the sergeant. "Any of you chaps got anything white?"

"Got my pantaloons, sir!" Arthur asked.

"Not that!" Captain Clark replied. "OK, give me something I can wave; what's this?" He grabbed a jacket that belonged to somebody, presumably, and stood on the firing step again. He waved the jacket and shouted. "What do you want, Fritz?"

"Englishmen!" came the voice again.

"Yes, we're Englishmen. What do you want?"

"Please don't shoot at us!"

"You do know we're at war, don't you?" the captain shouted back, bringing everybody in the company to grin at his humorous remark.

"Yes," replied the German officer. There was a long pause in the exchange of words.

The captain turned back to his men and shrugged his shoulders questioningly. "I have no idea what they want!" He shouted back at the German again. "I'm obliged to shoot at you! You're my enemy, and it's not Christmas!"

"Yes!" the German replied. "Please don't shoot me. I'm going to stand up. Do you promise not to shoot me?"

"I can promise that, but I doubt my men will!" The captain made everyone in the trench chuckle. Arthur knew the captain was only toying with the German, but he also understood that the German officer had no chance of understanding the joke.

"Are you an officer?" the German asked.

Captain Clark did not like that question, and he pondered for a while before answering.   "Yes," he answered reluctantly.

"I am also an officer. Please order your men not to shoot me."

"Just you? Or can we shoot your men?" The captain continued playing games with his German counterpart.

"Please don't shoot anybody!"

"Not going to win this war if we don't shoot you,

are we?"

"I'm not going to shoot at you!" the German shouted.

"Well then, why don't you go back to Berlin?" the captain asked once again, making everyone behind him smirk.

"I'm sorry, I do not understand you," the German officer shouted.

"If you're not going to shoot at us, then you might as well pack your bags and go back to Berlin."

"I'm not from Berlin. I'm from Cologne!"

Captain Clark realised that the German didn't understand that he was being toyed with.

"Right. We won't shoot you." the captain shouted back before turning to Sergeant Wignell and telling him to make sure nobody fired at the German officer.

"Here I come," the German shouted.

Captain Clark stood up on the parapet and raised his head. "If they shoot me now, please don't tell my mother I died a fool!" he said. He watched the German officer, who was filthy and weary-looking, walk past the barbed wire and right up to the first layer of sandbags.

"Good morning. I am Major Badstuebner," the German introduced himself politely.

"Captain Clark. 'Tis a pleasure on this fine summer morning. I think these belong to you," the captain said as he tossed an onion towards the German major.

"Danke. I mean, thank you. Is there a place we can

talk as officers? Away from the men?"

"Certainly not!" the captain remarked sternly. "My men are only in this because of you, and whatever you have to say to me, you can say to my men."

"Fine. Good morning to you all." The German nodded towards Arthur and the rest of the company, who were still poised for action, rifles ready. They were nervous. Except for Arthur, who'd met a German officer at Ypres, this was the first time the men had spoken with a German. They were a little surprised at how civilized the man was. They'd come to expect nothing but barbarity from the foe they'd been facing for months now. These were the people that had killed their friends and disrupted their peaceful, happy lives. They all stood nervously, wondering what was going to come out of his mouth next.

"I have a proposal for you Englishmen, and I hope you like it," Major Badstuebner added.

"Go on," Captain Clark prompted the German to continue.

"We, on the other side, are getting a little bored. Your attack in this area has failed. We are fighting Russians, too, so we won't be attacking you until we have finished with them. We must take advantage of the warm weather to the East."

"Is that not information which your superior officers would rather you didn't share?" Captain Clark asked.

"Possibly," Major Badstuebner answered.

"So as you've noticed, we're not attacking you, and

you're not attacking us. We're going to sit here in-
definitely until one of us cracks. What's your proposal?" the Captain asked, although he had already
guessed what the German Major was going to say.

"A truce."

Captain Clark had guessed right.

"We won't shoot you, and we won't order any artillery on your position here if you do the same for us.
Would it not be a nice break from all this misery if
we could go for a walk? We are a little tired of looking at the mud and the sky every day," the German
major admitted.

"A walk?" the captain asked. He turned to look at
his men, unsure if they were puzzled or if they liked
what they were hearing.

"Sergeant Wignell?" Clark called out.

"Yes, sir."

"Aim your rifle at this major's head. If something
happens to me, kill him. Steeples, Green, Corporal
Lindsay, you do the same, please. I'm going for a
walk."

"Yes, sir," they all replied.

Arthur raised his rifle and pointed it straight at the
major's forehead. The major looked back at him,
and Arthur smiled. "I would love to plug an officer,"
he said to the German.

"That will not be necessary," the major hastily replied. The two officers walked side by side into no
man's land.

"Your English is excellent; may I ask where you
studied?" Captain Clark thought a good compli-

ment would be a perfect way to break some more of the ice between them.

"I studied at university in my home town of Cologne, but most of my English was taught to me by a teacher in Vienna. He was a clever man who understood Italian and French and said his next language would be one of the countries to the North. Perhaps Swedish or Norwayish."

"Ah, it's Norwegian," Captain Clark corrected him.

"Norwegian—you see, my English is not perfect. But I travelled around quite a lot, and your language came in very useful. Your empire has had quite an impact on the world, I can tell you."

"That's not likely to change either, is it? You can't win. You're taking on the largest empire the world has ever known. And the French and the Russians, both powerful countries too." The captain began to feel at ease. It was clear the German was sincere in his quest for a truce.

"Well, we must leave that to kings and tsars."

"If not for them, we wouldn't be in this mess. If your Ferdinand hadn't tried to take control of the Serbs, we might have peace throughout the world," the captain was quick to respond.

"Well, actually, he was an Austrian. They are our allies, the same as the Muslims attacking your armies in Palestine. Also, we've heard the news of a British failure at Gallipoli. Do you think your vast empire can take on three empires?"

"We've got the Anzacs, Africans, Indians, and the Canadians."

"Yes, but the Americans will not commit," the German major said, raising his index finger.

"They will if you keep sinking their ships!" Captain Clark was again very quick with his comeback.

"It's a war. Accidents happen. Americans are only interested in money. However, they won't spend many millions of dollars, as they would need to send men to die for England. They're still annoyed at you for burning Washington," said the German major. The captain knew he was talking to a very well-educated man.

"That was a hundred years ago. Times have changed. We've got more in common with them than you and your kaiser."

"Yes, the kaiser. He's your king's cousin, is he not? It would be best if you were supporting us against those Russians. And the French? Your history with the French goes back how many years?" The German again displayed an array of knowledge which both impressed and stumped Captain Clark.

"Hundreds, but we've had no feud with them since we sent Bonaparte packing. We were allies in Crimea against the Russians, and do not forget that our king is also cousins with Tsar Nicholas."

"Queen Victoria would be—what's the phrase in English? Turning in her grave if she knew that our great nations were slaughtering each other like this."

"OK, Major, enough. What about this truce?" Captain Clark said, changing the subject quickly.

"We will fire a machine gun from that position over

there randomly between three o'clock and five o'clock every day, the German major said, pointing towards his front line, which they were walking towards. "We will also throw some bombs into some of these craters too. Keep your heads down."

"Fine, we will do the same between one o'clock and two forty-five. That gives a fifteen-minute changeover. But Major, how do I know you're going to keep your word? I want to be able to assure my men that they will be safe," Captain Clark questioned.

"I need the same assurances from you, Englishman! I think we are just going to have to trust one another," came the German's somewhat unsatisfactory answer.

"So be it. We will aim at the trees behind you. Then it's over to you. The rest of the time, it's a ceasefire."

"Very well," Badstuebner agreed.

"Good luck, Major," Captain Clark said.

"And good luck to you, Captain."

The two shook hands and gave each other a look which made it clear that neither fully trusted the other. Captain Clark hadn't realised that he had wandered almost to the German trenches. He could see German soldiers lined up in the trench, occasionally peering over enough for him to see the whites of their eyes. He had a look beyond the front trenches into the forest behind them. He could see firsthand the damage the British shelling had done. The forest was in a terrible state, with barely a tree left untouched. Long stumps stood in defiance of their human destructors, while nothing else could live through such ferocity.

On turning round, he began to walk quite slowly and calmly back to his front line, and it dawned on him that he had been walking amongst dead men for the past few minutes without even realising it. Death had become so much the norm that it now went unnoticed. At least the truce would be an opportunity to clear them. That's what he would tell his commanding officers if they asked him why the fighting had come to such an abrupt halt without orders from above.

Chapter 9

The truce which Captain Clark had negotiated with the German Major Badstuebner had held. It was now the middle of August, and for the past eight weeks, every day in the allocated times, there was sporadic gunfire and the throwing of bombs. For weeks A Company had barely taken a casualty and had only one death, a young Corporal Pearson who Arthur hadn't ever really gotten to know. One of the many thousands of unexploded shells had killed him after he stepped on it, totally unaware of its presence.

Arthur was sitting on the floor of the trench smoking a cigarette. "If it carries on like this, I'll be a happy man," he said to Corporal Lindsay.

"Maybe we really can just sit it out until it all blows over on some other front, and we can go home in peace, not pieces," Corporal Lindsay suggested.

"Well, who knows? We might all just give up, say neither side won, and agree to go home," Steeples said.

"It ain't likely. Too much at stake for the knobs at the top," Sergeant Wignell put in.

Arthur continued to smoke his cigarette and poked his head over the trench to look across no man's land. A German who had decided to do the same waved at Arthur, who returned the gesture with a smile. A feeling of peace and camaraderie drifted through the air. It was as if the war had just been a blip in their lives, and they could now all go home and continue to live happily. Arthur could sense no hatred coming from his enemy across the dotted, pock-scarred patch of wasteland dividing their worlds.

"This is my kind of war indeed," he spoke softly to himself. He turned around on stepping down from the parapet to see Captain Clark had come to join them. He looked at ease and greeted them with a warm smile.

"Good day to you, chaps," he said. "I've got some news." Arthur, Steeples, Corporal Lindsay, and Sergeant Wignell listened intently.

"I'm going on leave. I'm being sent back to London for a few weeks, and when I return, it will be with a new draft to bring the company back up to strength." He instantly received a few pats on the back and several words of sincere happiness for the man who had done his best for the men who served under him. He would certainly be missed out here in the dwellings of their underground wilderness.

"So, as a parting gift, here is a bottle of whisky I'm going to leave in your capable hands, Sergeant."

"Thank you very much, sir!" Sergeant Wignell said with a big smile, taking the bottle eagerly.

"We getting some new officers then, sir?" Arthur asked.

"Well, I need to talk to you about that." Captain Clark toned down his voice. "I'm to be replaced by a staff officer. He happens to be the son of a brigadier who is very close to our divisional commander, General Wilcox. So, as I'm off on leave, top brass wants to send him here in my stead so that he can get a bit more frontline experience. Rotten luck for you lot, really."

"Who is he then, sir? Do you know him?" Wignell asked.

"Yes, and so do these boys. His name is Captain Godwin!" Captain Clark answered. The boys exchanged tense looks with each other. They all remembered their encounter with Captain Godwin.

"You called him a prick, Jimmy. Do you remember him?" Clark reminded Steeples.

"Yeah, I remember him, sir," Steeples replied.

"And he remembers you, that's for sure. You've got to tread carefully with him. He's not seen action before. He might be a bit too eager, but at the same time, he might get bored and try to bully you. I won't be here to protect you. Any of you. Do you all understand what I'm saying?"

They all nodded and muttered, "Yes, sir" quietly. In truth, the boys knew that they'd been fortunate to have had Captain Clark as their company commander. Arthur would never forget how he had saved his life on the night of the battle, and Steeples suddenly remembered being let off lightly for his poor conduct when they had first met Captain Godwin. He had negotiated a truce that had kept them all alive, and now he was surrendering his whisky for them.

"Right, well, I'll be off then. I've got to hand everything over to Godwin this afternoon. Good luck, chaps. I will be back soon. Try to stay out of trouble!" He saluted his men, and they saluted back. Such formalities had been dropped in the past few weeks, but their respect for the captain had never faded. The mood with the entrenched men was already changing into an unwelcome resentment. The captain left, and Arthur looked at his watch.

"Nearly shooting time, Sarge," he informed Wignell.

"All right, I'll go give the nod to the machine gunners," Sergeant Wignell sighed. The machine gunners opened fire at the treetops behind the German trench and continued at random intervals for the next hour and three quarters. Arthur lobbed a bomb harmlessly into a crater. It was difficult for him to believe that the people at the top of the command chain still had no idea that in this sector of the lengthy lines of trenches, an agreement had been made with the enemy not to kill each other. At precisely three o'clock, the Germans started firing. Their bombs went off, and the sound of battle drifted pointlessly for nearly two hours.

During those two hours each day, the boys played cards. Whist was the usual game, but occasionally, they'd have a hand at poker. They'd started off playing for each other's money, but they'd lost count of who owed who what, and the chance of them getting their hands on the coin anyway never seemed to present itself.

At about ten minutes to five, Sergeant Wignell announced, "Officer coming through!"

The whole company, with mixed feelings towards a new commanding officer, stood to attention sloppily. They were dirty, smelly, unshaven, riddled with lice, and had dirty faces. Their breath was foul, and their teeth were turning brown.

"These men are dirty, Sergeant!" Godwin grumbled

"A true soldier to a man, sir!" Sergeant Wignell replied.

"A dirty soldier is not a good soldier. How am I supposed to distinguish who is who in battle when they all look alike like this?" Arthur stood to attention as Godwin approached him. The light brown-haired captain with a pointy nose and long dimpled chin was dressed with immaculate perfection. Arthur wondered how long it would be before he was also covered in dirt and stopped caring about his turnout.

"You," Godwin said as he stared coldly into Arthur's eyes. "We've met before."

"Yes, sir," Arthur replied.

Godwin turned to Steeples. "And you! Do you remember me, Private Steeples?"

"Vaguely, sir," Steeples answered, forcing Arthur to suppress a grin.

"Been killing Germans, have we?" Godwin asked Steeples.

"Not so many recently, sir," Steeples replied.

"Well, we'll have to remedy that, won't we? I'm to make a report on the situation this evening, which means you're going to go on a little patrol for me. I will stand here and watch how you kill Germans. Are those Germans I can hear firing now, Sergeant?" Godwin turned to face the big Sergeant Wignell.

"Yes, sir, that's German fire. Best keep our heads down if we want to keep them on our shoulders, eh Captain?" Arthur suddenly realised that this Captain Godwin, who sat behind a desk for the duration of the war thus far, had no idea about the truce.

"Nonsense, Sergeant!" Godwin spoke strongly. "Tell our machine gunners to return fire while these two, Steeples, and what's your name, Private?"

"Private Green, sir," Arthur replied.

"While Private Steeples and Private Green go on a reconnaissance raid. I'm going to make sure we win this war. Get your weapons and prepare for a combat patrol."

Arthur didn't know what to do. He knew that this officer was not one to be disobeyed, but at the same time, he couldn't break the ceasefire; it would be a death sentence for the entire company. Arthur had to think quickly.

"May I make a suggestion, sir?" he asked Godwin.

"You may."

"If we wait until it is dark, then we've much more chance of success." Arthur thought that to be a

smart way of avoiding what the captain was pro-
posing. That way, they could sneak across the field,
maybe even make contact with the Germans and
try to explain that they were going to let off a few
bombs just to please a new officer who wanted
some action.

"Well then, how will I see how you kill Germans,
Private? Seems like a poor thing for me to make a report on, does it not? What would it say? 'Two of our
boys attacked the German position, but I saw nothing and cannot report on how the attack went?' Absolutely not, Private Green, you're to go now in
broad daylight so that I can get a good picture of the
front for my report."

Arthur was lost. Steeples and Corporal Lindsay
were stood to attention, unmoving. Were either of
them going to say anything? Was Sergeant Wignell
going to tell Godwin about the unofficial truce?
Maybe Godwin would enjoy the fact that he might
be able to get through the war without being in any
serious danger. Arthur decided he would have to
come clean or the entire company would come
under attack, and they would have lost their lives
for nothing more than this ignorant imbecile to get
another step higher on his career ladder.

"I can't do it, sir!" Arthur told the shocked captain.

"What did you say to me?" Godwin thundered. His
long, white face had turned red with a mixture of
anger and embarrassment. A scruffy, low-born teenager had directly disobeyed his very first order on
the front line. Sergeant Wignell looked at Arthur

sympathetically, understanding his situation. The Germans suddenly stopped firing, indicating that it was five o'clock. Maybe Arthur could demonstrate.

"Let me show you, sir." Arthur looked at his wristwatch; indeed, it was five o'clock, so Arthur knew he would be safe. He turned around, climbed up onto the parapet, and lifted himself onto the top of the trench. In plain view, he could see the Germans looking at him without an ounce of concern for their safety, as they too felt protected by the cease-fire.

"What on Earth are you doing, Private? Get down, you're unarmed, and I've not given you the order to attack yet!" Godwin shouted. Arthur smiled and gave a thumbs-up to the Germans. Godwin stepped up to the parapet and cautiously lifted his eyes above the surface of the ground and could see the Germans who were not firing at Arthur.

"What is going on here?" he asked an aimless question.

"Watch me, sir." Arthur stood up fully and walked, unafraid, past the barbed wire and right into the middle of no man's land. Liberated by the peace that had descended, Arthur strolled on.

"He's going to be killed. Get ready with suppressing fire; tell the machine gunners to be ready!" Godwin barked. No one moved.

"Company, make ready!" he ordered, shouting. He turned his gaze back to Arthur, who was standing in no man's land, looking back at him. Godwin could not believe his eyes. There were Germans behind

Arthur in the open who weren't doing anything. They were allowing Arthur to wander freely. He looked back to the company and noticed that not one of them had their weapons ready.

"I ordered you to make ready. Who here would disobey an officer?" Godwin shouted. The men from the company started looking towards one another, not knowing what to do. Corporal Lindsay approached the new captain commanding the company.

"Sir, we have an arrangement," he sighed as he broke the news to Godwin.

"You've got a what?" he hissed, eyes wide open in disbelief

"We fire between one and clock and two forty-five. Then the Huns fire until five o'clock. After that, we live and let live."

"Give me your rifle, Corporal," Godwin ordered. But before Corporal Lindsay could offer the rifle to him, he had snatched it. With Arthur still standing in no man's land and more Germans starting to appear above ground, Captain Godwin stepped up to the parapet and aimed the rifle.

"Don't do that, sir!" Steeples begged.

"You're all going to be shot for cowardice, fraternising with the enemy, disobeying orders and treason, Private Steeples. Trust me, I'm going to do him a favour. His mother will receive a telegram stating the enemy killed him in action. Yours is going to get one that mightily disappoints her!"

At that, Godwin squeezed the trigger, breaking the

silence of the truce. Arthur jumped as the crack of the rifle rang out. His heart skipped a beat, and he turned around, looking towards the Germans, assuming they'd decided to shoot at him. They hadn't fired the shot, but one of their privates was on the ground, silently bleeding.

"Got the bastard!" Godwin exclaimed, pleased with his minor victory.

"Oh, you've done it now!" Sergeant Wignell pounced into life, taking the rifle from the captain and pushing him aside.

"Run, Arthur, run!" he shouted as loudly as he could.

Still in shock and confusion, Arthur jumped into a nearby shell hole, and what sounded like a thousand bullets, all with his name on them, flew over his head. "Shit-shit-shit!" he said to himself.

Sergeant Wignell took control of the company and ordered the machine gunners to give Arthur covering fire if he needed to run. Then the shelling started. The Germans had immediately ordered an artillery bombardment on the British position, precisely what Captain Clark had said he would do if the Germans broke the truce. Captain Godwin dived to the floor in sheer terror as the bombardment grew with intensity. There was no telling who it belonged to, but a forearm with a smashed wristwatch attached to it landed next to his head. He was unused to such sights.

Two Germans jumped into Arthur's shell hole. He immediately put his hands up and surrendered. He was unarmed, and it was all he could do.

"Tell them to stop!" he shouted at the Germans. They couldn't hear him. They just aimed their weapons at him and shouted incoherently in German.

After ten minutes, the shelling stopped. Still with his hands up, Arthur begged the Germans to let him go, but they couldn't understand him.

"Can I speak to Major Badstuebner?" He asked. One of them showed that he vaguely understood. "Badstuebner?" he repeated the name to Arthur.

"Ja Ja, Major Badstuebner!" Arthur nodded in fear. "I know Major Badstuebner." It was a lie; he'd only met him once, and that was weeks ago. Even then, he had pointed a gun in his face, but Arthur was in panic mode, and it was all he could think of to say.

"Kommen!" the German who had spoken said and gestured to Arthur to follow him. The other German grabbed Arthur's sleeve and dragged him along out of the shell hole, across no man's land, which had again turned eerily silent. He jumped into the German trench only a few feet away.

Several furious Germans gathered around Arthur. They spoke angrily to each other, and some shouted at him. Soon after, but still far too long for Arthur's liking, Major Badstuebner arrived.

"Are you the Tommy we just saw walking between the lines?" he asked, with no hesitation or introduction.

"Yes, sir," Arthur replied. "I was demonstrating to a new officer, not a very nice one, that we have this truce, and he didn't believe me, so I tried to show him, then somebody fired a shot, and I'm sorry."

"Your side broke the truce, which I agreed with your captain!"

"I know, sir, but we have a new officer. He doesn't know the rules," Arthur pleaded.

"One of my men is dead! Now I must write to his mother!" Badstuebner scowled angrily. Arthur tried his absolute hardest to appear sympathetic about the dead man, even though he had seen so much death in his few months at the front that he didn't have any sympathy at all. Especially for a German.

"I know, major. It's not my fault. I'm sorry. I was just demonstrating that we have this truce and that we will be safe if we keep to it."

"I understood you the first time, Private!" The German major was furious at the unchivalrous British.

"Green, sir. Private Arthur Green."

"Arthur Green," the major said as he stroked his chin in thought. "We have been enjoying this truce, Arthur Green. Do you think your new officer will agree to it?" he asked.

"I don't know, sir. We don't really know him too well. If we explain that Captain Clark had it arranged with you personally, then he might allow it to continue." Arthur had no idea how to answer the question, and so this was the best he could come up with. He was afraid. These Germans could rip him to pieces with their bare hands at any second, and from their point of view, they would justify it. Some of the other German soldiers had rifles pointing at his chest, and others stood with mallets and shovels ready to tear him up.

"Where is Captain Clark?" Major Badstuebner asked.

"He's been sent on leave and returned to London to bring back reinforcements for our battalion, sir. So we've been given this new one, Captain Godwin. He only arrived today, sir. He's arrived and not known our situation."

"Okay, Arthur Green, this is what will happen. Two of my men are going to be ready to shoot you as you stand in the centre of no man's land. You will request this new Captain Godwin meet with me in the middle of our lines. If he refuses, my men will shoot you and make sure your men see it!"

"That's an excellent plan, Major. I'm one hundred percent sure the captain will agree to meet you. I know he will. He's a British officer just like Captain Clark, sir. He was just unaware of what was happening, that's all."

After another exchange of words between the German officer and his men, two soldiers stepped forward and pointed their rifles at Arthur. They ushered him over the parapet and gestured for him to go forward. Arthur walked through the gap in the German barbed wire and into the cluttered mess of no man's land.

"That's far enough, Tommy!" Arthur heard the German major shout. Arthur didn't stop. He closed his eyes and continued to walk.

"I said that's far enough!" Major Badstuebner thundered. A warning shot rang out into the air, breaking the silence. The aimless bullet whizzed past Arthur's head, and he froze. Fear consumed him, and he felt the warm sensation of urine trickling down his leg. He could see the battered sandbags of his front line. There was smoke coming from his trenches where the shelling had been just a few moments ago. He could hear wounded men and a big commotion. He cursed Godwin and hoped he'd been hit.

"Call to your friends Tommy!" Major Badstuebner ordered.

Arthur didn't know what to say at first. "Hey!" he shouted through chattering teeth. There was no response.

"Hey!" he cried out again, more desperate this time as he felt the urine seep into his socks—still nothing. Inexplicably, the thought of Little Pimple popped into Arthur's head. He told himself there and then that as soon as this little episode was over, and he was safe, he would write home immediately.

"Hey!" Arthur called to his lines again. Thankfully, Sergeant Wignell's head appeared from behind the sandbags. He breathed a deep sigh of relief. "Sergeant Wignell, sir!" Arthur yelled at him.

"I'm not an officer, Arthur," Wignell shouted back, reminding him to stop saying sir. "What are you doing?"

"They want Captain Godwin to come and discuss continuing the truce!" Arthur replied abruptly.

"Speak up, Private. I can't hear you!"

"They're going to shoot me unless Godwin comes here to discuss the truce!" Arthur pleaded.

The wind had picked up slightly, and his voice, despite his shouting as loudly as possible, was carried away. The sergeant couldn't hear him. Arthur's eyes filled up, and he began to panic. He was sure that he was living his last moments. He thought about running for it, but he was able to prevent himself from doing so, knowing that he was more likely to be killed if he did. It would also mean an end to the ceasefire, and they would all have to go back to killing one another again.

"Godwin needs to come here, or they'll shoot me!" Arthur screamed but to no avail. It was clear that his words were failing to reach the sergeant. Arthur turned back to the German line. More of them had rifles aimed at him. On turning back to his lines, he saw Sergeant Wignell clamber out of the trench and make his way towards him.

"Are you hurt, Greeny?" the sergeant asked upon reaching Arthur.

"No, Sarge, I'm fine. But they're going to shoot me unless Godwin comes here to discuss a truce." Sergeant Wignell took a glance at the enemy trenches. He could see several men aiming their rifles at both of them now.

"OK, Greeny, sit tight. We'll get you out of this."

"Thanks, Sarge. I owe you one." Arthur smiled. "I swear to God, Sarge, if you get me out of this, I'll clean your boots every day for a year!"

"You and I both know that my boots haven't been

cleaned for weeks. You just take it easy now. We're both gonna get out of this, ok?"

Arthur nodded and was amazed at how terrifically calm Wignell was. The sergeant took a look towards the Germans and slowly called out to them. "I am going to get the captain. Don't shoot me! Understand?"

"I understand you," Badstuebner answered him. "But hurry up!"

As Sergeant Wignell turned to walk away, he whispered to Arthur, "Walk with me."

"What?" Arthur was not expecting this.

"Walk with me, and they'll think we're both going to get the captain. They'll be confused. Trust me!"

"No, they'll shoot me, Sarge!"

"No, they won't. They want a ceasefire. They won't get it if they shoot you. Come on!" the sergeant whispered impatiently.

Both Sergeant Wignell and Arthur started walking away from the German line and towards their own. Wignell was right. The Germans didn't shoot. They watched the pair walk away in the hope that they would return with Captain Godwin. As they approached the British front line, Godwin showed his face to the two young men.

"Stop right there! Not another step forward! What's going on, Sergeant?" he asked. Arthur and Wignell were stood still a few yards on the wrong side of the British barbed wire.

"They want you to go and meet with a German officer and discuss continuing the ceasefire, sir," Sergeant Wignell explained. "Please, sir, they have several rifles aimed at us right now. They will kill us both if you don't go and talk to them!" he explained again.

"You want me to go across no man's land and discuss a truce with the enemy?" Godwin laughed in disgust at the proposal.

"Yes, sir," Sergeant Wignell paced forward, and upon doing so, there was a fizzing sound and a few sparks from beneath his feet.

He had trodden on an unexploded shell. He knew it could go off in any second, and so did Arthur. Sergeant Wignell scoured the ground around him. He quickly saw a large piece of wood next to him that appeared to be from a broken wagon. It was as tall as he was and heavy, but the sergeant had enough strength to lift it and slam it down on top of the hissing explosive just in time.

The weight of the wood had the desired effect of suppressing the blast. The shell exploded, but although the sergeant was lifted high into the air, breaking both his legs and shattering his feet, Arthur, Godwin, and anyone else who might have been blown to smithereens were unharmed.

Sergeant Wignell landed awkwardly, dislocating his shoulder and breaking his clavicle. Arthur couldn't for the life of him understand how it was possible, but somehow, despite the injuries sustained, Sergeant Wignell was still breathing.

Arthur was able to crawl to the safety of the trench, dragging the broken body of his unconscious sergeant with him. Desperately wanting to continue the truce, the Germans hadn't fired a shot and Arthur was thankfully still alive.

Chapter 10

After another week had passed, they finally had a day off. Since the explosion that had taken Sergeant Wignell out of the war, there had been no serious action. The men from A Company could now rest, as they had been given a few days to spend back at the redoubt. Arthur and his two remaining friends, Steeples and Corporal Lindsay, requested a pass to visit the sergeant in the Casualty Clearing Station. They had gone straight over Godwin's head and requested the pass from Major Burnett, who permitted them to leave the front for twenty-four hours.

They were fortunate in being able to hitchhike a few miles on the back of a supply wagon that had been loaded with empty ammunition boxes to be refilled again back at some depot, which was miles behind the lines.

The driver had stopped the wagon at a junction, which was typically clogged with other wagons and troops and horse-drawn vehicles, and pointed them the way to Hazebrouck. It was a three-mile walk that went peacefully enough, although there was a constant stream of ambulances going towards the town, none of which would give them a lift.

The town was small but bustling with life. It

was also a typical layout with a traditional market-place in the square, a church with a clock tower, a town hall, and a school. British soldiers who were on leave filled the cobbled streets. Arthur couldn't understand who'd be mad enough to stay this close to the front.

Many men recovering from wounds were enjoying the day sitting outside a French café in the late August sun. Beers were brought to them by grateful waiters, and inside, Arthur could hear some music. There were too many men singing for Arthur to tell whether it was a gramophone or a real piano. Music was something he'd not heard for a long time. Turning towards the cafe and seeing the joyous smiles brought Arthur to do the same. Infectious laughter made him want to join in. Then, looking the other way across the street, the products of war lingered on in the form of maimed faces.

Finding the Casualty Clearing Station was not hard. All they'd had to do was follow the lines of the walking wounded. Everywhere outside, men were laid down on stretchers with blankets. Some of them were completely covered. Arthur understood that they had died and had yet to be taken away, probably to some mass grave on the town outskirts.

Some of the men were so severely wounded that they had to have their cigarettes removed from their mouths by a friend or a nurse between drags. Men on crutches practiced their hobbling, and men with arms in slings wandered aimlessly. One man lay on his back with a blanket up to his neck. It was apparent where the shape of the blanket changed that this man had no legs. His face was completely black with burns, and although he was breathing, he was not moving his eyes. He just glared upwards into the sky.

"Stop staring, you!" came a female voice. Arthur immediately took his eyes away from the man on the stretcher to see a middle-aged woman with her hands on her hips scowling angrily at him. "When your turn comes, you'll not want someone looking at you like that, will you?" she hissed.

"Sorry," Arthur said, although he wasn't.

"I should think so too, and you're gonna-" Before she finished scolding him, Arthur turned and walked away. She jabbered on behind him, but he didn't care for her words. The boys reached the entrance, and the smell of infected wounds creepily invited them in. Rotten meat or cheese was the first thing that came to Arthur's mind.

An orderly in a white coat flapping behind him approached them hastily with a clipboard. "Who you lot here to see?" he asked the boys.

"Sergeant Wignell," Corporal Lindsay told the man.

"Which unit?" he asked, looking at his clipboard.

"4th London."

"Oh, *that* Sergeant Wignell!" the orderly said, raising his eyebrows and no longer needing his clipboard.

"Yeah, how many Sergeant Wignells you got?" Corporal Lindsay asked jokingly.

"Pick a surname. We've got a hundred of each. Just take a look at that lot!" the orderly said, looking over his shoulder to a tremendous long hall filled with hundreds of people. Nurses, stretcher-bearers, ambulance crews, walking wounded, and of course, the hundreds of rows of beds each filled with a wounded man.

Some of them were unconscious, some of them were moaning. Some of them were both unconscious and moaning, completely delirious as their bodies succumbed to gangrene and septicaemia. Some of them sat up with friends around them, and Arthur noticed one man writing a letter while he smoked a pipe quite cheerily.

"You can't see *him* today!" the orderly said.

"Well, why not?" Steeples asked. "We're his friends!"

"Well..." The orderly was hesitant and reluctant to say.

"Just tell us which bed he is in, and we'll quickly pop in to say hello, and then we'll be off. We'll not be any bother!" Corporal Lindsay assured the orderly.

"No, he isn't in here!" the orderly replied. Arthur feared that the orderly would tell them that he'd died but hoped that the orderly would instead inform them that their sergeant was fine and had already gone to England. Neither of those guesses was right.

"He's in his own room," the orderly went on. "He's a bit of a special case, and he's slightly pre-occupied!" The three boys looked at the orderly, who gave a big sigh, indicating that he was giving in to the pressure. "Okay, he's with the general!" he half-whispered, as if it was a big secret.

"He's with the general?" Arthur repeated the orderly in a questioning tone.

"Yes, you've come at a strange time; the general is with him now. I don't know how long he will be."

"Hang on a minute, mate, why's he with the general?" Arthur asked.

"Well…"

"Come on, out with it!"

"Well, you see…your sergeant has been recommended the Victoria Cross, and the general wishes to congratulate him in person. He's arrived just a few minutes before you! I promise that when the General leaves, which will be out the back door, you will be able to visit Sergeant Wignell."

Dumbstruck and elated, the boys' eyebrows flew to the ceiling while their young jaws dropped to the floor.

"He's got the Victoria Cross?" Arthur exclaimed.

"Well, I'll be damned!" Corporal Lindsay spoke in astonishment. They were as happy as any man in France right now after hearing their friend had earned himself the highest medal a British soldier could earn.

"A bloody Victoria Cross?" Arthur said again with excitement.

"Right, thanks mate, we'll wait right outside," Corporal Lindsay assured the orderly.

The three boys went outside, almost jumping with

joy at the news. Arthur, half inspired by their sergeant's medal and half inspired by the man he'd seen
writing from his bed, decided to pull out a piece of
paper and a pen and write his own letter home. He
sat on a patch of grass and wrote away while
Steeples and Corporal Lindsay dozed next to him
lazily, surrounded by wounded men who had had to
be left on the outside of the overcrowded building.

One of them sat up and started to talk to the boys.
"All right, lads?" he said in a Scottish accent.

"Eh up mate, how ya doing?" Steeples replied.

"Failin' means yer playin'," the Scotsman answered
with a smile across his face. He had a bandage
around his head, a face covered with dirt and dried
blood, and another bandage around his left foot,
which was sticking out of the blanket.

"Ken ye give us a cigarette, littl'un?" the Scotsman
begged.

Steeples was struggling to understand the strong
accent. "You what, mate?" he asked in reply.

"Gie us a cigarette else I'll gie ye a skelpit lug!" The
Scotsman stared menacingly as he spoke. None of
the boys could tell what he'd just said, but he was
terrifying.

"I think he wants a cigarette, Jimmy," Corporal
Lindsay said to Steeples.

"Right, yeah, here you go." Steeples gave him a
cigarette.

The wounded Scotsman leaned forward to have
it lit by Steeples, who struck a match, and the movement made the Scotsman groan with pain as he

stretched his wounds. "Thanks, wee laddy," he said.

"No problem, mate."

"Aye, you're a good lad. I had a lad like you once. My wee Benjamin. He was a real skinny malinky long-legs, though. Must have got that from his mother's side coz I'm not too tall myself. Lovely lad."

"Who are you talking about?" Arthur asked as he tried to guess the man's age. He put it around forty.

"Aye, my wee Ben. But the baw's on the slates for that poor lad. At the end of the day, we're a' Jock Tamson's bairns."

Steeples looked at Arthur and shrugged his shoulders, indicating he had no idea what the man was talking about.

Suddenly the man began to cry. Not just a sob, but a downpour of emotion ran tears like waterfalls down the man's face. "My boy!" he wept as he glared at the three boys. "My boy!" he shouted. "My wee Benny!"

"You're talking about your son?" Arthur guessed.

"Yes, I am," the Scotsman cried.

"Well, you got plenty of time to write to him. I'm writing to my mum and sister now. I can give you some paper, if you'd like,"

"I cannae write!"

"Well, you can tell me what to write, and I'll write it for you?" Arthur suggested.

"Haud yer weesht, lad, I can write; I know how to do that! I cannot write to my boy. He's dead! I seen him go down." The man put his bandaged head in his hands and cried some more. "How can I go back to

Edinburgh and tell his ma that I let him die?"

The boys remained silent, but they all finally understood what he was getting at.

"Those fucking bastards! Those fucking sausage-eating fuckers! I'm gonna get myself well again, and I'm gonna avenge my Benny!" The Scotsman lay down and smoked, wiping the tears from his eyes. They had left marks where they had cleaned the mud and blood away. He was clearly distressed. Arthur looked at the man with pity. He remembered his brother and thought about what he'd say to his mum if he ever got home.

"Thanks for the cigarette," the Scotsman said quietly as he lay back down and smoked.

The orderly appeared again about twenty minutes later and told the boys they could go in and see the sergeant. Arthur put his half-written letter away neatly into his pocket to finish later.

On the other side of the great hall, which seemed to smell worse the farther they went in, was a door. A nurse had opened the door for them, and a pretty young woman was another thing that Arthur hadn't seen for a long time. However, this pretty young woman had blood smeared all down her front, which was supposed to be white. He thanked her for opening the door, and she bowed her head. There was a corridor with three or four rooms on either side, which appeared to be for important casualties. A colonel's uniform was hanging outside the door of one room, and inside, a man was shouting at a nurse for some mistake she must have made. The final room on the left was their destination, and the orderly showed them in.

Sitting up with an enormous grin on his face was Sergeant Wignell.

"Hello boys," He said. The first thing Arthur noticed about the sergeant was that he was clean. The nurses had shaved him, and even his teeth were whiter.

"Good to see you, Sergeant! They treat you right in here?" Corporal Lindsay asked.

"I'll say," Sergeant Wignell said, his voice having returned to its previous strength before spending weeks in the trenches.

"You've got officer status quarters. Look at you, Sarge!" Arthur said.

"I know, get a load of this!" He showed them a newspaper. On the back page, it read, "HERO SERGEANT GETS V.C. ON WESTERN FRONT!"

"Bloody hell, you're famous, Sergeant!" Arthur said as he read the headline.

"Aye, but look at me." The sergeant nodded sadly to his plastered limbs. Arthur looked him up and down. One arm was in a sling so close to his chest that he couldn't possibly move it. Both of his legs were in plaster. It was clear by his movement and mannerisms that he was still in a lot of discomfort.

"I don't even remember it. All I know is that I woke up in here after doing something heroic," Sergeant Wignell explained.

"You saved all of our lives, Sarge!" Arthur told the

sergeant.

"I've heard. Captain Giles from B Company came in the other day and told me all about it. He was the officer that recommended me for the medal. I didn't even know he was there."

"Me neither," said Arthur.

"No, neither did I," Corporal Lindsay added.

"Godwin been to see you?" Arthur asked.

"No, unlikely he will," the sergeant said, not caring much for Godwin.

"Shame you had to save his life 'n' all though," Steeples put in.

The others, including the sergeant, nodded in agreement. The banter between the men lasted about an hour, until some nurses appeared with food. The sergeant offered to share it with the men. They all accepted the kind invitation to eat, and for a few minutes at least, they all felt happy.

Chapter 11

Twenty-four hours away from the front seemed like a lifetime. After eating real fruit and drinking clean water with the Sergeant, they had gone for a beer in a French café. There were so many British soldiers in there that it would be forgivable to an outsider to have not known they were in France. However, the beer was weak and not plentiful, and so the four boys had gone off to sleep in a barn somewhere between the town and the front, which had real hay. It was warm and comfortable, and they all slept well.

In the morning, Corporal Lindsay had risen before the others and headed back into the town. When he returned, the others were awake, and he broke two French baguettes in half and shared amongst them for some breakfast. It was dry, but it was good.

Apart from the usual sounds of the war, the walk back to the front was uneventful. They arrived back at about ten o' clock in the morning, just in time for a roll call in the redoubt before the short march back into the trenches.

Since the truce had ended, the whole company

had been much more on guard. Extra care had to be taken to keep heads down. Everyone had to be much quieter and conceal smoke from cooking fires or cigarettes. Life became considerably harder. Arthur thought about Godwin and why such a mindless, uncompromising officer had been sent to replace Clark, who had been one of the best. He just had to accept that it was pure bad luck.

At midday, Major Burnett appeared at the front to give an inspection. It did not take long. The company was all well used to the drill by now and had learned what was important and what was not when it came to being presentable on the front line. Only Godwin could go to such lengths as to reprimand a soldier for having mud on his buttons or stubble beyond the accepted length. After the inspection, there came a surprise for Arthur. A corporal from B Company fumbled along the line asking for him.

"I'm here, sir," Arthur said.

"Sir?" the corporal replied. "I'm a corporal, you idiot. You don't 'sir' me."

"Sorry, Corporal. Force of habit," Arthur explained.

"Anyway, Major Burnett wants to see you at the redoubt. He's in the main dugout."

"He wants to see me?" The message made Arthur curious.

"That's right. Best get back there pronto."

"I've just bloody come from the redoubt!"

"Don't look at me. I'm just the messenger." the

corporal said.

Arthur looked at the others, who each looked back with blank expressions. Steeples shrugged his shoulders. "Maybe you're up for a V.C too!" he joked.

Arthur laughed. "Not likely. Right then, lads, back later, I s'pose."

And with that, Arthur gathered his rifle, pack, and webbing and made the short walk back to the redoubt.

Outside the dugout were two military police-men. Arthur didn't speak to them, but he recog-nized who they were by the red shoulder badges.

"Well, I hope they're not here for me!" Arthur said under his breath.

He entered the dugout and stood to attention be-fore Major Burnett.

"Private Green reporting, sir. You sent for me, Major?"

The major had his back to Arthur and was read-ing some sort of letter in his hand.

"Ah, Private Green," he said as he spun on his heel to face Arthur. "I'll keep this brief. You and I are to be taken to the general's headquarters in a chateau about thirty-five miles away under MP escort."

"I don't understand, sir!" Arthur said abruptly. "Those military policemen are here for me?"

"No," said the major. "They're here for us!"

"I'm sorry, sir, but may I ask why?"

"No, you may not," the major answered, putting his cap on his head and his cane under his arm.

"Leave your weapon and webbing here. Let's go, Private."

Arthur followed the major out of the dugout. He heard the major say, "Come on then, let's get on with it" to the two military policemen who were still in the entrance.

"After you, please, Major," one of them said as he gestured which direction to walk.

"Come on then, Private, follow me," Major Burnett said with a serious look on his face as he made eye contact with Arthur.

They walked for about five or six minutes by Arthur's reckoning, until they came out of the trenches to the same main road which had taken Arthur out of the front the day before.

They approached a very nice-looking staff car where one of the military policemen opened the major's door and asked him to get in. Arthur went round the other side, opened the door himself, and sat down.

The journey was bumpy as they drove over potholed roads and damaged lanes. Arthur had no idea what was happening, but he was worried.

What could military police and a general want with me? he thought.

The French countryside suddenly became peaceful. Fields turned from brown to green, and trees that actually resembled trees began to appear. It was just like the countryside in England.

Before long, they approached a huge castle-like

house, which Arthur assumed must be the chateau. The driveway was almost a hundred feet long, with great giant oaks lining its sides. This was one of the biggest houses Arthur had ever seen, with huge panes of glass standing tall in the front windows. Large white steps with gargoyles on pillars on either side led to a giant black front door. Two Scottish guardsmen wearing parade ground kilts stood to attention, perfectly still.

The police escorts guided Arthur and Major Burnett into the hallway, which had stuffed animal heads all along the walls. There was a stag and several other horned creatures, as well as a bearskin rug on the floor. It was an ominous place, and surreal. Arthur felt he would be more at home back in the trenches than in here.

The sound of boots on the dark varnished wooden floors echoed around the whole building. It made Arthur very uncomfortable. This was not his class at all. He'd never been in such pompous surroundings.

The military policemen ushered both Arthur and the major into what looked like some sort of dining room, where an older man in military uniform with too many medals to count stood.

"Thank you, gentlemen, you may leave us," the old man said to the military policemen.

They both saluted, spun around, and marched out of the room in perfect step.

"Good afternoon, Major," the elderly man said

softly.

"Good afternoon, sir," Major Burnett quickly replied.

Both the major and Arthur were at attention. Arthur's heart was beating heavily on the inside of his thin rib cage.

"And you must be a certain Private Green, if I am not mistaken?" the older man asked Arthur, looking at him with a deadly ferocious glare. His accent was very upper class. The sort which Arthur and his schoolmates would mock in the playground when pretending to be kings or queens as children.

"Yes, sir" was all Arthur could bring himself to say.

"Good. I don't believe we've ever met?"

"No, sir," Arthur replied, not understanding that the question was rhetorical.

"No," the old man added, "we have indeed never met. So allow me to introduce myself. I am General Wilcox. I command the whole division." The general turned to Major Burnett.

"You, however, Major, I have met lots of times. How long have you been at the front now?"

"Since April, sir, five months." Major Burnett spoke as if scripted.

"Five months, I say. And the fighting spirit of the men is still as enthusiastic as when you first arrived?" the general asked earnestly, as if he had no clue about the state of his own men.

"Yes, sir. Still ready to bash the Boche, as it were, sir."

"And what about you, Private Green? Still ready to 'bash the Boche?'"

"Yes, sir. Absolutely sir," Arthur answered clearly enough but was still unsure as to why he was here.

"Then both of you, regardless of your ranks, which are both equally below me, explain here and now why I have had a very different report from a certain Captain Godwin. I received word from Godwin that the 4th Battalion has for some time now been taking part in an unofficial, unauthorized truce with its enemy counterpart on the other side of no man's land? What the hell is going on?!" The general slammed his fists on the table before him and leaned forward, staring at the two men. "Major, this is your battalion, is it not?"

"Yes, sir, it is, sir," Major Burnett answered again.

"Then you had better make a formidable explanation, or I swear to God that you will be sent home in disgrace and shot for desertion." The general switched his eyes to Arthur. "And you, Private Green, you're likely to be shot for fraternisation anyway, so I sincerely hope you have got something good up your sleeve!"

"Sir, if I may?" asked the major.

"Yes, you may."

"The truce of which you speak was negotiated by Captain Clark of A Company."

"And you allowed it, Major?"

"I turned a blind eye as nothing was going on in our sector, sir. We had received no orders to attack, no orders whatsoever other than to hold the line.

As our line has thus far not moved one inch either forward or backward since receiving that order, we have successfully carried it out. I agreed with Captain Clark that convincing the enemy not to shoot at us would be quite a good strategy for defence, given that the battalion as a whole is now only a quarter of the size it was when we first arrived, sir."

Major Burnett had done well, although Arthur knew he was lying through his teeth.

"Convincing the enemy not to shoot. I like that, Major," the general said slowly as it became clear the cogs in his mind had started turning.

After a few seconds, the general spoke again. "Do you know where Captain Clark is now, Major?"

"He was sent to England to come back with a new draft, sir. I'm yet to be informed as to when he will return to us, sir."

"That's right, Major. You have not been informed. And that is because he is now Major Clark. He is now the commanding officer of the 4th Battalion, and you are to be transferred to another unit after you've had two weeks rest here in France. How does Paris sound, Major?"

The major's face filled with confusion. "Sorry, sir, are you saying I'm losing my command? A demotion?" He sounded genuinely concerned.

"No, you'll still be a major. But we've new battalions coming in, and they need experienced leadership. You've been in the front line for five months and need a rest. I'm doing you a huge favour, Major, and I suggest you accept it."

"But who will my new command be, sir?" Major Burnett asked, still with a look of shock and bemusement.

"That will be decided over the next week or so. In the meantime, Captain Godwin is to be the acting commander of the 4th Battalion until Major Clark returns. That will be all. My staff car will take you back to the front. Hand over the command to Godwin, say your farewells to the men. Then get yourself to wherever the hell you like, in Paris. Report to division HQ on the 1st October. Go now before I change my mind, Major."

The major saluted before giving a small glance to Arthur. "What about Private Green?" he asked.

"Private Green is now not your concern. Only mine," the general said.

Burnett turned to Arthur and held out his hand. "Well, good luck and goodbye from me, Private Green."

Before Arthur had the chance to take the major's hand and say goodbye, the general broke in. "Get out, Major!"

"Yes, sir." Burnett obeyed and walked away without shaking Arthur's hand.

Arthur stood to attention and waited for the door to close behind him after the major made his exit. The idea of being shot for treason was going through his head.

Will it be tomorrow at dawn? Will I be sent back to England first? Will there be a court-martial? It seemed too unfair that Major Burnett had just been sent to Paris for two weeks' rest when he was the commanding officer who had overlooked the truce, and Arthur was only one of the many men following orders. *I'm just an expendable private, and no one will ever know the truth. They're going to make an example out of me not to obey orders of truce or face the firing squad,* the voice inside his head told him. Arthur's emotions were a mix of rage, fear, and confusion. The anger was mainly for Godwin but also for this older man before him, who had the power of life and death over the entire division. The officer responsible had just walked away freely, and here was poor Arthur Green about to be shot for it!

"Take two paces forward, Private!" the general ordered. Arthur did.

"Do you see this chair in front of you, Private?"

"Yes, sir," Arthur answered as he looked at a dark wooden chair with red velvet smothering the seat.

"I am going to ask you to sit in it, Private, and when you accept my invitation, you will be the lowest ranking soldier in the entire British Army ever to have placed their backside upon it! Won't you sit down, Private?"

Arthur followed the order quickly. It was a surprisingly comfortable chair. Far comfier than anything else Arthur had sat on for the past five months.

"Been in the battalion long, Private?" the general asked, and the sudden eerie politeness made Arthur uneasy.

"Joined up last December, sir," Arthur answered.

"And you shipped out in April?"

"March, sir. Saw our first action at Wipers, sir. Been in France ever since."

"Yes, I do know where your battalion has been Private. I'm the general that ordered you to go there."

"Yes, sir," Arthur said.

"And have you been in the 'thick of it,' as it were?"

"I've seen action myself, sir, if that's what you mean, sir?"

"Yes, it is what I mean."

"I've killed Germans too, sir." Arthur tried to impress.

"Have you?"

"Yes, sir."

"Because it is my understanding that you lot weren't shooting at Germans; instead, you made friends with them and have been enjoying walks together!"

"It isn't quite like that, sir."

"I'm going to give you one chance to explain to me what it was like, Private!"

"Well, I was there, sir, when this German officer came to us and spoke with Captain Clark. Then the captain came and told us he'd made a deal that if we didn't shoot the Germans, then they wouldn't shoot us."

"As simple as that?"

"Yes, sir."

"And what's this about you going to the German trenches? Godwin tells me you went over to the Germans. What were you doing? Deserting? Having a picnic?"

Godwin's face appeared in Arthur's mind, and now more than ever, he wanted to punch it as many times as he could before his fingers broke. He hated Godwin more than he hated the Germans at this point.

"No, sir. I was trying to explain to Godwin that the Germans opposite us were..." Arthur couldn't think of the right word. 'Friendly' was what he was thinking, but he could hardly sit here and explain to the general that they had met some friendly Germans. "...They were...not...I just wanted to explain to Godwin that there was this truce, so I tried to show him that the Germans wouldn't shoot me if we wouldn't shoot them. Then Godwin started shooting at the Germans, and they started shooting back, and I tried to find cover, but these Germans grabbed me and took me to their trench, and then they let me go again after I'd explained to them that we had a new officer, Godwin, who wasn't aware of the rules..."

The general turned red in the face. "Rules?" he shouted as he slammed his fists down on the table, causing a pencil to jump. "You've come here to fight in the largest clash of arms the world has ever seen, and you thought you could make your own rules?"

"No, sir, they weren't *my* rules." Arthur desperately tried to defend himself.

"I've heard enough, Private. This is an outrage the likes of which I've never heard of!"

Arthur began to sweat. He was sure the next words he was about to hear would be along the lines of being shot at dawn, or court-martialed and shot, or sent back to England, disgraced and shot.

As she always did when he was in a precarious situation, Little Pimple popped up in his mind. What would she grow up thinking? Her eldest brother had died a hero, and the other was shot for fraternising? Or cowardice? Or desertion, treason, disobedience, or whatever the army wanted to pin on him?

The general spoke again. "You have put me in the most awkward situation I have ever been in in my entire life, Private. Forty years I've served, this is my third war and hopefully my last. I have never been in a predicament such as this."

Arthur didn't know what the General was talking about. It seemed simple from his point of view.

"You've really put a dilemma on me," the general said again.

"Sir," Arthur agreed, though still not understanding why.

"Back home, the army is going on the largest recruitment campaign in the history of the British armed forces. Do you know what inspires men to join up, Private?"

"No, sir. To fight for England, sir?" Arthur answered.

"Is that why you joined, Private?" the general asked. Arthur wasn't sure where this was going.

"Um, yes, sir. I don't know, sir. It was my duty, I suppose, sir. I don't really know why I joined up, sir. I just sort of wanted to do my bit. Be a part of it."

"I see. And now that the war is entering its second year, what do you think would inspire people back home who have yet to join the colours, Private?"

"I don't really know, sir. The same reasons, I suppose."

"Heroics," the general said. "Stories of courage and valour. Real inspirational tales of glory and bravery in the face of the enemy. Medals."

"Yes, sir," Arthur answered in blind agreement.

"Your sergeant, what's his name—Wignell, is it?"

"Yes, sir. Sergeant Wignell."

"He has just received the Victoria Cross, have you heard?"

"Yes, sir, I visited him in the hospital."

"As did I, Private. Did you know that his name and picture are in nearly every newspaper in the English-speaking world, let alone the empire?"

"No, sir. I saw him in a paper but didn't know he was all over the world, sir."

"Well, he's becoming somewhat of a national celebrity. We've made sure of that to encourage more volunteers. His story of saving the lives of his men while under fire, living to tell the tale, and receiving Great Britain's highest honour from the king himself is damn inspiring stuff, wouldn't you agree?"

"I do agree, sir." Arthur nodded.

"And what do you think the world press would make of it if they were to find out that Sergeant Wignell received this high honour while in the middle of a sincere act of total cowardice on our behalf?"

"Cowardice, sir? No one was a coward, sir!"

"The whole damn lot of you were cowering in your trenches making deals with the enemy not to be shot at! Cowardice is the only way to describe it! At least that's what my superiors will say, and that is exactly what the papers will say if they ever find out! I should have the whole bloody battalion shot, but I can't. Can I, Private?"

"No, sir," Arthur agreed, this time for the sake of his own life.

"I can't have an entire battalion disbanded and shot for cowardice just as we begin our recruitment campaign. It would be most discouraging for our potential volunteers. Just after the news of a well-deserved Victoria Cross would make your battalion, the regiment, me, and everyone else associated a complete laughingstock! Not to mention the enemy press having a field day with their propaganda. You really have put me in a difficult situation, Private!"

Arthur didn't speak. He didn't care for the politics behind what the general was implying; he only understood that he was not about to be shot! Arthur became slightly more at ease with that knowledge but was still tense as he was unsure what would happen to him.

"Captain Godwin is now *our* problem. I think I can trust a load of privates to keep their mouths shut, most of whom will be dead in the coming months if not weeks anyway, as will the NCOs."

Arthur was angry at the thought of how easy it

was for this man to dismiss hundreds of lives and class them as already dead.

The general continued, "Your officers, however... Giles, well, he'd be throwing away his commission if he admitted to being a part of this, and Clark is now the battalion commander, a position he won't want to lose. I'm under the impression you all think he's a bloody hero, as he spared many of your lives while refusing to fight, am I correct?"

"Captain Clark is well-respected, sir, yes."

"He is Major Clark now. So I'll be seeing him on his return with your battalion's new recruits, where I'll have a clandestine word with him about this. I believe I can trust him. So that leaves Godwin."

If there was one man in the entire British Expeditionary Force that Arthur would gladly have shot at dawn right now, it was Captain Godwin.

"Godwin is the son of a well-known and highly distinguished brigadier-general. Are you aware of this?"

"Yes, I'd heard something about him along those lines, sir," Arthur replied quickly.

"But you may not be aware that Godwin himself came to see me about all this truce nonsense, and he overstepped his mark somewhat, using his father's influence upon me. He told me that I must first recommend him for promotion to Major Godwin. That would make him the battalion commander. Then I have to recommend him for a second promotion to lieutenant colonel by Christmas. If I did not do this, he would immediately run to his father with the news that one of my battalions had made a secret pact with the Germans. It would be *my* life on the line! Forty years I've served, and I'm not being disgraced at this, the tail end of my career, because some bloody desk boy wants to blackmail his way to the top! Well, Private, this is what is going to happen. You had better bloody well listen carefully, because I am extremely unwilling to say this twice."

"Yes, sir. I'm listening, sir," Arthur assured the general.

"Good." The general leaned forward and squinted into Arthur's eyes. "In one week's time, maybe ten days, or at the very least the first week in October, your battalion is going into action a few miles to the south. The area is near Hulluchs, and you'll be facing the Hohenzollern redoubt."

"The what, sir?" Arthur asked.

"Just listen, please, Private. Captain Godwin is going to command that attack, and you're going to make sure-" the general lowered his voice to a whisper, "you're going to make sure that Captain Godwin does *not* survive!"

Arthur turned white. Had the general just ordered him to assassinate his commanding officer? He couldn't believe his ears.

"I don't care how you do it. I don't care if you have accomplices. I only care that Godwin is dead before his recommendation for promotion, which I will send shortly, is received in London." The general sat back in his chair and stroked his short black and grey moustache. "What will happen if you fail,

Private?"

"I-"

"I'll have you shot for cowardice!" the general growled before Arthur could answer.

"Yes, sir," Arthur said with a wobble in his tone.

"In the meantime, Private, I need you alive. You're to go on leave immediately without returning to the front. I'll see to it that you have sufficient pay to find accommodation not too far from here."

"Can I go to Paris, sir?" Arthur suddenly saw the opportunity of a lifetime. A week in Paris would be an adventure in itself.

"No, you bloody well can't!" the general said frustratedly. "I want you close to here so that you can be found and escorted to the frontline at a moment's notice. I also don't want you contacting anybody at all. Major Burnett has just gone to Paris, and I don't want him knowing about any of this. Is that clear?"

"Yes, sir. Clear."

"While you're enjoying your time off, if at any point Godwin is killed by pure fortune, then you will be called for and sent straight back to your battalion. Now, do you have any questions about this? Ask them now because after today, I never want to see you again!"

"Yes, sir. Um, won't the men back at the front ask where I've gone?"

"Yes, they probably will. I will send a letter to Godwin informing him that I've requested his promotion as promised and that you're being kept here for interrogation pending court-martial. That should put a smile on his face."

"OK, and one more thing, sir…" Arthur asked.

"Go on," the general said exasperatedly.

"What's the Hohenzollern redoubt?"

The General leaned forward again, intending to pour fear into Arthur's heart. "It is an area of particularly concentrated German strength. Hohenzollern, I'm sure you're aware, is the kaiser's surname. Only something of enormous value to the Hun would deserve such a prestigious name. It is going to get very hairy over there, and you, Private, are going to be right in the middle of it."

Arthur breathed in heavily, puffed out his cheeks, and blew an enormous sigh.

"Now, Private."

"Sir."

"Leave this room, leave this HQ. A car is waiting for you. Get yourself to the nearest town; I believe it is called Lillers. I will have my driver inform me of your whereabouts. He will help you find comfortable and secluded accommodation."

"Yes, sir. Thank you, sir."

And with that, Arthur, the lowest ever ranking soldier ever to sit in the general's chair, stood up and saluted the general who, to Arthur's surprise, saluted back. Arthur walked out of the room and out of the chateau, with a heavy burden weighing upon him.

Chapter 12

The driver of the staff car seemed to be in a hurry. Arthur and his military police escort slid and bashed into each other several times as they swerved this way and that to avoid the potholes. It had been seven days since he'd left the general's chateau. Military policemen had taken shifts in guarding the door of his small hotel where he had taken residence. There were some other guests, but Arthur had noticed that they were all officers and none of them, even during meal times, chose to speak to Arthur. Maybe they had been given special orders to avoid him. Perhaps they were just too high and mighty to stoop so low as to talk to a private.

Still, Arthur couldn't complain. A week indoors, in a bed, eating hot food was going to be missed. Even though a military policeman had followed him everywhere, he would miss the walks he'd taken either through the town or along one of the many country lanes. There didn't seem to be anything special about Lillers, but it was pleasant enough. Being forbidden to speak to anyone and always under surveillance doubled the dullness of his time off. He hadn't even been allowed to write home.

After one week had passed, Arthur received the call that he was to return to the front. A car was waiting for him outside his hotel with a brand-new rifle and ammunition. He had mixed feelings, glad to be doing something but unhappy to be going into battle. Extremely unhappy to be going into battle to murder his commanding officer. Arthur was more nervous than he'd ever been. He didn't consider it murder to kill the enemy. He had had the last week to think about what his mission was, and he *did* believe that to be murder, even if it was Captain Godwin.

Approximately thirty minutes into the journey, and with the roads turning to mud, they were forced to drive along wooden planks that the Royal Engineers were laying out ahead. The car slowed to walking speed. After half a mile of going painfully slow, the driver gave up.

"This is as far as I'm going, mate," the driver said as he brought the car to a stop.

Arthur looked at the military policeman, who was still under orders not to speak to Arthur, and he nodded. Arthur took that as his signal to get out. They were close to the front. Artillery was pounding away, drowning out all other sounds. Arthur left the car and would have to make the rest of the way back to his battalion without his escort.

"Thanks," Arthur said to the driver, and he gave a nod to the military policeman. He slung his rifle over his shoulder and walked along the mud track towards the activity ahead.

He didn't know where he was going; he followed the sounds and went in their general direction.

There were men everywhere working along the road carrying things, mainly big planks of wood to continue laying down. He thought about asking someone the way to the front but realised that it was a silly question.

Just follow the noise, Arthur told himself. He thought about what was going to happen today. How was he going to kill Godwin? What if the opportunity didn't present itself? What if someone saw him? What if he was wounded before he got the chance? Thinking back to his previous battles, Arthur knew how confusing they had been and how hard it was to find someone. At least this time, it would be daylight. Then his mind cast back to the brief but terrifying description the general had given him about the Hohenzollern Redoubt. It made Arthur shiver.

A T-Junction gave Arthur cause to speak to someone. A lieutenant holding a map and talking to a small group of NCOs seemed like the perfect person to ask.

"Excuse me, sir, I'm looking for the 4th Battalion," Arthur said to the lieutenant, who looked to be in his thirties. He also seemed to be lost, judging by how he looked at his map. There was a lot of umming and erring when he spoke to his men.

"Sir!?" Arthur tried again, louder, forcing the man to lower the map and engage Arthur.

"I'm looking for the 4th Battalion, sir."

"Which 4th Battalion?" the lieutenant sighed.

"Londoners, sir, fusiliers."

"I don't know," the lieutenant said and went back to his map. The sound of the sky tearing like an enormous piece of paper ripped above their heads. Arthur stood balancing his cap on his head for fear of a shrapnel shell bursting above him.

"I need to find the 4th Battalion, sir. I'm not sure where I am," he shouted.

The lieutenant, who was now half squatting and similarly holding his cap on his head, roared back to Arthur over the noise of the heavy guns, "I don't know where they are, lad."

A sergeant who appeared even younger than Arthur spoke up. "Aren't they over at Auchy way, sir?"

"Pardon?" the lieutenant shouted back.

"I think they're up Auchy way, sir," the sergeant yelled into the lieutenant's ear.

"Auchy?" the lieutenant cried to his sergeant.

"Yes, sir, I think the London lot were going into Auchy today!"

Arthur didn't know what the sergeant was talking about. "What's Auchy?" he asked as loudly as he could, just as another rip tore the sky above them.

"It's a village. It's on the northern tip of the Hohenzollern Redoubt," the sergeant yelled, almost breaking his voice.

"Yes, that's it!" Arthur said excitedly.

"Go up this road about half a mile until you come

to a sign saying 'Big Willie this way!'"

"Big Willie?" Arthur asked.

"Yes, it's a German trench named after the kaiser. It's huge—good luck taking that monster. We spent about a week in front of the redoubt last month. There're more Germans there than there are in Germany right now!"

"Well, I think our orders are to take it!" Arthur explained.

"Well, bloody good luck to you is all I can say!" the sergeant commented with a shake of his head.

"Thank you, sir."

Arthur immediately told himself to stop saying "sir" to those who were not officers.

The noise showed no signs of ceasing, and so Arthur, still with his hand on his cap, stood up and started to half walk, half jog in the direction the sergeant had given him.

Sure enough, half a mile down the road was a crudely erected sign made from two planks of wood saying "BIG WILLIE THIS WAY!!" and underneath in parentheses it read "(The Front Line!!)"

Arthur didn't like the look of the exclamation marks written in red. He followed the sign, brushing past hundreds of other men, all going in different directions. It reminded him of King's Cross station on a busy day, except all the men were soldiers, and no one was by any means in a friendly mood.

Following the sign, Arthur could see entry points into the trenches. There were signs all over the place, but Arthur had no idea which one to take. A group of privates sharing a cigarette caught Arthur's attention.

"Oy, lads, looking for the 4th Battalion. The London lot."

"That one," one of the boys said, nodding towards an entry point that had no steps into the trench. He had to lower himself in, excusing the men who were trying to come up the other way.

The trench seemed to go on for a very long way, with other grooves joining and forking off in other directions. He asked aimlessly at different groups of soldiers.

"Anyone know where I can find the 4th London?"

"Yeah, keep going," a random voice came back.

That was enough to encourage Arthur to continue until he asked again. "Straight on up that way," called out another anonymous voice.

One final sign which said "The Front Line" pointed towards a trench, which Arthur followed. After a few more twists and turns, he was suddenly amongst familiar faces.

"Morning, lads!" Arthur said as he passed some of his company's men. None of them spoke. They just stared at him, completely dumbfounded. It had only been a week. Had they all forgotten who he was?

"Remember me?" Arthur asked. Not one of the company soldiers made a sound. Arthur looked back in surprise and anxiety. Why was everyone staring at him? What was so weird about him coming back to join them?

"Arthur?" he heard someone say. Arthur turned his head and re-straightened his cap again.

"Corporal Lindsay!" Arthur said. He put out his hand to shake hands with his old comrade, but Lindsay didn't offer anything in return. He stood there staring at Arthur in amazement.

"What's going on?" Arthur asked.

"I don't know what to say, Arthur," Corporal Lindsay answered. Just then, a figure appeared behind Corporal Lindsay. He had a cap on, pulled down over his eyes, and held a rifle in front of himself so that Arthur couldn't see his face properly.

At first, Arthur ignored the figure and asked again, "What's the matter with everybody?"

Corporal Lindsay moved to one side and revealed who was behind him. The man lowered the rifle and lifted the cap by the peak, revealing his face.

Arthur's jaw hit the floor. He dropped his rifle and went weak at the knees. This was the last thing on Arthur's mind and the last thing he expected. Charlie was back!

"Charlie, you're alive!"

"But Arthur, you're alive!" Charlie replied.

The two brothers hugged, and at the same time, a shell burst in front of the trench, raining mud in clumps small and large onto the men. Neither brother flinched an inch. Neither brother could believe the other was alive.

"We were told you were dead, Arthur!" Charlie spoke first, still holding his brother's arms. "They told us you had been shot for cowardice, for fraternising with the enemy! There have been all sorts of rumours."

"What? And you believed them?" Arthur asked as if it were a joke. "Who told you that? Besides, don't you know that when you get shot for these things, it's your fellow company men who do the shooting?" Arthur pointed out.

"But Godwin told us that you'd been sent away for a court-martial. Everyone here testified that you went over to the Germans and became friends with them!"

"Who said that? That's certainly not what happened!" Arthur replied angrily at the false accusations. He turned to speak to his comrades. Corporal Lindsay said nothing but continued to stare in disbelief. "Or did you all blame me, saving your own skins?" Arthur asked, looking at everyone.

"So, where the hell have you been?" Charlie asked.

"Where the hell have you been, more like!" Arthur answered, patting his brother's arms. "It's been months—why haven't you written, why haven't you contacted anyone?"

"I got banged up in some French hospital! I had my clothes all burnt, my documents burnt, my paybook burnt. I lost everything except for my skin and my underpants after the Hun set me on fire. For weeks no one knew who I was! I can't speak French, and until a couple of weeks ago, they had me wrapped up in plaster so that I couldn't write anything!" Charlie explained.

"Have you written to Mum?"

"It's the first thing I did when I got out of the hospital," Charlie told his brother.

"Good. Hang on!" Arthur suddenly had a harrowing thought. "You haven't told her that I've been shot for cowardice, have you?"

"Of course not!" Charlie replied. "I've only been back here for three days. I was offered the chance to go home, but I didn't want to. They told me that we'd all be on leave soon anyway, so I decided to get back now in case they transferred me to a different unit."

"Well, it's bloody great to have you back, big brother! What a sight for sore eyes you are!" Arthur hugged his brother again and then turned to Corporal Lindsay. "Where's Steeps?"

"You haven't heard?" Corporal Lindsay responded. Something was different about Corporal Lindsay. His eyes weren't the same. Arthur knew it was going to be bad news and feared the worst.

"Oh no!" Arthur said. "Not Steeps. Not Holey Moley."

"He's not dead, Arthur, but..."

"But what?" Arthur became impatient.

"But he's going to wish he was," Corporal Lindsay remarked, followed by a big sigh.

"How bad is he?" Arthur asked.

"Well. He's totally without a limb. We got him to a dressing station, and they amputated his one remaining arm there and then." Arthur wanted to know more, and he could see Corporal Lindsay was struggling to re-tell the story as his eyes reddened and welled up. He continued nevertheless. "Both his ears were blown off completely, his nose and eyebrows aren't there anymore, and he is completely blind and deaf. I saw him in the hospital two days after it happened. I'd say the surgeon did a pretty good job on him. I don't know how they managed to save him. But he was just this limbless, faceless, miserable ball of burnt flesh the last time I saw him." Lindsay was stuttering as he described what had happened to his friend.

All those standing around listening stared at the floor. "No arms, no legs, no eyes, and no ears. Better off dead," Corporal Lindsay finished.

"Jesus Christ." Arthur added, "Better off dead."

"Officer coming through!" they heard someone shouting.

All the men stood to attention and faced the front of the trench with their rifles by their sides.

"Right then, men, let's get this done!" Captain Godwin spoke loudly in his usual pretentious manner for all to hear. "Up and over, remember your briefing. You all know your roles. No stopping. Capturing the slag heap is our objective. B Company to our left will take Big Willie! One minute to go." Godwin had been strolling past the troops lined up as he spoke, carefully inspecting the men, looking each of them up and down as if he hated them. He reached Arthur.

"Well, well, well!" He stood face to face with Arthur. "What have we got here? Arthur Green. Court-martialed and shot for cowardice, back from the dead and amongst my ranks!"

"Private Green reporting for duty, sir!" Arthur stood to attention, boldly facing the man he was going to kill.

"What is the meaning of this!" Godwin burst out.

"We've got forty seconds to go, sir!" said a sergeant behind Godwin, who was holding open a pocket watch. Arthur stood boldly and stared the cruel, thin-faced Captain in the eye. Godwin looked back as if Arthur was nothing but dirt.

"I'm going to have your guts for garters for this, Private Green. No one makes a mockery of me. Do you know who my father is?" Godwin probed.

"Thirty seconds, sir!" the sergeant said anxiously, trying to see why the captain had stopped walking.

"I'll not fight side by side with a traitor, you Boche-sympathizing scum!" Godwin snarled.

"Twenty seconds!" the sergeant called out. Godwin had nearly turned purple with anger at this private, who had somehow made it back to haunt him after being informed of his death.

"Private Green. You will go first! You're so good at avoiding death. You can show us how to do it. One pace forward!" Godwin ordered, but Arthur didn't move. "I said one pace forward, Private Green!" Godwin was bursting with fury.

"Ten seconds, sir!" the sergeant called out again. Three shells in less than a second successively landed along the trench to the left of where Arthur stood. Godwin ducked his head, but Arthur didn't shy away from the blast. He maintained his eye contact to stare the doomed captain dead in the eye.

"Sergeant Banks!" Godwin called to the man behind him.

"Five seconds, sir!" the sergeant nervously replied.

"You will record that Private Arthur Green, in the face of the enemy and at the onset of battle..."

Godwin hadn't finished his speech when whistles started blowing, and men began climbing over the top. He continued nevertheless. "...deliberately and cowardly disobeyed my orders..."

Arthur had heard enough. He pushed past the captain and followed his brother and Corporal Lindsay straight up over the parapet, leaving the captain behind. Arthur was amazed he could still hear the captain blabbing away as he was above ground. Even the sound of a heavy battle hadn't managed to silence the captain's pointless droning.

Getting through the barbed wire was easy enough. He followed his brother. Arthur suddenly wished he had had some sort of briefing. He had no idea what he was supposed to be doing. There was something that Godwin mentioned, something about capturing a slag heap, which was to his right about five hundred yards away. The ground he trod on was a mess. Wet mud clung to his boots, making it much harder to run. It was only when he was about thirty yards from his trench that Arthur realised that men were beginning to drop.

The Germans were lobbing shrapnel shells into the sky, bursting behind the charging men. He could see three men in front of him ripped open from their backs as a burst caught them. Down they went, as if an invisible force had pushed them. Their tunics instantly turned red, their bodies became swiftly lifeless as organs began to spill through their skin.

Arthur was still following his brother, who was setting one hell of a pace. He wasn't sure if he could keep up. He then remembered his mission. He had gone over the top while Godwin was still in the trench.

"He must be behind me?" Arthur spoke out loud to himself. He turned around and dropped to one knee. Roughly thirty yards behind him was the captain, bellowing loudly and incoherently at hapless men who paid him no attention as they stumbled forward. Arthur had a quick look to his left and right. There were far too many people around to witness the crime he had orders to commit.

He stood up, and his charge became an unrelenting run towards the slag heap, an enormous pile of coal which Arthur now reckoned was something like three hundred yards in front of him. His mind had been so fixated on the murder that he'd forgotten all about fear of battle. Bullets whizzed past, but still, Arthur remained unhurt. He continued loping on, though the mud was making his boots heavy. His webbing and rifle were weighing him down too. It was not long before he was totally out of breath, and a stitch began to ache in his side. He was one hundred yards from the foot of the giant slag heap which dominated the landscape. To his left at a similar distance lay the rows and rows of coiled barbed wire, which had already claimed the lives of the first British soldiers to reach it. Their bodies were flaying and seemingly hovering above the ground in unnatural positions. Some of them were wriggling, and some of them completely unmoving aside from bobbing like rag dolls as the wire went up and down.

Arthur had had enough for the time being. The enemy was still invisible save for the flash of a machine gun, which fortunately was sweeping way over to Arthur's left. He collapsed to his knees and then flopped into the prone position to catch his breath. There was a dead body on either side of him, and hundreds of wounded were screaming for help in dire pain. Out here, there was no such thing as safety. Bullets could hit you from anywhere, shells could land on you at any time, and shrapnel could pounce upon you like a cat on an unsuspecting baby mouse, helpless and unaware. Arthur just had to trust his luck. As he smelled the sweet smell of soil which his cheek pressed against, his thoughts turned to God.

"Please God, please God, please God," he found himself saying. He put his hands over his ears to block out the noise of the ensuing fire-fight, which was now all around him. Someone ran past him, accidentally kicking him in the forehead as he did. "Please God, please God, please God," he again shouted to himself, although he couldn't hear his own pathetic voice. Then his mind turned to Little Pimple, standing in the doorway of his home, autumn skies above with patches of grey, the breeze blowing brown, yellow, and red leaves through the street. A leaf was entangled on the laces of her pretty white shoes.

She was smiling. Appearing out of the darkness behind her was their mother. She smiled as well and put her arms over the top of Little Pimple's shoulders. It was such a peaceful day: nothing but love and happiness facing him, with his entire future to look forward to.

A solitary tear fell into the mud and soaked into the ground. The stitch had gone, and the tranquil red face of his dear little sister turned into dirt as reality invaded his thoughts.

The ground began to shake as what sounded like a thousand shells all landing at once churned up the earth behind him. It was time to get going. Not far to the slag heap, and maybe his brother was up there. Arthur still hadn't had time to allow it to set in, the fact that Charlie had been alive the whole time.

Up he got, and he strode as steadily and as quickly as his body would allow itself in the direction of the slag heap. He attached himself to a group of ten other soldiers who were also heading that way. Fifty yards to the slag heap, twenty yards, ten yards—almost there! A hidden machine gun nest on top of the pile spat its deadly gift down on them like a dragon breathing metal and fire.

Once more miraculously untouched by the flames and lead, Arthur dived to the ground. In front of him lay the bodies of his fallen comrades, sprawled over the side of the massive heap like a patchwork quilt on a slanted mattress. The black coal had turned into a sheet of blood. Red and black mixed to form a sea of maroon sticky liquid, which trickled towards the bottom of the slope. Some British soldiers to his right had also reached the heap without losing their lives. When the machine gun swept away from them, they knelt upward and started firing aimed shots towards the enemy nest of death.

Arthur rolled over and over, making his way towards them, again pleading with the almighty that the German vultures inside their nest wouldn't spot him. The machine gun continued to fire but was now only showing interest to the men on the left.

Arthur half crawled and half rolled in a clumsy sort of scramble towards the British men he'd seen. Through the second coincidence of the same nature in the same morning, Arthur was happy to find his brother amongst them.

"Charlie!!" Arthur called out to him. "Trimmer!!" he shouted again but had been unheard. He scrambled a few more feet and passed some of the other men who had lined up on the slope.

"Charlie!" he said over his brother's shoulder. Charlie turned towards him and acknowledged him. He turned back to his rifle and took several more carefully aimed shots. A German soldier in a field gray uniform, drenched with sweat, fell down the slope. He was sliding, rolling, and falling like a puppet who'd had his strings snipped away. He was dead before he stopped moving, but several bullets continued to pierce his body nevertheless. A chorus of obscenities was shouted at the dead German by nearly everyone who had witnessed the poor man fall.

"Have that you fucking Kraut bastard!" screamed Charlie, who put another round into the corpse.

"Keep moving!" came an order from an unseen officer. Unseen most definitely, unrecognized most definitely not. Arthur turned to confirm what he already knew. It was Captain Godwin.

"Get up that slope, you cowards!" he shouted again.

What is it with this man and calling everybody cowards? Arthur thought to himself. This desk boy, as the general had called him, had been at the front for a week, and this was his first big battle. Many men here had been fighting for months and seen plenty of action.

Two of the men gathering on the slope attempted to advance on Godwin's order, but it was useless. They were both dead with several bullet holes in a matter of seconds.

"This is useless, Charlie!" Arthur shouted to his brother. "We need to find another way!" A flare shot up into the sky over to the men's left.

Charlie turned to Godwin. "Orange flare, sir, look!" Charlie pointed towards the German trenches.

"We've taken the trenches, lads! That's the signal. B Company have got the trenches. Let's get up and take this mound!"

There was the sound of bullets splattering into the ground, followed by tiny pieces of coal springing up into the air in front of them.

"Sir!" Arthur shouted at Godwin. "We're never going to take this hill, sir!" We need to find another way! Perhaps we can try going around it, sir?"

Godwin looked at Arthur in disgust. "You really are one yellow-bellied lowdown shit, aren't you, Private Green?"

Arthur chose to ignore the ill-witted captain, who was now no use to anyone unless they wanted an insult.

"Get up that slope!" Godwin shouted to another man, who obeyed the order only to receive his share of lead through the chest. The man did not die instantly. He slumped next to Godwin, lay on his back, and panted ferociously, struggling through his punctured lungs to contain air. He gasped for about a minute, staring at Godwin the entire time until slowly, life faded from his eyes, and his chest let out one final breath. Arthur stared at the man and then looked around. He and Charlie were the only two left with the captain.

Now is as good a time as any! the voice inside Arthur's head told him. *If not now, then when? Bullets are coming in constantly; maybe I can make it look like one of them hit Godwin? Or maybe I can make it look like an accident. I'll pretend my rifle went off by mistake and shot the captain in the head. He won't know what's happened, and maybe I can explain everything to Charlie?* A hundred different ideas shot through his mind.

The machine gun stopped firing.

"They're reloading. Let's go!" Charlie shouted to his brother and the captain. "Or the barrel's too hot. Let's take it now!"

Arthur nodded and joined Charlie in the ascent up the slope. No one was firing at them.

Another chance to kill Godwin missed, Arthur thought.

As they edged closer and closer to the black sandbags which made up the nest, the two brothers could hear distinct voices speaking in German. It sounded like they were shouting at each other. There were at least three different voices. A glance down the side of the slope, and there was Captain Godwin, easy prey for Arthur, who could take the shot right now.

Charlie tapped his shoulder. He mouthed the words, "On three?" Arthur nodded back, quickly being able to lip-read what Charlie was on about. Charlie held up his index finger, then his middle finger, and a second later his ring finger, giving the signal to go.

Charlie was a second ahead of Arthur and managed to get his body over the sandbags and put a bullet into the first German's belly. He went down screaming. Charlie jumped into the nest, landing on top of the agonised German bent double holding his stomach area as he lay in the foetal position. It caused him to lose his footing. He fell, and the two other Germans scrambled for something to knock him out with. One of them held a bayonet and raised it above his head, ready to thrust into Charlie, who was trying to push himself back up.

Arthur's first shot went through the man's forehead, killing him instantly. The second man turned to climb out of the nest's back entrance in complete shock and panic, but Arthur quickly reloaded and sent a bullet into the man's spine. The shot went right through his body, spurting out the other side.

The first German to go down was still screaming. "Bitte, bitte, bitte!" he cried.

Charlie picked up the bayonet from the German Arthur had shot. It was still in his grasp. He thrust it into the pleading man's throat, spraying blood all over his face. Charlie sat down with his legs over the dead man's body and panted like a dog on a boiling hot day.

Arthur decided it was now or never. He spun around, put his elbows on top of the sandbags, put the butt of his rifle into his shoulder, and aimed directly at Captain Godwin's head. Not even a second of thought went by as he pulled the trigger. Godwin went down and lay motionless on the black slope of the slag heap. Arthur had no idea if he had killed him or not. He sent another bullet into the torso and, for good measure, sent a third.

"What the hell are you doing?" Charlie asked breathlessly. Arthur knelt down in his surroundings of sandbags and corpses and stared at Charlie. Charlie rose to his feet and peered back down the slope. There were a good few hundred bodies behind them, and not one of them a German to his estimation.

"Where's Godwin?" Charlie asked. Arthur stared back at him with nothing to say. "You've just shot him, haven't you?"

"Charlie, listen!" Arthur demanded.

"The rumours are true, aren't they?"

"What bloody rumours?" Arthur was still not aware of the detail of the gossip about himself.

"The whole company was talking about it," Charlie began to wheeze.

"About what, Trimmer?" Arthur asked.

"Don't deny it now, Arthur. I just saw you! You've killed the captain!"

"I had to!"

"Why? Because you made friends with Germans?"

"What? No! That's not what happened!" Arthur was mad.

"It all makes sense! That's why you were court-martialed!" Charlie went on.

"Charlie, I wasn't court-martialled!"

"Then where have you been this past week? In the German trenches?"

"I haven't been to any German trenches, Charlie, please listen to me!"

"The whole company said they saw you. Godwin saw you. That's why you've killed him! Everyone knows the truth, Arthur, that's why we thought you'd been shot!"

"I wasn't shot! Look, I'm right here. How is it that I can possibly have been shot if I'm still here?" Arthur was becoming angry at his brother's insistence. "I am not a traitor or a coward!" he added.

"That day back in Wipers. We thought you were dead then too. But you walked all the way across no man's land after being let go by a German officer, and not a single German fired at you."

Arthur had to rack his brains. It had been six months since the fighting in Ypres. "He let me go that day, yes, but…"

"Were you already on their payroll? Were you checking in?"

"Charlie, stop it!" Arthur begged.

"And that day we got to the front in France. You went on the night patrol. Interesting how you and Steeples somehow accidentally butchered one of our sergeants by mistake and funny how the new officer that went with you never came back!"

"Oh, for God's sake, Charlie, this is ridiculous!"

"The other lads told me that you went on a prisoner patrol with some Indians, and somehow you came back, but none of the Indian chaps did!"

"What? Who's been spreading this rubbish?" Arthur couldn't believe what he was hearing. He was infuriated.

"Everyone's been talking about it, Arthur. Some of the lads tried to defend you, but after the discussions we've been having, it all makes sense. Everyone knows you for what you are, Arthur. They all saw you go into no man's land one morning without a single German firing at you, then you came back across and threw a bomb at Sergeant Wignell!"

"Charlie, that is *not* what happened!"

"Oh no? And who can vouch for you? Steeples can't speak, see or hear, and Corporal Lindsay confirmed everything!"

"Yes, to save himself! The whole company entered into a truce with the Germans opposite us, negotiated by Clarky!"

"And where's he? Somehow he just disappeared!?" Charlie scorned.

"Charlie, you've got this all wrong. It's all idle gossip and people pointing their finger at me to get themselves off the hook!"

"That's bullshit, Arthur. I just watched you shoot Captain Godwin! You're not my brother; you're not my mother's son. You're a traitor and a coward!"

A thunderous roar descended upon the boys as a German counter-attack began at first in the form of an artillery barrage. When they were able to gather their senses through the dust, they both peered over the top of the sandbags towards the German lines. It was an incredible sight. Arthur watched in awe as he tried to understand the scale of what was obviously the Hohenzollern Redoubt below them. Thousands of ant-like men in German uniforms crawled towards the massive trench, which must have been Big Willie. There was no way they could hold it.

"We've got to get out of here, Charlie!" Arthur exclaimed.

"Why? Your brethren are coming. You'll be safe as houses!" Charlie spat.

"Don't be a fool, Charlie, let's get going—look!"

He pointed to the bottom of the coal mountain.

Germans were crawling all over it. Nothing more needed to be said. The two brothers leapt from the captured machine gun nest as they flung their bodies down the slope and rolled over the dead, there being no choice but to stand on them to get away.

Wounded groaned and moaned and pleaded for the brothers to carry them back, but there was no time. Looking back up the colossal coal slag heap, Arthur could see some Germans had already made it to the top and were preparing to start firing on the retreating men.

They ran as fast as they could, being fortunate enough to avoid the thousands of pieces of metal that had started being sent their way.

The brothers jumped back into the relative safety of their front-line trench just in time to see fresh troops from a different regiment filling up the parapet in preparation for another attack. They sat on the floor of the trench and stared at each other.

"Traitor and coward!" Charlie hissed in his brother's ear.

Chapter 13

By the end of October, the weather had started to turn. The sky was dark most of the time, the autumn rains had come, and the wind blew relentlessly. Fortune, too, had come their way in the form of fresh troops arriving from different units. The 4th Battalion was finally relieved and ordered to make their way to the rear to depart by train to Western France for rest.

The march to the train had been without incident. The train journey itself was incredibly dull, and the troop carriages were cold, which added to the sombre mood. So few of them were being taken out of the line alive. Now that Corporal Lindsay had been missing since the day of the attack on the Hohenzollern Redoubt, the Green brothers were the last of their small band still fit for action. Arthur overheard one man talking as the train rocked.

"Did you know I've been in the line since our arrival in March? I've fought in every action this company has been a part of, and we haven't been out of the range of German guns for two hundred and fifty-five days," the man said. Most of the men appeared surprised by this fact, but it showed to be true. They were filthy. No one's clothing was fully intact. Everyone's faces were dirty, wrinkled, and thoroughly worn. Fingernails were black right up to the cuticles. They wore battered boots. Some of the older men still only in their mid-twenties were going grey in the hair. Teeth were yellow and black with bleeding gums. Everyone had bloodshot eyes, and now that they were out of the line and into cleaner surroundings, the smell began to be more noticeable.

Arthur closed his eyes and listened to the sound of the wheels on the tracks rumble beneath him. They reminded him of machine guns. Now and then, the train would jostle, which brought to his mind the feeling of a shell exploding nearby, the way it made the earth tremble.

He drifted into a slumber and had another dream about Little Pimple. This time they were running through a park, and Arthur was in civilian clothes. His little sister kicked a mound of gathered leaves and laughed. The leaves flew up into the air the same way earth flung when a shell landed. She kicked and kicked again, sending leaves all over the place. Arthur shouted at her to stop and ran towards her. Although he couldn't exactly identify what it was, he could sense she was in danger. Conkers started dropping from the tree. They landed all around her, splattering mud on her white dress as they landed in puddles that had appeared from nowhere.

Suddenly the brown splashes against the white dress turned blood red, and she fell into his arms. He held her like a wounded comrade. Her hair covered her pale white face completely. As he brushed it away to reveal her eyes, he noticed they were completely black instead of blue. Her ears slid away, and she lay there soaked red. As he stared at her, she gradually changed until the body he held was not his sister's. It was Private James Steeples. He was now in military uniform, and the pleasant park they were in was a mass of shell holes and explosions. The rain poured and poured until it soaked Arthur to the bone. Looking once more into the face of his fallen pal, it had changed again. This time it was his brother. He was staring directly into his eyes with blood gurgling from his mouth. Slowly but clearly, he whispered, "Traitor. Coward!"

Arthur woke up on the train in a cold sweat. No one else had seemed to notice he had been asleep, and indeed others had also drifted off. Some were talking to each other, but Arthur didn't bother to try and listen.

He stared across his dark carriage to a boy who he had known for a while but had never really gotten to know properly. Danny Thompson was his name. Arthur couldn't help notice that the poor boy's left arm kept twitching. He was holding it with his other arm, but it moved uncontrollably. Their eyes met. Another jerk of the boy's arm and, "What you looking at?" came out of his mouth.

Arthur looked away. He no longer had any friends in the company. Even his own brother didn't trust him and wouldn't sit next to him in the carriage.

Stupid rumours, he thought. *How can they honestly think I have been working for the Germans? It's ludicrous. They'd have had me shot for it, and men from my company would have been the firing squad. Most of them were there too. They were aware of the truce, and they all abided by it, same as me.*

Alone with his thoughts, he tried to sum up the last six months. It was true that at Ypres, a German officer had captured him and let him go. It was also true that he and Steeples were responsible for killing one of their own sergeants and that Lieutenant Chapman was killed on his first patrol. It was true that they had gone on a patrol to capture German prisoners with some Indian soldiers. Incidentally, none of the Indian soldiers had come back, save for one who came back the next day, but the men had forgotten about it, and Charlie hadn't been there to witness it.

The only people who could vouch for him were Salt, Steeples, and Corporal Lindsay, who were all with them that day. Salt had a blighty, and Steeples was in the worst place imaginable. Lindsay had lied through his teeth to save his skin, which made Arthur angry to be betrayed by his friend. Now Lindsay was missing too, and probably dead.

Sergeant Wignell would have been a useful ally, but he was also out of the war. Before he'd had a chance to convince his brother that the rumours weren't true, he had shot and killed Captain Godwin right before Charlie's eyes.

I've fought well, Arthur convinced himself. *I've lost*

count of how many Germans I've killed. I've not had a single wound. I've been in action more than most! Why am I being punished? I'm as loyal a soldier as any!

When the train finally stopped, Arthur was the last to disembark the carriage. He did not know and did not care to learn the name of the town. There was an unfamiliar sight of French civilians going about their day on the train platform. Well-dressed children holding their well-dressed mother's hands caught Arthur's eye.

British soldiers had entirely occupied Lillers, and even in a week spent there, Arthur hadn't come across women or children. His hotel staff were French men too old to take part in the fighting. Serving British allies was their contribution to the war effort. Arthur stared at a French child who saw Arthur staring at him. French soldiers wandered the place too, standing out in sky blue uniforms.

"This way, 4th Londons." Arthur followed the voice and shuffled away from the platform. They marched through the town until orders were dished out and passed along by exhausted NCOs. They were good orders.

They had been designated a building to serve as a barracks. They rolled out blankets and slept indoors. The building was large enough to have been a town hall or a school before the war. Arthur didn't bother to find out what it had been, and he was too tired and uninterested in anything other than getting the rest that they desperately needed. He and his company stayed on the first floor in a large hall.

Darkness arrived, and on the floor with about one hundred other men, neatly laid out, Arthur fell asleep. Charlie had chosen to go up a floor, disassociating himself from Arthur.

Early the next morning, the battalion's shattered remnants received the order for a parade, which meant once again cleaning everything they had. After a brief but monotonous routine, they all lined up outside the building on a closed road. They were stood to attention for far too long in a drizzle of rain. The four companies looked appallingly small. At a glance, they looked more like a single company lined up in four platoons, not an entire battalion. That was about to change, though.

Several more minutes passed and taking them all by surprise, their long-awaited replacements came marching down the road. There were a fair few hundred of them by Arthur's reckoning. At the head of the line was a welcome face. Clark was back. He was now a major, and Arthur knew full well he would be able to count on him to prove his innocence. At last, his brother would see the truth.

The newly-promoted major stood around his battalion, now a mixture of experienced and raw soldiers. He gave lengthy speeches about what he expected of his men. It was the usual drab cliché of everyone doing their duty and not letting the side down. It turned to 'blah–blah-blah' in most of the experienced troops' heads, but Arthur understood that the new recruits needed to hear such heartwarming patriotic words. Then the men were given a training schedule.

Some rest this is going to be, Arthur thought. *Parades every day and more training.*

There was some thread of excitement when the major told them about a new weapon they would be training with. All the men wondered what it could be.

The parade ended, and the men went back to their boring day. They had forty-eight hours off until training began, with only a morning and evening roll call for them to attend each day.

In the meantime, Arthur intended to patch things up with his brother. Now that Clark was back, he was sure that he would be able to clear the air.

The battalion HQ had been set up in an adjacent building to the one the men had slept in. It was a large brown stone building that had been a hotel before the war.

Clark was standing at the window when Arthur knocked on the door, which was ajar. The major turned around and was pleased to see his old comrade. It had been a few months since they were last together, and the major was quick to remember the night he had saved Arthur's life. That seemed like an age ago.

"So what have you come to see me for?" Major Clark asked Arthur after the small talk had faded away naturally.

"It's my brother, sir."

"Ah yes, I couldn't believe all that time he was

missing, he was in a French hospital unable to contact anyone. Glad he made it back," the major remarked.

"Yes, sir. Incredible story, really. But there's a bit of an issue with him, sir."

"Go on," the major spoke with his hands, gesturing to Arthur to continue the issue.

"Well, you know how he was wounded some months ago, and now he's back? A lot has changed, sir. He's heard these rumours, you see. He wasn't there when you agreed that truce with that German officer, so when he came back to the front, Captain Godwin told him that I was a coward and a traitor for my part in the truce, and I was going to be court-martialed and shot. People have been saying all sorts of things about me, that I'm responsible for the deaths of our boys, that I collaborated with the enemy..."

"Private!" Major Clark interrupted.

"Yes, sir," Arthur sighed impatiently.

"I have just arrived here with over three hundred brand new recruits. I am NOT going to have it known that I arranged a truce with the Germans. As far as you and I are concerned, the truce never happened. It is just a rumour. It will go away."

"But my brother, sir, he saw me...."

"He saw what, Private?" The major didn't have time for this.

Arthur suddenly realised that he had to speak carefully. Was Clark aware that Arthur had killed Godwin?

"Godwin, sir," he said very quickly.

"What about Godwin? I heard he was killed in action during the battalion's attack on the Hohenzollern Redoubt."

"Yes, sir." Arthur was stuck. It appeared that Clark had no idea about Arthur's encounter with the general or the murder he had committed against his former company commander.

"I'm afraid, Private, that your family affairs are not my concern. Your brother was away for a long time, and when he came back, neither you nor he was the same person as before. War changes people, Private. Now, when we got back into action next month, I will need experienced troops like you and your brother, and I need you on the same side. I will not tolerate squabbling amongst my men when the enemy shall be our biggest worry. The world stands on a knife-edge. I'll not have any part in our downfall should we be the ones to slip. If you can't make it up with your brother, then I'll have one of you transferred to a different battalion."

All hope was gone. The major was not going to admit to anybody, even Charlie, that he negotiated the truce, and there was now no legitimate excuse Arthur would be able to give Charlie as to why he'd killed Godwin. He knew that if he were to start blaming generals and other higher-ranking officers, then he would be marched away and shot for whatever reason they liked.

"Thank you, sir. That's all, sir." Arthur saluted.

"Thank you, Private, and it's good to see you."

Chapter 14

The cold November frosty mornings were a nuisance. Standing still on a parade ground, they waited every day for the officer taking roll call to shout out their names in the freezing, biting wind that endured far too often for the men's liking. It was okay if they were doing something active, but standing still was a chore. Arthur found it hard to resist rubbing his hands together or stamping his feet gently to get some blood back into his toes.

Then one morning after roll call, they were marched off to a new training ground. Shallowly dug practice trenches were created with poorly crafted fake shell craters around the edge to mimic a battlefield. It was obvious what it was supposed to be, but it looked nothing like the real experience. There was still grass, for one thing. The lack of shelling allowed the men to hear themselves think, for another. There was no stinking latrine or random limb or torso lying around. There were no piles of rotting human corpses or horse carcasses swarmed with bloated, greedy flies or filled with maggots. No rats were scurrying over everything the second somebody put anything down.

Their new company commander, Captain Fair-bridge, and second in command, Lieutenant Colli-son, had the men lined up. Collison, who looked to be the older of the two new officers even if the jun-ior in rank, opened a wooden box. He pulled out a small round object about the size of an apple with a ring going through the stalk at the top.

"This, gentlemen, is the new prototype hand-held bomb—a hand-grenade. I will give a simple demon-stration and then," there was a murmur of excite-ment from the onlooking men, "it's your turn." The lieutenant continued. "Our job over the next few weeks is to practice hard and develop trench clear-ing tactics. The German trenches are getting deeper and deeper, and they've got to be flushed out. Watch and learn, lads!"

The lieutenant pulled the ring from the top of the apple-like object and lobbed it as if he were bowl-ing for a cricket team. The eyes of the spectating men followed the round device as it landed in the trench. Two seconds later, there was an enormous bang, which made nearly everyone jump. There was a flash, and a small mushroom cloud rose upward. Arthur was excited. It suddenly looked like a lot of fun throwing such novelty weapons into holes in the ground. In groups of four, the whole company took turns lobbing hand grenades.

For the next two weeks, they trained relentlessly with the new weapon. They practiced throwing with rocks and other objects if there were not enough live explosives to go around or if they were waiting their turn. Then they practiced taking the trench in teams. About ten men were acting as the Germans, and a group half that size were the attackers throwing dummy bombs into the trenches. They practiced night attacks as well as early morning attacks, afternoon attacks, and dusk attacks.

Inevitably there were accidents, but all the weapons used were dummies. One corporal emerged from a trench with a broken nose, and a new private was stretchered away after twisting his ankle badly while practicing jumping into the ditch. Although the training was intense, it was enjoyable and occupied a lot of their time. For Arthur, memories of the real fighting began to push themselves to the back of his mind, and the rumours about him faded away.

Some of the new recruits were taking a liking to him. He had been in battle, and they therefore looked up to him. He had killed Germans, and that earned him some respect. When demonstrations of how to throw the bomb correctly were needed, the officers always picked Arthur. He was becoming a real soldier of inspiration to these fresh boys who were yet to see their first action.

"Private Green, show them how it is done, would you?" Lieutenant Collison or Captain Fairbridge would say. "If any of you still don't get it, just watch Private Green."

He was proud of himself. Soon, everyone would forget about the previous months' mishaps, and one day, he and his brother would look back and laugh.

Even though his brother never volunteered to be in a team with him and thus far they had slept in different rooms, Arthur held onto the faith that the day would come when they would forgive each other.

Then on one icy morning, Arthur was woken up by his brother. It was still dark, but Charlie had a torch.

"What are you doing?" Arthur grumbled as he sat up, wrapping blankets around his shoulders.

"Got this from Mum," Charlie showed him an open parcel.

"We got mail?" Arthur asked, confused.

"Actually, we got it a few days ago, but I kept it," Charlie said.

"What? Why would you do that?" Arthur questioned his brother as he rubbed his eyes to take a look into the parcel.

"I wanted to give it to you today," Charlie explained.

"Why today?" Arthur asked.

"Are you serious?"

"Yes, why?"

"Arthur, it's your birthday!" Charlie told his surprised younger sibling.

"Today?" Arthur had forgotten. He had been at war for so long that days had become meaningless to him.

"There's a letter from Mum and Dad. Dad's gone back to work, and there's even a note from that girl of yours, Florence."

Arthur had forgotten all about her; she was a long-gone, distant memory. Arthur picked up the note and read it. On the back was his new age, nineteen, written inside a heart.

"It is my birthday today?" Arthur was still stunned. "Well, I never..."

"So tonight, little bro, you and I are going out. We've no drills or training tomorrow, only daytime trench bombing drills later today. B Company are out at the training ground tonight, so after evening roll call, we're going to the pub! There's a joint across the town square where a lovely French girl sings and plays piano to you. She'll be sure to do something nice just for you on your big day!"

"Okay, that sounds great. Let's do that!" Arthur agreed. Charlie ruffled Arthur's hair and left abruptly.

Wow, Arthur thought. *I knew it. Sooner or later, Charlie would forget all about it.* He smiled and lay back down. A sense of peace drifted over his body. He was away from the fighting, and his brother had finally seen sense. Arthur fell back to sleep with a feeling of warm hope that all this would be a thing of the past one day.

Training that day had started as usual—a brief roll call, followed by the thirty minute march to the training ground trenches. Captain Fairbridge chose Arthur for another demonstration, and to Arthur's surprise, Charlie volunteered to be in his group. The two brothers and Lieutenant Collison prepared to show the onlooking men how to take a German dug-in position. The company stood well back as the trio slipped into the trench.

"Proceed if you will, Lieutenant," Fairbridge instructed.

Their job was to take out some scarecrows acting as practice dummy Germans, propped up in the trench with funny spiked helmets on. It looked and sounded easy.

The three men manoeuvred through the trench. They did it exactly how they were shown and how they had practiced daily for the past few weeks. They were very good at it. Lieutenant Collison threw his bomb first, and two scarecrows about fifteen yards away around the trench corner blew up into pieces. The company cheered. Arthur went next, shuffling along the trench, and he took out another scarecrow. They continued to move through the ditch with professionalism. Charlie lobbed and sent two more of the practice dummies up in the air, prompting another cheer.

The lieutenant raced ahead and round the corner of the trench. He had gone on too far and too quickly. Arthur had already thrown his next bomb over the top of the sandbags ahead of him, and before he could tell the lieutenant to come back or get down, the bomb exploded. The cheers went silent as the smoke cleared. Lieutenant Collison lay on the floor bleeding and burnt.

"Oh my God, Arthur!" Charlie gasped. "You did that on purpose, didn't you?!"

"Don't just stand there. Get him out!" Captain Fairbridge shouted.

"What are you talking about, Charlie? Of course I didn't do that on purpose!" Arthur seethed at the absurd accusation. Arthur and Charlie lifted the unconscious lieutenant out of the trench and laid him on the ground.

"Yes, you did!" Charlie lashed venomously.

Fortunately, the wounded lieutenant wasn't dead.

Captain Fairbridge decided to cancel the rest of the day's training and marched the company back to the town, summoning Arthur and Charlie to his quarters upon their arrival. The boys stood to attention as Captain Fairbridge addressed them.

"He isn't dead, fortunately, but these accidents to an officer cannot go unnoticed and without inquiry. Now Major Clark is going to press me for a written report as to why one of his officers has been sent back to blighty without even seeing the enemy."

"It was an accident, sir," Arthur interrupted.

"That may be the case, but why were you so reckless? You've been at this for weeks. If it was an accident, then it was gross incompetence, and I understand that you, Private Green, have been in the war for quite some time and have seen more action than most," Captain Fairbridge responded.

"It was just an accident, sir!" was all that Arthur could muster. He could hear the cogs in his brother's mind going round and round and round. Would he dare tell the captain that he believed Arthur had done this deliberately?

"One of my most experienced soldiers accidentally threw a bomb at one of my platoon commanders...is that what's going into my report?"

The frustration rose through Arthur's body like heat in a barrage balloon. He wanted to explode and shout out all of his pent-up anger at the captain and his brother, but he knew he couldn't do it. He knew that he had only done it by mistake, and that the lieutenant should have known better than to run ahead before Arthur had thrown his next bomb.

"No, sir. I am a competent soldier. I have been fighting in this war since March. I have fought and fought and fought, and I have done more than my fair share of time in the line. But Lieutenant Collison has not, sir. He's had hardly any experience of warfare at all, much less than any of us. An officer he may be, but an experienced soldier he is not, sir." Arthur could not believe he'd been brave enough to come out with such words.

The captain looked shocked and furious—a private soldier pointing his finger and blaming an officer for his own lack of diligence. However, Fairbridge took in what Arthur had said.

"I think...I think you might be right, Private."

Arthur was more than relieved and appreciated the captain showing some understanding. After all, the captain had been watching the demonstration and could have seen for himself that it wasn't Arthur's fault. The tone in the room suddenly seemed to change to a much lighter one. "What do you think, Lance Corporal Green?" the captain asked, looking to Charlie.

"I don't know, sir. I was at the rear of the drill and didn't see what happened."

Although satisfied with Charlie's response, Arthur was perplexed. Why was his brother so awkward? He'd already accused Arthur of doing it on purpose merely a few hours after coming to see him to say happy birthday. Just when Arthur thought the past was behind them, an accident happened in training, and Charlie was accusing him once more.

Thankfully for the boys, the captain's meeting was short, and Arthur could go without punishment. Captain Fairbridge was satisfied that Lieutenant Collison was to blame for his own injuries in training and agreed with Arthur that it was down to a lack of experience. Charlie, on the other hand, had not been convinced. Arthur had tried to speak to him after they'd left the captain's quarters.

"You see, Trimmer? It was an accident!" Arthur said. Charlie didn't respond. He turned and walked away into the town. Arthur watched him until he was out of sight. He could no longer make sense of his brother since he had returned. He just wasn't the same person anymore. Major Clark had been right in saying that the war had changed them both.

By evening Arthur was bored. He'd written half a letter home but was not happy with its content, so he had scrunched it up and thrown it away. He had truly felt happy earlier that morning when Charlie had come to see him and given him the letters from home. Arthur was pleased, too, when Charlie had volunteered to do the training exercise alongside him, then the stupid accident happened.

Sitting on a pile of his blankets in the large hall, Arthur decided he'd had enough. He would go and find that pub Charlie had been talking about and have that drink. After all, it was his birthday, and he was going to celebrate.

The pub was easy to find. Arthur had an inkling of where it was anyway. There was singing and dancing, and indeed a French girl was playing the piano, just as Charlie had said there would be. She was receiving one hell of a lot of attention. There were other girls in there too. They were also dancing away and sitting on the laps of young soldiers. Arthur walked to the bar to get a drink. Before he reached it, he was intercepted.

"HAPPY BIRTHDAY TO YOU!" Charlie raised his voice above that of the singing and the piano.

Arthur looked up and saw his brother was completely drunk. Charlie slurred his voice, and he was struggling to stand upright. He put his hand on Arthur's shoulder and shouted, "Hey, lads! It's Arthur's birthday!"

The noise in the room died down and a circle formed around them.

"It is my little brother's nineteenth birthday today, lads! Let's get him a drink!"

A raucous cheer followed, and a pint glass full of beer found its way into Arthur's hand. He started to drink, and several others put their arms around Arthur. The music and the singing continued, and someone raised Arthur onto someone else's shoulders. The drink ended up on the floor, and two French girls took hold of Arthur's hands, spinning him and the man carrying him round and round.

The clumsy footing of the man beneath him sent all four of them to the floor. Laughter erupted, and another drink ended up in Arthur's hands. Charlie put out his hand to help Arthur to his feet. He accepted the hand, and they stood facing each other. As Arthur laughed, Charlie's face dropped. His mood had changed again.

"What's the matter now, Trimmer?" Arthur asked, sensing something was afoot.

"You!"

"Oh come on, it's my birthday, drink with me! Let's enjoy the night!"

"You killed Godwin!"

"Let's have a drink on Mum, Charlie!"

"You threw that bomb at Collison!"

"Let's drink to Little Pimple!"

"You killed that sergeant of engineers!"

"That was Steeples; come on, Charlie, let's have a drink on Dad as well!"

"You tried to kill Wignell!"

"Let's get two pints!" Arthur was desperate for Charlie to stop this nonsense before someone overheard him.

"You've been bought by the Hun!"

Arthur turned to the bar "Two pints over here!"

"You killed those Indians and bargained for a ceasefire, you traitor!"

"Trimmer, watch your lip. You're drunk!"

"You killed Chapman!" Charlie refused to stop.

"Charlie, have you lost your mind completely? You weren't there, and you saw nothing!" Arthur felt anger brewing inside him.

"TRAITOR!" Charlie shouted and swung his right arm at his brother's face, catching him on the chin. Arthur swung back, punching Charlie on the forehead. The brief exchange of fists turned into a full brawl between the two brothers, who grabbed each other into headlocks and wrestled themselves to the floor. Neither held the advantage over the other. Charlie was slightly bigger, but he was also drunk, and eventually, Arthur was able to wriggle free and lay a knockout blow into Charlie's face, leaving him flat on his back in the middle of the pub floor.

The music had stopped, and all the other boys and girls in the pub had made space for them. Some of them had stood on chairs and tables to get a better look at the punch-up.

Then the brawling duo was grabbed by the scruffs of their necks by a sergeant who was enormous. They were both turfed out onto the street.

There was another enormous cheer as the door slammed shut behind them. The party inside did not miss the fighting pair, and the music and cheering started up again.

The street was dark and cold. A few other British soldiers wandering the town that night had turned their heads to see what was happening. Arthur chose to ignore them.

Still out of breath, he spoke to his brother. "What is the matter with you, Charlie? You're not the same!"

"I'm not the same? I saw you with my very own eyes shoot our captain. There are so many rumours about you," Charlie panted.

"But they're rumours, Charlie, they're not true!" Arthur could see his breath firing out of his mouth in great plumes. It was ever so cold.

"Shooting Godwin wasn't a rumour. I saw it! I came back from being in the hospital for weeks on end to find that you'd been taken away for treason. Then you suddenly appear out of nowhere and shoot one of our officers! If you're not fighting for the enemy, then who are you fighting for?" Charlie argued.

"If you're so convinced, then why haven't you done anything? Why haven't you gone to any other officers and told them that the Hun has somehow bought me? I don't think you really believe it!"

"I don't want to believe it, Arthur. But then I saw what I saw, and I don't know what to do. They'll have you shot, and I'll be part of the firing squad. Then how can I go home to Mum, Dad, and Little Pimple? If, God willing, I survive this war, people are going to ask me about it one day. All I'm going to be able to say is that the war made me shoot my own brother!"

Arthur noticed tears appearing in Charlie's eyes. "That's not going to happen! You'll see. When we get back into the line, you'll see," Arthur tried to reassure his brother.

"I'm not going into the line with you, Arthur. I don't trust you. Major Clark said one of us could transfer if we're unable to get on. I'm going to see him in the morning."

Arthur looked to the sky. The first flakes of snow had appeared in the air. He thought about what his brother had just said. A transfer might not be a bad idea.

"Fine. Get a transfer. If that's what it's going to take to get you off of my case for some bullshit trench whispers, then do it." Arthur hoped the bluff would work.

What a birthday, he kept thinking as he lay in his crude bed. Hopefully, his next birthday would be a happier time. The war would surely have ended, and all this would finally be over. Wrapped in his goatskin and under several blankets, Arthur shivered himself to sleep.

Another morning came. The snow had fallen all night, and there were still a few small flakes floating softly to the ground during the morning roll call. Arthur saw that Charlie had deliberately chosen to stand as far away from him as possible. He tried to catch his eye, but it was in vain. There was a dark ring under Charlie's left eye.

"Did I do that?" Arthur asked himself.

Upon being dispersed, Arthur received a summons from Major Clark. He went there directly.

"Good morning, Private," the major began.

"Good morning, sir."

"I've heard a bit of a rumour about you, Private."

Oh no...don't tell me you know about Godwin, please don't tell me you know about Godwin! I swear I'll kill you for this, Charlie! The voice inside Arthur's head panicked.

"Rumour, sir?" Arthur asked pathetically, trying to act normal.

"Something about a bar brawl last night involving you and a certain lance corporal." Major Clark looked at Arthur with raised eyebrows. Arthur took in a deep breath.

"I hope that the lance corporal was not by the name of Green?" the major asked.

"No, sir," Arthur lied.

"Then why is it that when he came to see me earlier this morning before roll call, that he had a black eye and came with the request of a transfer?"

Arthur now did not need to lie. "I'm sorry, sir. Yes, it was my brother. He was drunk, and we had an argument."

"And what were you arguing about Private?"

Now Arthur genuinely did need to lie, and he needed to do it well. He couldn't come out with the truth. "Just about stuff, sir."

"Stuff? What stuff? I always thought you two got on quite well."

"We did, sir, but... as I said already, since he's been back from the hospital, he isn't the same," Arthur attempted to explain.

"None of us are the same, Private. It doesn't matter anyhow. I summoned you here to inform you that I granted him his transfer."

"So soon, sir?"

"Yes, he is leaving today. He's joining the 22nd Battalion. They require replacements and, in particular, experienced NCOs. He will be a full corporal in a few days," Major Clark informed Arthur.

"Right. That's that, then. He's off to join the 22nd," Arthur commented.

"That's right. The 22nd will be adjacent to us in the line when we go back anyhow, so you'll be close."

Arthur was somewhat astonished by the sudden news and that it had happened so quickly. He suspiciously thought that Charlie might have been planning this for a while. Arthur had heard enough. Charlie would be leaving later that day, and Arthur wanted to catch him before he left.

"OK, will that be all, sir?"

"That will be all, Private."

Arthur saluted the well-respected officer and ran across to the barracks. It was too late. Charlie had packed and gone before Arthur had had the chance to say farewell and good luck.

"We'll meet again someday soon," Arthur said to himself as he stared at the empty space where his brother's bed had been. "Good luck, brother."

Chapter 15

Snow had been falling for days. Out in the fields where it was unmolested, it had piled at least two feet deep. The trenches offered little shelter as the company shivered as one. Everybody had white eyebrows and white moustaches. The ground was frozen too. To sit down meant a numb backside within minutes; to stand meant near exhaustion. Every day men were being taken away with frost-bitten toes. Fingertips were black. Some men managed to get fires going, but they could expect a shell if an enemy spotted the smoke.

Coming back into the line was different than it had been before. More than three-quarters of the battalion were newly recruited, fresh-faced newcomers. It was an unforgiving introduction to those who had never been near a war before. Inexperience had already cost them several casualties. Some of the luckier ones would be home in a week, just in time for Christmas, where they could brag about how they'd done their part and could show off their wounds. They'd only served a week in the line, if that. Arthur was now in his ninth month away from home. With Christmas being only a week away, he decided to exercise his fingers and do his best to write a letter.

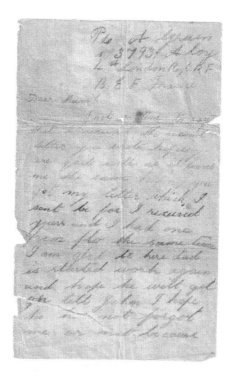

Pte A Green
No. 3793, A coy.
4th London Regiment RF

B.E.F France

Dear Mum,
    Just a line to say that I received the second letter you wrote hoping are quite well as it leaves me the same, hoping you got my letter which I sent be for I received yours, and I had one from flo the same time.
I am glad to hear Dad is started work again and hope he has not forgot me because you know I never here any thing about him. He might send me some fags, as he gets more than I do, and I hope you will all have a happy x-mas and a prosperous new year.
as I expect I shall spend mine in action facing those ugly broutes of huns.
Well, give my love to Granddad and Mar and all at home, Little Pimple and Dolly—hoping she will have a happy x-mas.

Dear Mum, excused me not writing be for, as we are attached to the R.E for 8 days and of cause you know it is mostly night work as well as day, so you know I have not got much time, so excused short letter this time as I have

to shave be for I got to fight for the night.
So goodnight to all. Hoping you all a happy x-mas from
your loving son A.G

XXXX

Arthur had to put his pen down after a few lines. It had stopped working several times, and he'd had to lick the nib to get it going again. He kept the letter short. It was getting dark, and it was too cold to continue.

He uncomfortably leaned against the trench and imagined the look on his mother's face as she received the letter. What gift would he like to give Little Pimple right now? What food would they all be eating around the kitchen table, singing songs in front of the fire in the living room? What would he give to spend Christmas at home? At least his thoughts were warm, even if reality was the stark opposite.

"Arthur!" someone called out.

"What?" he cried back without bothering to turn to see who it was.

"Fairbridge wants you in his dugout."

"Fine," Arthur replied. He stood up and brushed himself down. Snow had covered him so that he was completely white.

"Can you read a map, Private?" Captain Fairbridge asked Arthur upon his entry to the dugout. Arthur certainly hoped that it was a rhetorical question; if not, this new captain would face the same fate as

Godwin.

"Yes, sir!" he answered. He had tried not to sound insulted by Fairbridge's question but failed miserably.

"Look at this then," Fairbridge said, ushering Arthur over to a table in the centre of the underground room. It was a trench map. It was also self-explanatory—black lines for British trenches and red lines for German trenches.

"Right, look here," Captain Fairbridge said, pointing to the first trench in the system of mazes. It was a very detailed map, and each trench on both sides of no man's land was named.

"This is Essex trench." Arthur nodded in frustrated agreement. He didn't like the captain treating him like he was a simpleton. "It's important to us!" Fairbridge told Arthur.

Well, of course it is fucking important to us. It's one of our trenches, and no doubt it's full of our men, Arthur thought, only *just* managing to suppress the urge to speak out loud.

"Yes, sir," he replied.

"Well, it's important to the Hun too," Fairbridge told Arthur.

"Okay," Arthur said, quite simply not caring much for that information.

"If you look here, the trench turns sharply and doubles back on itself. That's why we call it the hairpin." The captain pointed to a turn in the trench which, sure enough, had "hairpin" written on it.

Does this man seriously think I'm a fool? Arthur

thought. "Yes, sir, I can see that!" he said, showing a little exasperation.

"Well, the Germans have captured it!"

Now Arthur was listening. His ears pricked up like a guard dog hearing the front gate swinging open.

"We're in a spot of bother. You see underneath the 'hairpin' we've been tunnelling to the German lines with the intention of detonating a mine. We're attached to the engineers, who are in a real pickle down there. If the Germans were to capture any more of the trench, then we'd be in danger of losing the mine. Weeks of work will be undone. More importantly, our intention of an offensive in this area will be known to the enemy."

Arthur understood the seriousness of the situation but was slightly concerned as to why Captain Fairbridge was sharing this information with him. "Okay, sir. But what's this got to do with me?" he asked.

"Well, Private, this is what we've been training you for. Bombing parties. Clearing out trenches. So you and your platoon are going to retake the lost trench. My officers have already received their briefings, and I'm telling you this because you are one of the only men within your platoon to have seen action. Even the officers are going to learn something from you. I've enough NCOs and other ranks, but that's no substitute for experience. You're going to lead the attack."

Arthur stood flabbergasted. He was just a private. How was he supposed to lead anything? Were all the officers seriously considered that incompetent that they needed to rely on the advice and leadership of a lowly private such as himself?

"I'm not with you at all, sir," Arthur said desperately. "Surely one of the officers shall lead? Even the sergeants—I can't be the only person..."

Fairbridge cut him short. "No, Private Green, you're not the only one. But you're the recommended one."

"Recommended by who, sir?"

"By Major Clark, if you must know. I asked him who he recommended for such a job, and he said that the best soldier he has worked with within the company is you, Private. He thinks you're a capable soldier and one he trusts to get the job done. We discussed it at length, and he is confident that you can do it successfully. My confidence lies within his confidence, and so that's our decision."

Arthur didn't know if he should feel honoured by the major's kind words or distraught that the major may have just issued a death sentence. Arthur chose the latter.

"Get the job done, I will, sir!" He felt a shimmer of pride overcome his previous feelings of frustration and belittlement.

"That's what we like to hear. As I said, our engineers are using this area working in tunnelling parties. We've been attached to them, as the mine is our main priority. So you'll be going in here," Fairbridge said, pointing to the map again. "You join the trench here along this communication trench. It's called the Shipka Pass. Do you need a map to take with you?"

Arthur stared at the map. He didn't need to take this map with him; he knew where Shipka Pass was. "No, sir. I know the way from here."

"Good. You better get going then. Report to Lieutenant Thew. He'll be the platoon commander while you're over there. Good luck, Private!"

"Thank you, sir." Arthur saluted as he made his way out of the dugout.

As he meandered his way through the cold white trenches to the Shipka Pass, he still felt flabbergasted that he had been chosen to lead an attack. He could understand that his experience was invaluable to the new recruits; they'd shown through the previous month of training that they looked up to the battle-hardened survivors of the original battalion, but for commanders to give leadership roles to privates above officers? Surely this was unheard of.

On reaching the Shipka Pass, Arthur found his platoon with ease. It had been several weeks since Major Clark had arrived with the new men, but Arthur still hadn't really gotten to know all their names and still hadn't spoken much with them. He'd been somewhat depressed since his brother's departure, which had flared up rumours again, and had therefore kept to himself. All his old friends were gone. Indeed, this would present an opportunity to erase what he believed everyone thought about him.

"Lieutenant Thew anyone?" he asked openly.

"Here, Private!"

"Lieutenant Thew, I'm Private Green, sir." Arthur stood to attention as he introduced himself.

"Yes, I know who you are," the tall, dark-haired lieutenant said with a deep voice. "Now I assume Captain Fairbridge has briefed you on the situation, and he tells me you're our bombing party expert."

Expert? Arthur had certainly been in several firefights, but he was no bombing party expert. He'd only been training with handheld bombs for a few weeks, and during that time, he'd accidentally blown up one of his own officers.

"Yes, sir!" he decided to say, immediately regretting it.

"Come with me then, Private," Lieutenant Thew said, leading Arthur into another dugout. There was another trench map almost identical to the one Arthur had seen previously with Captain Fairbridge. Lieutenant Thew began the briefing. "So you can see that we're here, and this here is our mine shaft."

That information was not on the other map.

"The Germans attacked about thirty-six hours ago and managed to capture this area here, the hairpin, adjoining to Essex trench. We've barricaded it, but we need it back before they can reinforce it, which we believe they intend to do either by digging a communication trench back to their lines or by rushing men into it under cover of darkness. If they gather the strength to push on to where we are now, then we'll lose the mine."

"How far away are the Germans now then, sir?" Arthur asked.

"About fifty feet."

"Fifty feet?" Arthur repeated with surprise.

"Yes."

"From where we're standing right now, the Germans are fifty feet away?"

"That's right." Lieutenant Thew nodded. Arthur was suddenly terrified. The initial excitement shot out of him like a shell from a cannon.

"So what do you suggest, Private?" Thew asked.

Arthur was stumped. He could never have imagined officers asking for his advice. He did his best to remember the training they had just gone through. "Well, sir, what's our strength?"

"You'll have fifty men, one large platoon."

"I say we should attack at night," Arthur suggested

"Yes, that's a given," Thew retorted.

"At the training camp, they told us that the best way to take a trench was from three sides. So I suggest three groups with fifteen men in each, the first group to attack from where we are now on the right flank. Then another group attacking at the same time from the left. The group attacking head-on will need to cover the open ground, but they shouldn't begin their assault until after the attacks on the flanks have started. That way, the Germans will be less concentrated in the centre."

"If that's what you suggest, Private." Thew nodded again.

"That's only forty-five men. We should leave five

behind to act as runners between each group should we need to contact each other." What was happening? Arthur was sounding like he knew what he was talking about.

"They told me you had excelled in the bombing training. Private, it does sound like you know what to do. You have impressed me. You could almost pass for an officer," Thew complimented the still-astounded private. "So we're going to go in at, let's say, midnight? Does that suit you, Private?"

"Umm, yes, midnight sounds good, sir." Arthur nodded.

Ammunition was passed around the fifty chosen men. The starting positions had been selected carefully, and everybody synchronized their watches. It was a very calm night. Clouds covered the sky, making it darker still. However, there was no wind, and every crunch of feet on the snow-covered ground seemed to echo and drift.

Arthur edged along the trench, still in disbelief that Germans were occupying a section of the British line only fifty feet away. He came to the barricaded section of the trench, which divided the two enemies. The barricade itself was a mere collection of planks of wood, sheets of metal, broken chairs, empty crates, and other random objects piled high to block the trench.

He acknowledged the fifteen other privates who had drawn short straws in joining him by patting them each on the shoulder as he passed them. They looked scared. They looked young. They seemed too innocent to be doing what they were about to do. At only nineteen himself, Arthur felt the same as they did. He was not an officer and still did not understand why he had to take on this responsibility. He knew it was too late to do anything about it.

"Do it for Little Pimple," he said to himself as the thought of her crept into his mind, as she did whenever he was in danger. He checked his watch and counted the last few seconds until midnight.

"Okay, boys, you know what to do!" he whispered as he turned to the other privates behind him. "Let's go!"

Just as he'd played it out in his mind dozens of times already in the previous few hours, Arthur pulled the pin of his first bomb and lobbed it as far as he could over the barricade and along the trench. Three others did the same, and four explosions came in quick succession, ending the calm before the coming storm of battle.

As the soldiers at the back lobbed more bombs, the barricade began to be torn down and clambered over. It was such a crude collection of objects. It was about ten feet deep and very unsteady, but Arthur made it across without receiving enemy fire. The bombs were doing their job and keeping the enemy's heads down. It seemed the Germans were still unaware that they were under attack. As the next few bombs exploded, the tell-tale signs of their success made their presence known as panicked screams in German scattered into the air. A German machine gun opened fire up ahead. Arthur took that as a sign that the left flank's attack had got going exactly as it should have done.

Arthur looked back over the barricade and signalled for more of the men to clamber across. The first two made it safely into the trench, but the next two were killed by bullets to their chests. The following two came using the dead bodies as a bridge to traverse the uneven heap beneath them. Voices in German could be heard shouting up ahead, far too close for comfort.

Suddenly, over the top of the curve of the trench came the Germans' response in their own hand-held bombs. A series of wild explosions hammered the barricade, blowing it to smithereens. The poor boys who were still on it at the time vanished with the fire and smoke into oblivion.

"Let's return the favour, lads!" Arthur called out to the remaining four boys behind him. Arthur knew that this was their first battle, and it showed by the sheer look of terror in their eyes. One boy, who indeed was still only a boy in his mid-teens by Arthur's reckoning, fumbled with a bomb. His nerves were gone already as he pulled at the ring, dislodging the pin. Arthur grabbed it from him and threw it hastily. It exploded harmlessly in the air.

"Don't worry about that. Get the next one ready," Arthur urged the trembling boy. The boy's legs were soaked in urine, but he gathered enough of his senses to correctly throw the next bomb. Around the corner of the trench came German soldiers. One of them thrust a bayonet straight into the stomach of one of Arthur's new young comrades. It was just pure bad luck for the boy that he had chosen to stand where he had, allowing himself to be spotted first. The Germans fought their way past the dying teenager.

The first enemy soldier to reach Arthur was a pathetic resemblance of his own comrades. Nowhere near the age of being able to grow stubble on his chin, he seemed disorientated, and his face was panic-stricken. Arthur grabbed the German child by his clothing and flung him to the floor. As the whimpering foe lay on his back, he stared into Arthur's eyes, displaying only fear and sorrow. Arthur raised his leg and stamped his heavy boot down onto the boy's face. Blood splattered onto his cheeks. Arthur stamped again and again until the young fresh face was nothing but a slippery pulp. Hand-to-hand fighting ensued. Everyone, both British and German, desperately grabbed hold of what they could to use as a weapon.

Arthur found himself gripped by a fierce rage that let loose an unforgiving demon within him. He saw only red. No mercy existed in this fearsome state. Anger and hatred flowed through him as he glanced upward to witness another of his fellow boy soldiers go down. The lifeless body of the boy collapsed as his face received the pointed end of a shovel thrust through it. Blood, brains, and broken bits of bone oozed and flowed out where a nose and a pair of eyes had just been.

Arthur soon took revenge on the boy's behalf and

let the German have it by ramming a bayonet into
his mouth. Blood sprayed relentlessly, turning the
snow around them red. Arthur shouted to his remaining two boys to fall back across the broken
barricade. They both quickly turned and obeyed
the welcome order. One of them had burns covering
his face and was only recognizable by his uniform.
Arthur grimaced as the boy clambered past him and
back across the stretch of trench where the barricade had been moments earlier. Thankfully the Germans did not pursue them.

Arthur stood on the parapet and tried to make
sense of the carnage. He was not sure of what was
happening in different sections of the attack.

To his complete frustration, the frontal assault had
still not begun. He grabbed the boy with the burnt
face and told him to send one of the runners with instructions for the frontal attack to hurry up. The
burnt boy disappeared back through the trench.

Arthur and the last of his chosen fifteen privates
crouched and waited with racing hearts. They
could hear fighting up ahead, but it was useless even
to try and guess what was happening.

"I think the Germans have gone back the other
way," Arthur said to his petrified companion. "Get
your rifle. We'll go forward and have another look,"
he instructed. The boy did as he was told, and the
pair crept back to the position they had just fled
from.

They had to walk across the bodies of the dead to
make any progress along the trench. Looking down

beneath his feet, Arthur saw he was standing on the rib cage of the poor infant-like private who had taken a shovel to his face.

The smell was already beginning to rise. Dead bodies that had loosened their bowels upon succumbing to their deaths reeked the air and filled the ground with squalor. Arthur and the boy crouched down in the slush. They waited for the frontal attack to start. When Arthur heard a machine gun open up, he took that as a sign that the assault had finally got underway. He was furious that it had taken so long.

"Let's go!" he said to the boy, whose name he still didn't know. They meandered on again a few more paces. They stopped when they found a gap in the trench where the wall had collapsed after a shell had hit it. Arthur looked out towards the land between the hairpin-shaped trench and their main front line. He gazed in despair as he saw the fallen bodies of those who had been part of the frontal attack. Clearly dead, they lay there like tree stumps or bleeding boulders. The bullets continued to tear into their flesh, ripping apart their torsos and limbs. Faces disintegrated, muscle and clothing became merged as the machine gun ripped through them, puncturing the visible intestines and other organs that had become exposed. Arthur continued to watch in horror and awe at this, the ghastliest of sights yet witnessed in all his months fighting this sickening war.

Eventually, quietness descended, leaving a pond of

skin, flesh, blood, and broken bone. A soup of mangled people, as if Hades himself had made his presence known to deliver the dance of death upon this Hell on Earth.

Arthur had seen enough of this pitiful debacle. Entirely shaken by what he had just seen, he stood up fully to get a glimpse of the machine gun in its nest of sandbags. Something caught his eye, and so Arthur took a look towards the German front line. He almost lost control of his bladder when through the flashes of a distant fire, he saw hundreds of men in field grey silhouetted with those damned spiky helmets, and they were all coming Arthur's way.

"Oh shit!" he said to the other boy.

"What is it?" the boy asked with tears mixed with sweat streaming down his face.

"Let's get out of here. Quick!" There was no time for explaining. Arthur and the boy ran as fast as they could, clumsily through the trench, tripping and stumbling all the way. They could hear the Germans arriving and jumping into the long crevasse behind them. They made it back to the debris which was once the barricade and crossed it. Men from the battalion were already waiting with bayonets fixed.

"Quickly, put the barricade back up! Grab anything, anything at all!" Arthur shouted.

Out of the darkness came Lieutenant Thew.

"What's going on here, Private?" he asked eagerly.
"There are hundreds of Germans, sir. We fought as best we could along the trench, but they've filled it up again with too many. Hundreds of them. We can't

hold them like this, sir; if they come this way, we won't be able to stop them!"

"All right, Private, don't panic. I'll send a runner to bring up more men. Are we under attack?"

Arthur thought that was a grossly daft question. Of course, they were under attack. The ready men started tearing down their trench sandbags, attempting to resurrect the barricade, which their enemy had blown apart minutes earlier.

"What happened, Private? Were we unable to retake the trench?" Lieutenant Thew was eager for more information.

"I don't know, sir. My section got blasted to hell by German bombs, and the frontal assault came too late. They got caught up in the machine-gun fire, sir. They're all dead. I sent a runner to them, but he hasn't come back yet. I don't know where he is, and I haven't had any contact from the left flank," Arthur explained in a crazed panic.

"Okay, Private, what do you suggest we do now?" Lieutenant Thew asked hastily.

Arthur was amazed by the question. He wasn't the platoon commander; he wasn't even an NCO. So why was all this seemingly his responsibility? "We'll need more bombs, sir. Do we have any?" he asked Thew.

"Plenty, Private, we've got massive boxes of them all stored in the mine shaft."

"Get them up here. We will need to put down a heavy defence of the barricade when the Germans come," Arthur ordered his ill-experienced superior officer. Thew obeyed the command and set his men to bringing forward the boxes of the new explosive weapons as well as the more desperately needed rifle ammunition.

Inexplicably, the Germans didn't come that night. They'd had enough for the time being. They had suffered their fair share of casualties. Arthur and Lieutenant Thew remained alert right through until mid-morning. Several times there had been cause for alarm. The sound of a twig snapping or something which resembled footsteps gave the very jumpy boys below the ground reason to believe they were under attack. After it became apparent that it was probably just the wind, the boys laughed it off nervously.

Arthur had never been so cold in his life. He checked his water bottle, but it had completely frozen. His toes were numb, and he shivered furiously. Lighting a fire was impossible. He would just have to suffer in silence for now, as would everybody else. Welcome reinforcements had made their way into the trench, but every single one of them was a private, straight out of the training camps.

So fresh. So unprepared. So stupid, Arthur thought as he studied what he assumed would be the next layer of bodies before the day was out. Arthur wasn't sure if they were going to be attacking or defending. Maybe nothing. Maybe they'd all just sit here and freeze to death instead.

Upon that thought and as light gently crept into the trench, Arthur looked at the newly reconstructed barricade. It was just sandbags and more broken planks. There was an arm sticking out of it. The skin of the crooked fingers had turned a pale blue. Any blood left inside had frozen.

He turned around to look at the boys behind him, all leaning against the wall of the trench. They huddled in a line like a queue of frozen schoolboys waiting for fate to serve up their deaths. The sound of heavy breathing filled the quiet morning, everybody able to see their breath upon each outward puff.

By midday, Arthur's stomach was rumbling. His throat desired liquid, but the water in his canister was solid ice, and he was unable to unscrew the frozen lid. His fingers were too cold to unscrew the cap anyhow. He thought he would have to get moving, just go for a little walk up and down the short Shipka Pass, but it wasn't necessary. The first German hand-held bomb exploded just above them, sending the recruits into a state of shock.

That's woken them up, Arthur thought.

"Stand to!" ordered Lieutenant Thew.

Arthur immediately pushed the cold to the back of his mind and stood up onto the parapet, exposing his head to see if there was an attack or not. No man's land looked empty, completely white with snow, but something was stirring along the trench and beyond the barricade. He knew that both the British and the Germans occupied different parts of the same trench; neither side would call in artillery for support. The fighting would have to be an extremely close quarter.

Another German bomb flew towards their position, and Arthur was able to see where it had come from. It exploded prematurely in the air but still managed to make the fresh-faced boys jump. Arthur asked one of them to hand him a bomb. He took it and threw it roughly where he saw the German one come from. The flash and the explosion sent a German helmet up into the air. They watched and waited for a response. It came far too suddenly. German soldiers began clambering out of the trench at either side from all along it. Then Arthur could see the spikes of enemy helmets bobbing up and down along the jagged trench, shaped like a set of teeth.

There was going to be no mercy here, and Arthur knew it. His main worry was that the majority of boys behind him did not know it. Their baptism of battle was going to be very bitter.

"Get up, get up, get up!" Arthur shouted at his startled comrades. A bomb landed roughly twenty feet behind Arthur, shredding apart several boys who never even got a chance to blink. He saw that they were in a death pit and probably stood more chance out in the open than down in the ground, where the Germans could fire upon them like rats in a barrel.

"Out of the trench!" he called out. Arthur stood on the sandbags and fired his rifle from his hip, sending one German down into the barbed wire. It was clear the man wasn't dead, but Arthur had no time and fired again, sending a bullet into the kneecap of another German who dropped his rifle, yelling out as he fell, putting both of his hands over his broken patella. Several British soldiers had managed to make it out of the trench, but most of them were still down below receiving bullets and bombs pitilessly as the attack overwhelmed the defenders.

The merciless morning went on into a bloodbath. Arthur felt no fear; pure adrenalin was forcing its way through his body. He fought on relentlessly. Desperation and the sheer will to survive possessed him. No pity or shame could prevent him from the menace that he had become. He swung this way and that with his rifle and bayonet, slicing the cheeks of one enemy soldier before thrusting the blade into the belly of another. Arthur struggled to dislodge the bayonet from the man's stomach, and so he let the man drop, taking the rifle with him.

Arthur reached for the nearest possible weapon, a piece of broken wood about a yard in length. His next victim received the wood's blunt end in the throat, forcing him to gargle and struggle for air as his windpipe collapsed. The choking man went down onto his knees, clutching his neck with both hands. Arthur clubbed him again, this time over the back of the neck, snapping the spinal cord. The body fell onto the snowy soil as his fearful soul began its painful journey to lifelessness.

Arthur went on into the bloody madness, choosing his next victim. A German, caught in a patch of barbed wire, who had no helmet and no weapon.

One of his arms was loose, but the other was tangled, and he was unable to use it. Arthur ran up to the struggling target and swung his wooden club viciously at him. The trapped man raised his free arm to block the blow, but his coordination was out. The wood struck his hand and broke all four of his fingers. Arthur swung again, hitting the man on the hand in the same place. The German cried out in pain before Arthur rammed the wood into his face, breaking his nose. The man crumpled into a heap, still unable to move for the wire around him. Arthur, fuelled by rage and hatred, uncoiled a piece of wire and wrapped it around the crying man's neck. He strung it around twice and then pulled as hard as he could, using his boot on the man's shoulder to aid the strangulation. Barbs pierced the skin, and blood began to spurt.

The man's purple face bulged at the eyes, and his tongue slithered out of his mouth like a slug. Arthur held on until the man had taken his final gasp, then he let go, allowing another fatality to join the ranks of the dead. The frenzy went on all around Arthur. He stood and watched the chaos surrounding him, the catastrophe of inhumanity that was unfolding before his manic eyes.

Something hit him in the head, and he spun around dizzily, hitting the pink snow. A pair of arms grabbed hold of his legs and dragged him down into the trench.

Suddenly the trench filled with smoke from a series of explosions behind him. Through the black cloud came a British officer firing in nearly all directions with his pistol. Behind the officer were more British soldiers. Reinforcements had finally arrived. As the officer got closer to Arthur, he could see that it was Major Clark! This was the second time this man had rescued him! British troops swarmed the area. Some of them dropped down as a machine gun from the Germans front line opened up. Arthur rolled to his knees, surrounded by dead men.

"Private Green?" the major asked.

"Sir!" Arthur panted.

"My God, look at this place!" Major Clark grimaced. Further along towards the hairpin and far beyond the old barricades, Arthur heard the fighting continue.

"Easy now, Private Green," Major Clark put a hand on Arthur's shoulder. "We'll handle it from here. You get back to the rear, boy; you've done more than enough."

Chapter 16

The fighting from Essex trench into the hair-pin continued relentlessly. Days and nights blurred into one. Time became non-existent. Arthur had no idea how many days he'd gone without sleep. He was both physically and mentally exhausted as he fought on.

However, the long-awaited order to leave the frontline and take up positions in reserve trenches finally came. When he arrived in the reserve trench, Arthur managed to find sufficient space on the cold hard floor to sit down.

He listened to two sentries chatting away idly. One of them mentioned that it was Christmas Eve, which was Arthur's first surprise. The second was that they had been replaced in the firing line at Essex trench by Arthur's brother's new battalion, the 22nd.

Battered and broken, bruised and beaten down, Arthur sat in the reserve trenches shivering and sipping on tea. He'd been awake for so long that he couldn't sleep now, even if he wanted to. He'd forgotten how to do it. Closing his eyes filled the dark lids with images of bombs exploding and boys screaming as they writhed in pain. His mind kept reverting to him peering through a box telescope a few days ago. He had seen a small group of German soldiers filling a crater with limbs in a useless and futile effort to create some space for the living just so that they could continue the slaughter: British legs, German arms, someone's head, someone else's feet. Bits of half-buried bodies lay scattered across a forest of broken bones that poked out through the top of the equally unforgiving snow.

The tea was good, at least. It was warm and had some sugar in it, which he greatly appreciated. Bread had been handed out, but it was frozen. Arthur had received some hard slices, but he had refused to eat them. They had blood on them. Everything had blood on it. His stomach was aching with hunger, but the very thought of putting something in his mouth and swallowing made him sick. He'd eat soon enough. He knew that much. There were some biscuits in his pack, and he'd eat them later. Not now, though. For the time being, he just wanted to sit. If he fell asleep and never woke up, it would be a blessing.

When Arthur snapped out of his daze, it was light again. He didn't feel like he had slept. He felt awful and grotty, unclean and stiff at every joint. But it was light, and he had no recollection of where the last few hours had gone, so he must have been asleep. Someone else was sleeping on his legs. He didn't care, as it was keeping him warm.

"Merry Christmas, Private!" a croaky half-whisper came at him from behind. He turned to see Captain Fairbridge. He didn't look right. Something about his face and the way he moved was different. Then Arthur noticed the half-empty whisky bottle in his hand. He was drunk.

"Come celebrate with me, Private. It's fucking Christmas! Come to my dugout, boy!" the captain slurred.

There was no way Arthur was going to miss this opportunity. The chance to get underground, drink some alcohol and possibly have a chance in hell of getting warm!

The dugout was cold. There were icicles in the entrance, hanging down. They were just like the rest of the soldiers, clinging on to their fragile existence whenever a shell exploded. Arthur could see a tin cup filled with ice where the water had frozen. The captain picked up the cup and smashed the ice out of it with a knife. Then he poured in some whisky and handed it to Arthur.

"Sit down, boy." He gestured to a chair. The dugout was remarkably well kitted out. The captain had the luxury of a few wooden planks with blankets on as a bed. There was electric lighting inside and a lantern that flickered randomly.

"Thank you, sir!" Arthur said as he took up the captain's offer. The captain's speech was slow.

"Do you know what day it is, boy?"

"It's Christmas Day, sir!" Arthur remarked through chattering teeth.

"That's right, Merry Christmas!"

"Same to you, sir, thanks for the drink. It's been a while since I had whisky, sir. My dad didn't drink it all that much. He preferred rum. I tried that a few times."

"Rum? You're in luck, boy; I've got a bottle of that too!" Fairbridge exclaimed excitedly.

"Wow, well, it is Christmas after all, sir!" Arthur smiled.

"Christmas in France. I suppose this is one Christmas we won't forget, boy. You'll be telling your grandkids how you spent Christmas 1915 in action against the Hun. Mighty proud they'll be too. You know we're going to win the war, don't you, Private?" the captain asked as he swayed in his chair.

"Let's hope so, sir." Arthur sipped at his whisky.

"Don't worry, boy, I'll admit we have taken longer than I first thought we would, but we're going to win it in the end. Christmas, they told me, it'll be over by Christmas! Do you remember? Everyone saying it'd be over by Christmas?"

"I do remember, sir. Well, I think they meant Christmas 1916, sir. It'll be over by next Christmas, sir."

"That's right, boy. Christmas 1916, it will all be over." The captain took a massive gulp of whisky, and Arthur took another sip. As it slid down his throat, the warmth of the alcohol was sincerely welcome. Then Arthur decided to gulp it too. Fairbridge filled Arthur's cup again without invitation.

"How old are you, boy?" the inebriated captain

asked.

"I was nineteen last month, sir."

"Nineteen! Still a nipper. I was thirty on my last birthday. What a day that was. I'm August born, you see, always had beautiful weather for my birthdays."

"I see." Arthur didn't have anything else to say to the captain.

"Do you want to know a secret, Private?" Fairbridge asked.

"Umm, yes, sir!" Arthur tried to sound eager. In truth, there was very little that he cared to listen to but supposed anything in some sort of shelter to drown out the incessant droning of shells would do.

"There's not going to be any football matches with the Huns this year, boy."

"No, sir," Arthur hadn't for a second supposed there would be.

"Our divisional artillery is sending them a gift today. They're going to fire three hundred shells as a gesture. Just to let them know that we're not playing games anymore," the captain continued as he swallowed another mouthful of whisky.

"No, sir." Arthur had run out of things to say.

"Well, there's another reason I wanted you in here today. There's someone else coming to see you, and here he is!"

With miraculous timing, Major Clark ducked into the dugout. Blocking the dim light from the entrance, he sent an icicle to a shattering end.

"At ease, and Merry Christmas, gentlemen!" the

major said with a smile. "I said at ease—that means don't stand up, Arthur; you stay put and finish whatever it is you've got there. What is it, gin?"

"Whisky, sir," Arthur answered. "Christmas with Captain Fairbridge, sir." Arthur could feel that it was having a slight effect on him. He was getting a little tipsy as Fairbridge again topped up his cup before pouring one for the major.

The three cups chinked, and everyone said "Cheers" and "Merry Christmas" once more.
Major Clark pulled up a chair and put his hand on Arthur's shoulder.

"How are you doing, Greeny?" he asked sincerely.

"I'm okay, sir. I had a bit of rest this morning, and it's warmer in here than it is out there. I must give thanks to Captain Fairbridge for bringing me in here," Arthur said, turning towards Fairbridge, who didn't speak but nodded an acceptance before finishing off yet another swig.

"That's good. Have you eaten?" the major asked.

"Not really, sir. Haven't felt like eating," Arthur responded.

"Well, here, have this." The kind major gave Arthur a bar of chocolate.

Arthur raised his eyebrows at the sight of the unexpected gift. "Wow, thank you very much, sir!" he said appreciatively.

"I gave you a terrible gift last week with that bombing party, didn't I?" the major admitted. "A bar of chocolate is the least I can do. And that's why I'm going to do more."

"What do you mean to do more, sir?" Arthur queried.

"Well, you're up for a medal, lad," Major Clark announced to Arthur.

Arthur's heart started racing. He had no idea that those words were going to come out of the major's mouth. Was the whisky playing games with his mind?

"A medal, sir?" Arthur was stunned.

Fairbridge spoke next as he sat back down. "Private, you led the attack on the hairpin and fought solidly for what, six days? I've never seen such gallantry, and here you are alive to tell the tale."

"I..." Arthur was lost. "I didn't know you were there, sir. Lieutenant Thew was the platoon commander, sir."

"Yes, he was. But Lieutenant Thew took himself out of the battle, only lightly wounded but exhausted. You were ordered to do the same several times and get back for some rest, but you refused and continued fighting. Do you know how many Germans you killed?"

"No, sir."

"Do you know how many British lives you've saved?"

"No, sir."

"You also saved the mine, Arthur; you're a bloody hero. There's a whole company of dead Germans out there who were brought down by your hand. You inspired the lads to keep fighting, and you belittled the officers who wanted to withdraw. If it weren't for you, we would not be sitting here now. The line may well have collapsed, the mine gone with it, and Germany would have had a minor victory just on the brink of Christmas. Instead, they're back in their lines cowering with a bloody nose!"

Fairbridge drank again.

He must be very drunk by now, Arthur thought. *He was drunk when he came to get me! He's had nearly five cups of whisky since then!*

"So I've been thinking of a citation. How does this sound?" the major continued: "*Private Arthur Green heroically steadied the line and rallied the troops on his own initiative in the face of heavy and merciless enemy attack. Thanks to his quick thinking and valour under fire, the enemy was repulsed with heavy loss.* I haven't finished it yet. Some things will need changing. It needs to have more detail, but it also needs to be short and to the point. So it's a DCM for you, Arthur, that's Distinguished Conduct Medal. I think it'd have been a VC if you'd have been killed, but you weren't. Better a DCM and alive than a posthumous Victoria Cross, eh?" Clark said.

Arthur was smiling by the time the major had stopped talking. He knew he'd fought bravely but had he distinguished himself? Well, maybe. It all seemed like a blur now. Had he really killed so many people?

"You've been nicknamed the 'Hero of Shipka Pass!'" Clark added.

"The Hero of Shipka Pass!" Arthur repeated his new title.

Six days of sleepless ongoing battle had forced Arthur to forget about the old rumours, and he could not wait to go and tell Charlie.

"Will I be able to see my brother, sir? I want to tell him; he'll be pleased to hear the news, sir!"

"Not today, sadly. I believe the 22nd are up at the front trenches now. We don't want to get you killed before you receive the medal. We'll be moving out of the line again tomorrow, but we'll have word passed along."

"Where are we going, sir?" Arthur asked eagerly. "Will my medal be sent to me?"

"Ha-ha, no, boy," Fairbridge said with a smile on his face. "We've got a real Christmas present for the whole battalion."

"What's that then, sir?" Arthur asked again. He was completely awake now. The combination of whisky and such praise from up high had seen to that. The major spoke next.

"Well, we're leaving the frontline tomorrow. We're going to spend about three weeks continuing our work with the engineers, mainly in carrying and fetching supplies for the mine, and then...would you like to deliver the news, Captain Fairbridge?" The major smiled.

"Thank you, sir," Fairbridge took on the baton of news. "And then, Private, you're going home!"

Arthur's face lit up with excitement and surprise. His jaw dropped open. He had to put down the whisky and hold his head in his hands.

"Keep it to yourself, for now, Private. We're going

to tell the rest of the men tonight at roll call."

"Thank you, Captain," Major Clark intervened once more. "We'll be home in London by the first week of February. You'll be summoned to receive your medal, and you'll be able to bring your family along to see the ceremony."

"My family, sir?" Arthur had forgotten about them.

"That's right, I'm sure you've got a mother and father who are missing you as much as any parent would right now, and I'm sure they're going to be very proud parents when they see you get your medal."

"And sir?" Arthur asked hesitantly.

"Yes, Private?" answered the major, who had helped himself to more whisky.

"What about my brother, sir?"

"Not your brother, sadly. The 22nd is staying for a while longer yet. Plus, your brother had what, four months in a French hospital, didn't he?"

"He did, sir."

"And he was offered the chance to go home, but he turned it down."

"I see, sir."

"You'll have plenty of time to see your brother when all this is over, ok, Private?"

"Yes, sir, thank you very much, sir."

"I feel it is us thanking you, Private. Dare I say, no one has earned a trip home more than you have, Arthur Green, DCM!" the major said, adding the medal to his name.

Arthur was overcome with emotion. He didn't care much for the medal after being told he was going home. He'd eat his mother's hot food and sleep in a real bed again! A tear nearly broke out onto his cheek from his swollen eyelids when he imagined picking up Little Pimple to give her the biggest of hugs.

"Would you like more whisky, Private?" Fairbridge asked. He didn't give Arthur the chance to answer. He filled his tin cup to about halfway, which also finished the bottle. "Bugger!" Fairbridge exclaimed. "Well, we'll have to move onto the rum now, won't we?"

Arthur was drunk. Not just on alcohol but on excitement and happiness. What news! He knocked back the whisky like a dedicated drinker, slamming the cup on the wooden table in front of him. He burped, looked at the curly-haired captain, and said loudly and drunkenly, "I'm going home!"

Chapter 17

The cold January snow remained crisp beneath the soldiers' feet without letting up. Vehicles slid along the tracks, horses collapsed from exhaustion or froze to death in the night. Survival in the fight against the bitter winter became the battalion's number one objective. Here, several miles behind the frontline, away from the shells and the bullets, nature was their enemy.

Arthur had been assigned to a logging party. Although he preferred it to frontline action, of which he'd seen plenty, he was no skilled lumberjack. Chopping down trees was not easy work. Rolling the logs and lifting them onto trucks to be taken to the front was tough going. It was not without its hazards either. Many of his pals had received wounds from the forest. Sores opened on their hands, which were not used to tools such as saws and axes. Splinters and grazes were commonplace all along their arms and shoulders from lifting jagged pieces of wood.

Then one day in late January, Arthur, along with several others, was ordered to get into a truck, which he had loaded with logs, and go with the driver to the front line to help unload them into the reserve trenches.

The road was icy, and the crude truck they were sitting in frequently slid, almost spinning several times. It was fortunate that they were unable to go much faster. If they were to come off the frozen road at any sort of speed, they'd all be killed by the sheer weight of wood that would hurtle into their bodies.

Arthur sat in the front of the truck, sandwiched between a new arrival who'd only been at the front a few weeks and an uneasy driver who was concentrating fiercely. The sound of the front line getting closer and closer brought back recent memories of fear. A nervous chill shot through Arthur and his legs began to shake.

"Can you stop that!" the driver said rudely to Arthur.

"Stop what?" Arthur asked.

"Doing that thing with your legs. It's putting me off. You're making me nervous."

"I can't help it. It's the front. It has that effect on you when you've been here as long as I have," Arthur explained bitterly.

"As long as you have? You must be joking. I've been here since September 1914, pal."

"But have you been in the trenches? Or are you just a driver?" Arthur fired back condescendingly.

"Just a driver? Ha!" the driver laughed. "You see that on the horizon?" The driver nodded ahead as he managed to turn a sharp corner in the snow.

"See what?" Arthur questioned the man begrudgingly.

"That. On the horizon, and over there another one," the driver repeated, pointing to his right but having to quickly bring his hand back to the steering wheel to steady the vehicle.   "Those balloons. You can't miss them, those bloody great big fat things in the sky. Do you see them?"

"Yes, I can see them. What about them?" Arthur wondered.

"They're spotters for Hun artillery. You'll probably find out in a few minutes. Whenever they see supply trucks going forward in convoy like this, they let us have it. Just as dangerous as being in the line. Worse in the summer, though. Dirt tracks kick up the dust. We stand out like sore thumbs. Six of us drivers got killed in one trip last week. Plus another seven or eight wounded. We were taking supplies, and we got ourselves spotted all right. The first three trucks got hit directly, the road got blocked, and we couldn't go back fast enough. The whole convoy got caught up in it. Worse for the horse-drawn, though. Once them horses start panicking and rearing up, it's bloody murderous. We shouldn't be doing that to animals, in my opinion, but what else are we supposed to do?" the driver told Arthur and the new boy, who had also started to shake.

"Oh Christ, don't you start!" The driver turned his attention to the new boy. "You been here long an' all?"

"Not really," the boy spoke in a tiny, high-pitched,

pathetic whine.

Arthur looked at the boy. There was a familiarity to the way he spoke and his body language. Arthur thought about it for a few moments, then realized what it was. This newcomer was almost a replica of Arthur when he'd first arrived. The nervousness, the innocent, childlike naivety of a boy who wanted to be a man.

"Hey," Arthur spoke to the boy, grabbing his attention by clicking his fingers. "How old are you?"

"I'm seventeen," the boy whimpered.

"Well, I'm not much older, but let me tell you. I used to be just like you, terrified. I still am. You can see I'm shaking too. But you've got to conquer the fear first. When you can do that, you'll be all right."

"How long have you been here?" the boy asked Arthur.

"I joined up in December 1914 and got shipped out last March."

"That's almost a year," the boy commented.

"That's right. I was at Ypres just after they used gas for the first time. Been in the line pretty much the whole time since. But, as I said, I used to be just like you. Helpless. Ah, you'll be all right," Arthur tried to reassure the boy, who seemed to have aged even since getting in the vehicle. The dark frown which drew itself across the boy's forehead, combined with his clenched fists, gave his body a stance and mannerism beyond his years.

"Here we go!" shouted the driver. Shells that came from nowhere started to burst about half a mile in front of the convoy. Slowly they crept closer and closer, one after the other, like the harmless flickers of an infant in the sand. Soon the rumbles and the booms followed, and the deafening explosions racked the ears of everyone around. Stones and ice flung towards the vehicle, smashing the windscreen. Another earth-shattering thud blew the side of the truck, throwing the three men inside from side to side like rag dolls.

"Get out, get out, get out!" the driver shouted to the new boy, who was already fighting with the handle.

After a few seconds of struggling with the door, it opened. The boy managed to jump free, but another shell struck close by, tipping the truck over. Arthur jumped from the open door as the whole thing capsized. He scrambled away, thinking he would not be quick enough, but the new boy had managed to grab hold of part of Arthur's clothing and pulled him into an adjacent field, just before the truck would have landed on top of him.

Arthur was half a second from being crushed to death. The logs from the truck came free from their bindings and rolled into the field.

Gathering his breath, Arthur had a look around him. He counted at least seven other trucks, all loaded with logs, that the short shelling had also destroyed. It had all only lasted a few moments. Other survivors were still clambering out of broken windows or doors. One overturned truck had a dead body next to it, and screaming was coming from within. Others were already on their way to help, so Arthur didn't bother going over to try and free the fellow trapped inside.

He looked on towards the road ahead and watched the rest of the convoy continue on its way. Not one of the trucks stopped to help anyone at all. There was no sign of their driver. Either he was underneath the truck and dead, or he'd run away somewhere. Although where he'd have run to was anybody's guess.

"Well, I suppose that means we're walking back!" Arthur said to the boy, who was shaking ferociously with a mixture of fear and cold. Some snowflakes began to fall, rendering their situation even worse than it already was.

"Come on. Let's get going," Arthur sighed.

"I'm Anthony Roberts," the boy said, offering Arthur a hand.

"I'm Arthur. Arthur Green, Private."

The two shook hands and plodded on back the same way they came.

"You're the hero of Shipka Pass, aren't you?" Roberts asked.

"Ha. Yeah, that's what they've started calling me," Arthur grinned. "Well, Anthony, I think I should thank you for saving my life back there. All this time at the front, and I've been thinking that being a driver was a luxury job. Apparently not. Jesus Christ, would you look at that lot."

Arthur had turned to look back at the convoy. Most of the undamaged trucks were now gently roll-

ing out of sight. The fields they were in were another close reminder of where they were. Broken
vehicles of all kinds dotted the roads and the fields.
Beneath the snow and the craters, the roads were
barely visible anyhow.

"Say, where are you from?" Arthur asked his new-
found friend.

"London, North-end, just by Tottenham High
Street."

"Really?" Arthur's face lit up. "That's where I'm
from! 11 High Street, Tottenham!" The recalling of
his address made him think of Little Pimple.

"Well then, we're practically neighbours, aren't
we?" Roberts smiled back. The conversation trun-
dled on about home, and soon after, both of them
had stopped shaking.

The walk back to their makeshift barracks was
long, and it was dark by the time they arrived there.

"Right, how about you and I hit the town tonight?" Arthur suggested to Roberts.

"I'm in!" came a quick-fire response.

Bethune was bustling, a large town full of night-
life typically symbolized by drunken English soldiers filling the music halls, bars, and brothels.

Arthur and his new friend Anthony Roberts
crawled the town from bar to bar, singing and dancing the night away. They danced with local French
girls, who were more than happy to accommodate
young English soldiers. According to two of the girls
they were chatting to earlier on in the night, the

English had better manners than their French coun-
terparts, and they found it flattering that the English always insisted on paying for everything.

The pair stumbled along towards the next bar,
laughing and joking drunkenly. Upon entry, Arthur
overheard two sergeants talking.

"Blown to kingdom come, it was," said the first
sergeant, a large fat man with a red nose and a
monobrow.

"I was up there just a week ago. Sheer murder t'was. To be honest, I'm glad they've blown it
up," the second commented. He was a skinny little
fellow with a high, squeaky northern accent.

Arthur was intrigued as to what they were talking about and listened closer.

"Them London lot got it bad. I heard about three
hundred were taken prisoner," the squeaky north-
erner went on. "I'm not one to know much about
grand strategy, but I can tell thee, brass are gonna be
kickin' themselves, t'amount of soldiers lost upon
that bloody hairpin."

Arthur's ears pricked up. As far as he knew, his
brother was still on the hairpin. He had to find out
what they were talking about.

"Did I just overhear you say they've blown up the
hairpin?" Arthur interrupted.

"Aye lad, Boche blew their own mine before we
could detonate ours. T'ole lot's gone up, t'least
that's what I 'eard."

"Charlie!" Arthur had to find out if Charlie was all
right. He turned to run.

"Where are you going?" Roberts shouted after him.

"I've got to find out about my brother!" he shouted back.

Arthur ran as fast as he could towards the battalion HQ, which was in the town in an old hotel. He ran in and was slightly concerned by the amount of activity going on in there. The lobby was full of officers going this way and that way, orderlies and batmen running around and carrying things. It was chaotic.

Arthur could sense something was up. He burst into Major Clark's HQ to find both Captain Fairbridge and Lieutenant Thew arguing with two different people about something. Major Clark himself was yelling down the phone.

"No, we cannot. It is impossible. It will take another day to get the battalion ready to march!" Major Clark said. He paused and waited for the person on the other end of the line to stop talking. "Then send in the 1st or 2nd Battalions. Mine is not ready... Because they're all over the town; they've got their passes, and they're using them!"

Arthur did not like the sound of what was going on. It was obviously serious.

"What the hell are you doing in here, Private?" Captain Fairbridge demanded from Arthur.

"I came to find out about my brother, sir, thought one of the officers would know."

"You don't come barging into HQ like that. What the hell do you need to know about your brother for?" the captain said with a raised, angry voice.

"I heard something about the hairpin. I wanted to know if he was still up there."

"What unit is your brother with?"

"22nd Battalion, sir," Arthur panted.

"I don't know. The hairpin which we spent God knows how many lives defending no longer exists. Boche detonated their own mine underneath it, and now the line is collapsing. Our leave to England may be put on hold."

The entire HQ was chaotic, with several phones ringing and all of them being answered by staff officers who didn't know what to say.

"May I ask what's going on, sir?" Arthur asked

Major Clark slammed the phone down and looked at Arthur. "What are you doing in here, Private? This is an Officers' HQ." He was furious.

"Sorry, sir, I just heard about the hairpin, sir, and wanted to find out about my brother."

"Get out!" Major Clark was red in the face, with veins about to burst.

"Yes, sir." Arthur walked away from the room as he heard the major pick up the phone and demand to be put through to the general.

Arthur was going to have to wait. He left the panic-stricken HQ, went back to his barracks, sat on his bed, and hoped his brother was ok. He'd learned not to accept idle gossip, so he discounted the figures of three hundred prisoners he'd heard the sergeants talking about. However, after hearing it from his company captain, he knew that the hairpin's destruction was not trench whispers.

The next morning, the twenty-sixth day of the new year, the battalion was ordered up for a parade in the town centre. They marched in fours in full parade gear. It was bitterly cold, and none of the men had any idea why it was necessary to practice a pointless drill, simply walking one direction in step and then turning to head off in another. Still, it wasn't as bad as being in the line, and it wasn't as bad as logging, so no one complained; they just questioned its purpose. As far as they were concerned, they would start preparing to leave in a week. Excitement was rife throughout all the ranks. Like a belated Christmas, the atmosphere spread itself around them. It was a warm, intangible blanket of comfort and joy. Only Arthur had any inkling that this might not be the case.

The order to halt was given, followed by hundreds of boots stamping and coming to an abrupt stop in the brown, slushy snow.

Major Clark slowly walked to the centre of the long line of men. He opened a piece of paper and started to read. Putting down the paper and with a serious look on his face, he addressed the battalion.

"I'm sorry to say...that we have to do another brief stint in the line before we go home."

Grumbles and moans made their way from each direction.

"Quiet, please, quiet now, lads!" Captain Fairbridge ordered.

It was clear that Major Clark had no desire to be the bearer of such bad news to his beloved men, but like them, he had to obey his orders from above, and so he continued reluctantly. "Yesterday, the Germans detonated their mine underneath the hairpin, completely destroying it. Men of the Londons suffered heavy casualties, and we've managed to rush replacements in from men closer to the line farther south. In turn, this has weakened our southern flank, which needs strengthening, and we are the sorry sods who have been chosen to do it. We'll be at the extreme end of the British line, occupying former French positions. We, officers included, are to prepare for the twenty-mile march to Lens, setting off no later than thirteen hundred hours, to occupy the line no later than midnight tonight. We're to march with weapons and ammo only. There is a supply dump with food en route just past a village called Noeux Les Mines. Get back to your billets and prepare for roll call here at midday. Battalion dismissed!"

The major immediately walked away with his head down towards HQ, and to anyone who was watching him, it was apparent he was in distress about what he had had to say. Arthur felt somewhat sorry for the poor major.

Roll call took place at midday, precisely as ordered. The whole battalion was ready to begin the long, cold march.

Captain Fairbridge left his standing position just

after the last name had been called and walked towards his company. "Private Green."

"Sir." Arthur had to speak loudly as the captain couldn't see where he was standing amongst the men.

"News from the front."

"About my brother, sir?"

"No, about his unit. They're marching south as we speak. They're to be on our left flank when we get to Lens; after we're billeted, you can go and find them and see if your brother is there, ok?"

Arthur sincerely appreciated the news and the permission to go and search for Charlie. He was also glad to be next to his good new friend Roberts as the company received the order to march back into the madness.

Chapter 18

The trenches they'd occupied went straight through a built-up area. The buildings were gone save for piles of bricks and random remains of walls. The cellars were usable, and they had been incorporated into the trench system. It was reasonably comfortable. French soldiers had previously occupied these trenches. The French had a habit of keeping them much tidier than the British. It showed, too, even after they'd gone. They'd drilled or hammered hooks into the bricks to hang clothes, carefully carved out neat fireplaces and cooking areas, and they'd made far more of an effort to make some sort of seating areas. Arthur lazed around, pondering about it. He thought it was something the British could learn from.

"Heads down, lads, keep your heads down," Captain Fairbridge told the boys as he moved, crouching through the mixture of brick and mud. "Right, listen closely."

Arthur and some others gathered around inside the trench. It was light again. They'd arrived into the line on schedule and fumbled about the ruined area finding their new billets uneasily in the dark.

Fairbridge went on to describe their position and that it was South Maroc, a suburb of Lens. Half a mile to their north were the 22nd battalion, and directly behind them was the 6th London Field Ambulance service.

The Germans were dug in, four hundred yards ahead of them across the rubble, and they held most of the city. There was also a pair of slag heaps, the double crassier, which the captain had described as a pair of tits as if they were on the stomach of a giant, sleeping woman. Arthur hoped they weren't about to receive orders to attack slag heaps again. He convinced himself it was unlikely.

The captain explained that they were only here to fill in the gap left behind after the previous occupiers had been sent farther North to prevent a German breakthrough at the hairpin. They'd only be here a few days anyhow, and there was no significant action being fought here. Arthur was eager to go and look for Charlie. As Captain Fairbridge drew his briefing to a close, he asked if anyone had any questions.

"Sir, can I go and find my brother?" Arthur asked.

"Yes, of course, you can, but keep your head down. It's quiet out there. Hun's got snipers everywhere."

"Yes, sir, I'll be steady, sir," Arthur assured the captain.

Arthur clumsily clogged his way through the trench. There was strange surrealism to having trenches going straight through a town. Every so often, the trench's wall turned into a genuine red brick wall and a real cellar with large beige bricks curving over in a perfect archway sheltering as many men as could fit under it.

After carefully negotiating several corners, he found the 22nd Battalion. He excused himself through them, prompting one private to give him an obscenity as he accidentally trod on his toes.

Then, amongst the boys, with a cigarette in one hand and a mess tin in the other, Charlie was there. Their eyes met instantly. Charlie's face relaxed its cheek muscles, and his smile became a surprised stare.

"Well, well, well!" he said, "look here, boys, it's the hero of Shipka Pass!"

"Hello, Charlie!" Arthur pointlessly whispered.

"What the bloody hell are you doing in this neck of the woods? Thought they'd sent you home!"

"Change of plan!" Arthur said with a smile

"So I see. Well, we heard all about your exploits up at the hairpin. Now you're getting a medal?"

"That's right. Got sent here last night and got told the 22nd were on our left, so I thought I'd pop over and see if you were here," Arthur said.

"Well, here I am," Charlie frowned.

"I heard about the hairpin and feared the worst, so I had to come and find you," Arthur explained.

"Come for a walk, brother. Let's not stand about making idle chit-chat. It's cold. Do you want some tea?" Charlie offered him his mess tin, but Arthur declined. He followed Charlie down some steps into an empty cellar.

"Look, Charlie, I thought that now I've proven I'm not a coward or a traitor, we might put the past behind us," Arthur declared quickly to the point.

"The past will be behind us when this damn war is finished. Then you can prance about with your medal as much as you like," Charlie fired back.

"Charlie, I don't know where I'm at with you. I've been here and fought just as long as you have. I've been in action and faced death every day for nearly a year. Why can't you admit you were wrong about me?" Arthur pleaded in exasperation.

"Because I will always remember what I saw with my own eyes that day you killed Godwin," Charlie said, throwing his mess tin on the floor.

"Right, let's sit down. It's time for you to know the truth," Arthur exclaimed. The brothers sat down, and Arthur told Charlie the entire story. He explained everything in as much detail as he could since the day Charlie first went missing. He told him about the first encounter with Godwin when Burnham had died, how they hadn't recognised his face as it was so dismantled, and had had to check his paybook for his name.

Then Arthur went on about the patrol with Ashpreet and the other Indian soldiers. The onions were thrown at them from the German Major Badstuebner, followed by Clark's truce. He spoke about Godwin replacing Clark to take over the company, Wignell's VC, the meeting with the General, and Major Burnett's dismissal. Everything Arthur could remember right up to the day he had been forced to kill Godwin to prevent the truth of the truce ever being known to the general public after Godwin had blackmailed the general. After he'd finished the long story, Arthur couldn't tell if Charlie had believed him.

"All right," Charlie eventually said. "We've really been in the thick of it, haven't we?"

"Yes, we have." Arthur nodded solemnly.

"Strange to think that we're the last of all our lot still around, including all our friends we met after Ypres. Do you remember shipping out?" Charlie asked with a smile.

"Of course I do, Wilson and Yates getting seasick across the channel and spewing on my boots." The brothers smiled as they reminisced.

"Do you remember back at Neuve Chapelle when Steeples couldn't times eight by ten?" Arthur thought back with a chuckle.

"Ha, I remember. Poor Steeples. What a life he has now. I wonder where he is."

"He's in Hell all right, living like that. And what about poor old Gareth Ellmer. He was alive when I lay down at Ypres and dead when I sat up again," Arthur reminded him. "Lindsay's still missing, Wignell's back in Blighty with Salt and Yates."

"We've had that many new officers come and go too. It's a miracle Clark's still with us. Am I forgiven, Arthur?" Charlie asked his brother.

"Of course you are. I can't wait to go home. Mum, Dad, and Little Pimple are going to come and watch me get my medal."

"Well, from what I heard, you certainly earned it. I'm sorry I called you a coward," Charlie spoke sincerely.

"Yeah, well, I'll not deny there have been times when I've been petrified stiff," Arthur admitted.

"So have I. That first battle back in Wipers, I pissed myself but didn't tell anyone!" Charlie said, laughing about it. "It got easier after that, when I knew what to expect. But the hairpin last week, when the German mine went up—that shook me up somewhat," Charlie remarked.

"Is it true the Germans took three hundred prisoners?" Arthur asked.

"It's true. I saw it. I wasn't in the hairpin. Luckily for me, I was in Essex trench behind it when the whole lot went up. I don't know exactly how many, but we were told three hundred of us were caught on the other side of the crater when the Germans rushed into it," Charlie said.

"Jesus. You know, I asked if you could be there to see me get my medal, but I heard the 22nd are staying for a little while longer yet," Arthur said, trying to change the subject to a more positive one.

"Just a few weeks longer. Then we'll be off home too," Charlie said, crossing his fingers.

"Maybe you can get re-transferred to the 4th?" Arthur suggested.

"No. I like it here. The 22nd isn't so bad, and look, I'm a full corporal now. See?" Charlie showed Arthur the two stripes on his upper sleeve. "But once I'm home, then that will be it. The war will surely end before we're re-deployed."

"Do you honestly believe that? Even after all this time at the front?" Arthur asked.

"Well, one can always hope," Charlie said, knowing that his belief might well be fantasy.

"All the fighting we've seen and neither us nor the Germans have either advanced or retreated. We're going to be stuck here forever," Arthur groaned.

"No, we're not. You're going home in a few days, and I'm going to be following in a few weeks. I suppose it'd be nice for Mum to have us both home together, but that's out of the question now," said Charlie

"Not to worry. When it's over, we'll all be together again. I wonder what home is like? What do you think has changed?" Arthur asked.

"I don't know. I hear them Zeppelin thingies have been bombing London. There might not be anything left of it!" Charlie replied.

"Don't talk like that. I'll be there soon, and I'll let you know what it's like. Shall I send you anything?" Arthur offered.

"Socks. Fags," Charlie answered.

"Okay. Right, well, I need to get back to the 4th," Arthur said, ending the conversation, happy with the outcome.

"Yeah, I've got things to do too. We've got an inspection soon," Charlie said.

"I'm glad we could talk."

"Me too," said Charlie sincerely. The brothers

hugged and shook hands.

"Good luck, Charlie." Arthur patted his older brother on the shoulder as he turned away to return to the 4th battalion.

"Good luck to you, Hero of Shipka Pass!" Charlie called after him.

The rest of the day passed quietly, only a few sporadic shells landing harmlessly between the two static enemy lines. Several Royal Flying Corps planes could be seen in the sky circling above. Their engines hummed away over them, but apart from that, there was no excitement. Rations arrived as promised, tins of bully beef, white bread with plum jam, and some ration pack biscuits. A few more days of this and Arthur's war would soon be over.

Disturbing Arthur from his day of doing very little other than snooze, Lieutenant Thew came along to talk with the men.

He was holding a helmet in his hand. He explained that this was the new edition steel helmet that would soon be distributed to the whole BEF. However, there was such a short supply at the moment that this particular helmet was given to whoever was on sentry duty. The boys had a bit of a chin wag with the lieutenant about how ridiculous it was that the company had been given only one helmet.

"Right, and there's a bit more to tell you. Bad news, unfortunately. Well, not necessarily bad, but potentially bad," Lieutenant Thew added.

Smiles faded, and the mood changed. Arthur stood

anxiously, waiting for what was about to be said.

"Okay, so here's the deal. Today is January 27th. It might not mean much to you, but to the Hun, it's a big deal."

Eyes looked up as brains were racked, but no one could guess why.

"It's the kaiser's birthday. We can probably expect some big spectacle or gesture from the Germans," Lieutenant Thew explained. Groans and moans rumbled amongst the listeners.

"That being said, we've been told by HQ that four days is the longest we have to wait until we're relieved, for good this time."

"Just four more days?" Roberts asked excitedly.

"That's right. Just four more. It's just a bit of bad luck on our part that the kaiser's birthday just happens to be today. Well, there's not much we can do about it, so we're just gonna have to sit it out. If we're unlucky, we might have to fight it out, but I have faith that you boys will see it through. So, as of eighteen hundred hours this evening, the whole line is to stand to in preparation for an imminent German attack. Questions?" There were none.

The groaning and mumbles cursed all along the trench as Lieutenant Thew moved farther down the line.

Six o'clock came, and Arthur went on sentry duty first. He got to wear the special new helmet for a couple of hours. It was heavy, but it gave him a lot of comfort, knowing that the thickness would provide extra protection from shrapnel and bullets.

His shift as sentry passed, and he handed over the helmet to his successor as he stepped away from the firing bay.

Another morning came, and with it came the all too familiar sounds of shelling. It seemed to be far away, but now and then, there would be one or two which landed close enough to indicate that the hapless bunch of troops might not be let off. Judging by the sound, it was German artillery firing a mixture of earthworks and shrapnel shells. Arthur had been at the front for so long now that he could tell such details by ear.

By midday, the shelling was continuing. Thankfully for the young boys in the 4th Battalion, it hadn't gotten that much closer to their trenches. It seemed to be concentrating about half a mile north of their position in North Maroc.

Arthur overheard Thew and Fairbridge talking.

"That's the 15th Battalion taking a pounding," Fairbridge told the lieutenant.

"They're gonna get it all bloody day long, aren't they?" Thew replied.

"As long as they leave us alone," Arthur said quietly but still loud enough for the captain to hear him.

"Don't lose your nerve now, Private Green. Three more days, that's all we've got to do. Three more days, boy." Fairbridge patted him on the back as he spoke.

"Yes, sir," Arthur muttered.

The captain stood upon the parapet looking out

through his periscope. It wasn't Arthur's place to ask, but he was keen to know, so he asked anyway.

"Anything going on out there, sir?"

"I'm not sure. They're giving the 15th one hell of a barrage. I can't see much, just broken walls and some poor chap's arm in front of us." The captain stood peering out for several more minutes. "Hang on!" he said suddenly. "Something's afoot!"

Several eyes and ears lent themselves to the captain. The atmosphere was immensely intense; everyone was so eager to avoid action.

"Okay, boys, stand to, we've got activity going ahead. Bugger!" announced Captain Fairbridge.

Arthur felt a panic go right through his body. Why, so close to the end, would they have to see action again? There inevitably would be casualties, and they all knew it.

"Okay, lads, fix bayonets!" came the captain's orders.

The sound of multiple bayonets being unsheathed and clipped onto the ends of their Lee Enfield rifles filled the trench.

"Get ready to give them Hell one last time, lads!" the captain shouted before giving the men the order to stand upon the firing step and aim their rifles over the parapet.

The shelling had stopped, and the sound of rifles cracking and machine-gun fire drifted to them from their left where the unlucky lads of the 15th Battalion were taking the brunt of the onslaught.

Arthur was standing next to Roberts, who was

trembling terribly. There was a slight whine coming out of his throat, and Arthur saw that he was crying. It was clear Roberts was finding the situation hard. The anticipation of a pending fire-fight was tearing away at his nerves.

"Keep it together, mate. They might not come this way!" Arthur reassured the relative newcomer. Roberts had been in the line at the hairpin, but that was now nearly a month ago, and they'd all spent the past few weeks under the illusion they were going home without having to fight again. It had played badly on their morale and, in particular, their willingness to go into battle.

"Listen up, men of the 4th Battalion!" came the voice of Major Clark. "Listen up!" he shouted again. "Keep your eyes forward but listen carefully. The 15th are being pulverised. We, that's us and the 22nd, have been ordered to get ourselves to their aid. We're going out into no man's land to attack the German advance on its left flank. Nothing is covering the double crassier in front of us, so don't expect any resistance. The rubble of the town will give us sufficient cover from small arms fire if the Germans engage us from up ahead. Pass it along the line, and prepare to advance!"

Wow, that was a quick briefing, Arthur thought.

"What the Hell's happening, Arthur?" Roberts asked, shaking like a leaf.

"We're attacking the Germans in the open as they attack our positions farther up. Use the broken walls and rubble as cover. Stick with me and you'll be right as rain, okay?" Arthur advised his friend.

"Okay, I'm going into battle with the hero of Shipka Pass!" Roberts laughed as tears streamed down his face.

"That's right." Arthur smiled at the pathetic excuse for a man in front of him with absolute pity. Roberts had urine shamelessly gushing down his legs. It had become the norm, and he wasn't the only one.

A whistle went, and with confidence in his abilities as a soldier and as a survivor, Arthur was one of the first over the top. Through the wire, typically marked with little white ribbons, and into the all too familiar desolate scene of man's inhumanity to man, no-man's land.

Months of fighting had utterly destroyed the town. To look at it, one could see its destruction, but now that Arthur was walking through, it hit home even harder what an unforgiving, cruel art war truly was. These were the remains of peoples' homes. As refugees, their lives had been left behind. Wardrobes, beds, kitchen utensils, everything associated with the interior of a household littered the landscape on which he now trod.

A whistle blew off to his left, and he could distinctly make out Captain Fairbridge and Lieutenant Thew ushering men to their left. Arthur turned and joined the herd, who stampeded where their officers directed them. The enormous double crassier, which certainly did dominate the skyline, was leaning towards them. The Germans were well behind it, or so they had been told, and therefore not to expect any fire from it.

Scrambling over the broken town, which didn't have a single building or wall more than four feet high left standing, Arthur found himself in a mixture of men from the 4th Battalion and the 22nd as they approached the battle zone together. A fast walk was all anyone could muster. Arthur had his pack, his webbing, and his rifle. All of it was weighing him down. He couldn't decide what was worse—trampling along bricks and broken homes, almost twisting his ankles with every step or the mud that had hampered him back in Belgium.

As expected, when the Germans realised what was happening, the sound of shrapnel shells above their heads appeared.

At least someone got the best helmet in the entire battalion, Arthur thought. Strange that humour had wormed its way into his mind again.

Up and over a small ridgeline, Arthur had a first-class view of the German attack. The British trenches defending the suburban town of Maroc, which had been equally reduced to rubble, snaked along the outskirts. There were little figures all in khaki firing up towards attackers, wearing field grey. To his right appeared the German trenches, which had just released their second wave of human cattle into the fury.

Some troops from Arthur's company started firing at them, but they were still too far away, so Arthur continued several more paces to get a better shot at his target. A shell landed about fifty feet in front of him, disintegrating the few British soldiers standing there a second before. They now belonged to oblivion. Their names were sure to appear on the 'missing, presumed dead' list that would follow in a day or two.

Arthur unslung his rifle, took a knee, and took aim. He fired two or three times but barely even bothered to check if his target had gone down. There were so many of them he would hardly have to aim at all if he could get closer. Then it would be easy pickings.

"Found you!"

Arthur jumped as Roberts appeared from behind him.

"Come on, Arthur, we've got them on the run!" he shouted excitedly.

"Let's get a bit closer," Arthur told the unexpectedly optimistic private whose damp trousers reeked of urine. He was somewhat baffled by Roberts commenting that the enemy was on the run. Anyone could see that they were indeed not.

The sky was ripping above them, and more shells flew their way. They were in danger of being caught in the open if they went within accurate range of German machine guns. Arthur decided to stop again, taking Roberts down with him as shells filled the air in front of them.

Whoever ordered this attack is a bloody butcher, Arthur thought.

Men of both the 22nd and the 4th battalions were now unable to get closer. The shellfire had honed in on them and was cutting them to pieces. The screaming and calling out for stretchers and mothers had already begun, but now it was all around them. Heading back was just as dangerous as moving forward, so both Arthur and Roberts hugged the rubble-based ground, which shook beneath them. Hundreds of tiny stones and smashed bricks were jumping up into the air with each vibration of the earth.

Arthur looked to Roberts, who was flat on his back with his hands over his ears, screaming uncontrollably like a child. He slapped him on the chest to get his attention, but it didn't work. Arthur thought about leaving him to his own luck but decided to help him come back down to earth. Standing up and grabbing him by his boots, Arthur dragged Roberts to steps that took them into a cellar. He knew that if the entrance were to take a direct hit, then they'd both be buried alive, but it was still safer than being in the open.

Dirt fell from the cellar ceiling, and Arthur feared it would collapse at any moment. Dust choked both of them as they huddled in the dark, damp corner. It was almost pitch black down there. Only the broken entrance with about eight steps leading back into the inferno of the outside world gave them any light. Roberts had calmed down somewhat but was still shaking terribly.

The shelling lasted another half hour at least. At

first, it seemed to move away from the area, but then it came back again before moving off in a different direction again. The cellar managed to stay strong before the barrage petered out.

Above ground, anything could have been happening. Neither of the two boys had any idea. They were both disorientated, unaware of which way their lines were.

"You all right?" Arthur asked his nerve-stricken friend. Roberts could only nod unconvincingly and stare Arthur in the eyes. His naturally black hair was white with dust, which also clung to his sweat-stained forehead and eyebrows, giving him the humorous appearance of an old man.

As the dust and smoke settled and their eyes adjusted to their dark surroundings, the cellar became lighter and more navigable. Some old glass jars had somehow managed to survive the war, and there was an old broken wooden chair with only three legs. Odd to think that this was once some French towns-folk's house.

"I'm going to have a look. You stay here," Arthur told his fragile companion. Ascending the stairs and into the light, nothing could be seen other than the town's pure ruin. The shelling had been murderously destructive. Arthur didn't dare to poke his head up any further. He couldn't tell where he was anyway, so he went back down into the cellar to think about his next move.

Waiting until dark seemed the obvious choice, but that was hours away. The Germans might open up the shelling again, and they might not be so lucky next time. Being buried alive didn't sound appealing, so he concluded that the option to stay put was no longer viable.

Arthur wasn't that keen on waiting at all. Typically, after an attack such as the one they'd just taken part in would come the anticipated counter-attack. That meant Germans might find themselves in the same cellar, and then they'd be for it. Maybe they'd have more luck if they split up. If one went one way and one went the other, one might go the right way. That meant one of them for sure going the wrong way, if not both of them if they went along no man's land instead of across it.

What would Clark do? What would Fairbridge or Thew do? They might not even be amongst the living right now, so he chose not to imagine he was one of them. Arthur ran out of ideas.

"We're just going to have to slowly make our way out of here until we see something that can give us a clue as to where we are," he told Roberts, who had been unhelpful with regards to solutions to their situation.

Arthur remembered the double crassier. If he managed to find out where that was in relation to their current position, then he should be able to get at least an idea of where British lines lay.

"Come on, let's go. When we get up there, keep your head down and just go where I go, okay?"

Roberts nodded, but it wasn't enough to convince Arthur. If Roberts was to become a burden, Arthur decided he would leave him. After being at the front for almost a year, Arthur was going home in two or three days. He wasn't going to get himself killed because of some untrained newcomer, even if he had become his friend.

"Let's go!" Arthur said. Just as he scrambled the steps into the open, there was a thwack and a thud. A hissing sound startled them a second later. Then came two others behind them, and another landed a few yards from the entrance to the cellar. Green fumes billowed out of the bronze cylinder which had hit the ground before them.

"Back into the cellar! Gas!" Arthur shouted at Roberts. He was slow in turning around, and Arthur pounded straight into him and lost his footing. Both of them tumbled back to the cellar floor as the greenish-yellow cloud crept after them into the blackness.

"Get your mask on, you idiot!" Arthur shouted at Roberts as he fumbled around for his own.

"My mask?" Roberts panicked.

"Yes, get it on!" Arthur impatiently scowled back.

"I haven't got it!"

"You what?"

Arthur slid the mask, which was more like a rubber bag, over his head and put the respirator's mouthpiece between his teeth.

The mask dampened his hearing, and through his barely visible eye sockets, he couldn't make out what Roberts was saying. He couldn't understand why he wasn't putting his mask on. Arthur slowly stepped back to the rear of the cellar, trying his best to stay away from the cloud as it came closer.

Roberts dived to the ground, put his face down to the floor, and tried to hold his breath. After several seconds he emptied his lungs and tried to suck in a final breath of clean air. The gas cloud swallowed the pair of them. Arthur could feel his hands begin to burn. He tucked them away under his armpits and slumped on the floor against the wall.

In front of him, Roberts squirmed. It was impossible to hear him, but he was shouting something to Arthur, who could only watch as the poor boy's face began to burn and blister. Moments later, Roberts lost control of his arms and legs. They twitched uncontrollably, and he started to cough. He lay on the floor, and his eyes began to bulge. The struggle turned into a frenzied hysteria as blood and froth fountained from his wide-open mouth. Blood trickled out of his ears and nose. His face was now a kind of pale blue-white with yellow boils appearing on his forehead. His tongue grew out of his mouth and down his chin, bathing in a white lather. It was purple and black. More gunk bubbled out of his nose, mixing with blood. His eyes soon looked in different directions, one pupil twice the size of the other.

After a few minutes of watching his last friend slowly die horrifically, Arthur had had enough. He felt his way to the cellar entrance taking one last look at Roberts, who was in his last few merciless heartbeats. He crawled on all fours up the steps and out of the cellar. The green haze had given Arthur some sort of sufficient cover. Although his hands were burning from the chemical mist and his neck was starting to feel it too, he was still alive.

He stumbled aimlessly, tripping on loose bricks and other pieces of broken housing. The deathly fog began to clear as Arthur kept going. He decided to crawl when the cover of the cloud was no longer there. He still didn't want to remove his mask, although he knew it was now safe to do so. A gentle breeze was blowing the gas away from him. Arthur turned and watched it waft with an almost innocent characteristic softly away from where he was crouching.

He got to his knees and lifted the mask away from his face. At first, he only smelled the air with his nose, and upon taking in a nostril full of crisp air, he inhaled a huge lungful. His face had been sweating inside the mask from fear and heat, and he briefly enjoyed the cold on his face. The sounds and groans of dying and wounded men were drifting through the air. He could hear someone calling for help, but he couldn't make out where it was coming from.

He had a look behind him but couldn't recognise where he'd come from. He had no idea where the cellar was.

Poor Roberts, down there in the dark. It was a sight to forget, however unlikely. Arthur had become familiar with death but watching his friend die from poisonous gas was an excruciating trauma.

He had a look around—desolation in every form at

every angle. Two hind legs of a brown horse lay about fifteen feet from him. This wasn't just a case of man's inhumanity to man, he thought. This was man's inhumanity to everything that existed.

He peered over a broken piece of wall and let out a sigh of relief. He had seen the double crassier of the coal mine. The Germans were on the other side of it, which meant his lines were opposite. He walked bent over, desperate not to be seen at this last moment of the days' fighting. At least he hoped it would be.

"Back to my lines, straight to the reserve trenches, find my unit, wolf down a tin of bully beef, have a good night's kip or two, and then I'm going home!" he told himself. He quickened his pace, and over a few mounds of Earth and brick, the British wire became visible. One hundred yards, or maybe one hundred and twenty. Not too far at all. He took off his pack.

His heart skipped a beat as a stray shell landed somewhere to his left. He hadn't heard it coming, but he certainly felt the impact.

One hundred yards. Ninety yards, eighty. Another shell burst, this time to his right. Seventy yards to go. Arthur unbuckled his webbing, and his fast walk was able to become a jog. Sixty yards and he dropped his rifle; fifty yards to go—he was now running and panting like a mad dog. At forty yards, he could make out the round caps of British infantrymen who watched him from the parapet. Thirty yards away, he could make out the white markers of the gaps in the wire. Twenty yards left, and he could hear his fellow countrymen egging him on, shouting and waving, beckoning him to safety. He ran through the gap in his own wire ten yards in front of his trench. He'd made it! He could see the sandbags and where to jump into the trench! Home! Mum, Dad, Little Pimple!

The shell exploded behind Arthur as he lunged forward to the soldiers' outreached arms, trying to catch him. The pain of the shrapnel piercing through his back and lodging itself deep into his ribcage was like nothing he'd ever known. He let out an almighty scream, which almost ruptured his larynx. The agony paralysed him, and although it seemed to grip his whole body, he couldn't feel his legs. A second piece of shrapnel had severed his spine.

"ARTHUR!" he heard his brother's voice. "Arthur, you made it!"

Charlie pushed another soldier out of his way. "He's my brother!" he explained. "Are you hurt, Arthur?"

Arthur tried to speak but could only shout a few words. "M-m-m-my b-b-back. Arrrrgggghhhh!" he cried out.

"Get some stretcher-bearers, will you?" Charlie yelled in a panic at some of the other men who'd come to have a look at what was happening.

Charlie held his brother's hand and noticed blood dripping out of the sleeve.

"Don't worry, Arthur. We're right next to the ambulances. We'll have you in the CCS as soon as we can. You'll be okay, got it?"

Arthur smiled at his brother and felt warmed by the reassurance. Two stretcher-bearers appeared and lumped him onto the stretcher.

"I'm coming with him; he's my brother!" Charlie told them. They nodded and were very quick to get their way out of the trench and into the reserve lines, leading them straight to the trench entrances and onto a dusty road that was littered with casualties. Ambulances were chaotically going back and forth all over the place. They were certainly busy in this sector of the war.

The bearers took Arthur straight to an ambulance whose doors were open.

"Only those who are going to make it!" bellowed one driver.

"Put that one over there. He's a goner," one man with a red cross on his arm told two other stretcher-bearers who uncouthly dumped the man who was still alive by the side of the road. The man was crying hysterically and whimpered, as the medic had indirectly told him that he would die. The scene put a lump straight into Charlie's throat.

"Come on, Arthur, let's get you onto this one," he said as he helped the bearers slide the stretcher onto the ambulance floor. There were two other casualties in there. Both were silent, but Charlie could see they were breathing.

"You coming too? Get on if you are. We ain't got time to sit about all day," said the stretcher-bearer, who was sitting in the back of the ambulance.

Charlie climbed on board and sat down on the rickety bench. The equally unstable vehicle pulled away, jostling and bouncing.

"Where are we going?" Charlie asked the ambulance crewman.

"Bethune, 33rd Casualty Clearing Station," was the reply.

It meant nothing to Charlie, who couldn't even point out on a map where they were or where Bethune was.

The road became sturdier the farther they got from the front. The thuds and booms of the war began to fade, and soon, the only sounds were the tune the ambulance crewman was humming, along with the engine's rumbling.

Charlie looked out of the window. "Your war's done, Arthur. You're going home! You lucky bastard! Got yourself a blighty, didn't ya? Gonna show that off to all the lasses back home. You jammy sod!" he chuckled.

"Halt the vehicle!" the crewman called out.

The vehicle came to an abrupt stop.

"His war's over, all right. Give us a hand; this one's snuffed it." The crewman opened the back doors and took hold of the stretcher handle.

"Come on, don't just sit there. Let's get him out!"

"What?" Charlie was in a state of disbelief.

"He's dead..." the crewman shrugged. "Give us a hand, will ya!"

"What do you mean he's dead? He's not dead. He's

my brother!"

The crewman didn't bother to show an ounce of emotion. "I've seen a hundred brothers kick the bucket this morning, and these two will be joining him if you don't let me get this one out now! He's dead. I'm not taking him to the CCS. There are places up there for the ones who will make it. He's a goner, snuffed it, light's out, stone-cold dead! Now you don't have to come with me the rest of the way, but help me get him off of this ambulance for the sake of someone else!"

Charlie took hold of the stretcher and lowered Arthur's white body down from the ambulance. Blood was dripping through the canvas where he'd lost his blood, which had poured out of his back.

"Ready?" the crewman asked. "One, two, three!"

They tossed the body to the side of the road.

"I need the stretcher!" the crewman said, staring at Charlie, who despised the way this man was treating the dead. The crewman shrugged again. "I've got a hundred more coming!" he explained. He jumped on the ambulance, tapped twice on the ceiling, and it drove away, leaving Charlie with his brother's corpse by the side of the road.

More bodies were lying just beyond him, and Charlie saw two gravediggers in khaki picking one of the corpses up. They had face masks on, and it was necessary, as Charlie was almost knocked back by the smell as soon as the fumes from the ambulance had gone.

The two gravediggers looked at Charlie.

"Eh up, this one's not dead!" one of them joked to the other.

Charlie looked at the gravediggers, and they soon stopped smiling when they saw the sadness in Charlie's eyes.

"You all right, mate?" the same one asked.

"Where are we?" Charlie asked.

"Nouex-Les-Mines," he replied. "Where those who die in the ambulances get chucked out."

"Okay, thanks," he said. He looked down at Arthur's pale white face. His eyes were closed shut, and already a fly had appeared on one.

"Noeux-Les-Mines," he repeated.

"That's right," the other gravedigger spoke.

Charlie knelt next to his brother and held his head. A tear rolled down his face. He sat there crying for quite a few minutes before a slight drizzle began to fall. The gravediggers worked around, taking all the bodies one by one. Eventually, they approached Charlie.

"We gotta take that one too now, Corporal," one of them said. Charlie nodded. The two gravediggers lifted Arthur by his hands and legs and tossed him into a hole. Charlie couldn't bring himself to watch the soil cover Arthur's face as he lay there lifeless in the shallow grave.

As soon as he heard them finish covering Arthur by hammering a wooden cross as a marker, two more ambulances arrived. Six or seven bodies rolled and flopped out of the back of each ambulance. Then the vehicles, in all their desperation, sped away.

"There's no end to it," one of the gravediggers muttered.

"Let's just get on with it," the other replied.

"You gonna stand there all day?" the first one asked Charlie.

"Ummm...No," Charlie answered hesitantly.

"What you doing then?" the second gravedigger asked.

"I'm going back to the front," Charlie said numbly.

And at that, Charlie turned around and headed towards the war that had no end in sight. He marched alone.

Arthur Green died on 28th January 1916 aged nineteen. He is buried at Noeux-Les-Mines Communal Cemetary, France.

Plot I
Row G
Headstone 8

Printed in Great Britain
by Amazon